D0891826

# DEAD SLOW AHEAD

# DEAD SLOW AHEAD

A Casey Jones Cruise Ship Mystery

## Stella Whitelaw

This first world edition published 2008
in Great Britain and the USA by
SEVERN HOUSE PUBLISHERS LTD of
9–15 High Street, Sutton, Surrey, England, SM1 1DF.

British Library Cataloguing in Publication Data

Whitelaw, Stella
  Dead slow ahead. - (A Casey Jones cruise ship mystery)
  1. Cruise ships - Fiction 2. Detective and mystery stories
  I. Title
  823.9'14[F]



ISBN-13: 978-0-7278-6678-3    (cased)

*All Severn House titles are printed on acid-free paper.*

Printed and bound in Great Britain by
MPG Books Ltd., Bodmin, Cornwall.

To Jeanne Newman of Epsom, a long-time fan of
Jordan Lacey, who tracked me down like a true-born PI

Many thanks to the ever patient staff of both Oxted and Worthing libraries who never fail to find answers to the strangest queries. To Nigel also, who glued together the perfect map.

To Fran and Neil Reynolds who recently produced and choreographed *Copacabana* and still found time to steer me in the right direction. And thanks to Dr David Thomas for medical advice despite working long hours in Australia. The wonders of email.

Lastly, I sincerely thank my excellent editor, Anna Telfer, for her enthusiasm, hard work and helpful comments.

As always, any nautical errors are entirely mine.
Throw me a lifebelt, please.

# Casey's Ten Commandments

- Always listen sympathetically

- Always listen with patience

- Never look bored

- Never discuss politics or religion

- Never mention illness

- Never ask personal questions – even if the passenger offers answers

- Never boast – exude authority and confidence

- Always be tidy

- Always be sober

- Smile

# One

# Southampton

The train from Worthing to Southampton shunted along the line like a nervous beginner at a cha-cha-cha class. It was already half an hour late and I was due back aboard the MV *Countess Georgina* by lunch time. I'd picked up a smudge on my sleeve and that was enough to have me biting my nails.

I stared out of the window, taking slow, deep breaths, watching cud-chewing cows sauntering about rain-sodden fields. They were moving faster than the train.

The reasons for the delay were relayed to passengers in what could have been a foreign language. It could have been leaves on the line, snow, frozen points, signal failure, damaged rolling stock or a wild cat strike. When the guard had finished his announcement, we were none the wiser.

'Why do we keep stopping?' a little old lady asked me. People always thought I knew the answer to everything. Keep calm, Casey.

'Trouble with the signals,' I said with a serene smile. She was reassured.

It would be my own fault if I was late. Six hours ashore seemed enough time to get to my flat in Worthing and back. My optimism was limitless. All I'd gone for was to water my plants and remind myself that I had a base on terra firma and was not doomed to sail the seven seas forever like the ancient mariner.

Normally my time calculations are faultless. My working day is ruled by the clock. Every event is regulated by those hands, tick-tocking time away. Six hours was ample time to water a few plants, check the flat for wildlife, shuffle mail.

I could smell the sea, salty and fresh. We were nearly there. I shot out of Southampton Central station and fell into a taxi. Passengers would be arriving by now in their masses, with mountains of luggage, living out the pre-holiday travel hell.

'Conway Blue Line docks, please,' I said.

'Lucky you,' said the taxi driver. 'Wish I was going on a cruise.'

'Do I look like a passenger?' This was off-duty me, low-key in jeans, T-shirt, denim jacket and smudge. A thousand sea miles away from the posh as paint entertainments director who sashayed round the decks all hours, 24/7. How I hate that tabloid phrase. Say all day and every day.

It was time to cast off. I felt a tremor of apprehension, almost fear, strike at my heart. My second cruise on the MV *Countess Georgina* was about to begin. Calm down, Casey, nothing's going to happen this time. The brass band was assembling on the quayside to play us away. Flags were snapping in the breeze. Passengers were leaning over the rails to wave goodbye to their friends.

'Bye, Mum. Bye, Dad.'

'Have a wonderful time!'

The elegant white ship never failed to fascinate me, with her clean lines, sweeping bow and striking blue funnel. She was beautiful. I hoped this Mediterranean cruise would not be as eventful as my first.

No more unexpected deaths and men overboard, please. I wanted the quiet life. Nothing more exciting than a new deputy entertainments director to ease into the team with me. The previous one was now safely behind bars, in custody, probably losing weight, courtesy of HM Prison Service. Susan Brook ought to be grateful, send me a thank you card.

It was a great job and satisfied my innate yearning for the sea, that cool blue expanse, the raging waves, the troughs of iridescence. My birth sign was Cancer. I was a sea-groupie, without the fins.

'Did you enjoy your shore leave, Miss Jones?' asked one of the immaculate officers as I went up the gangway, crew card in hand.

'Leave? It was six hours,' I said. 'I spent most of it sitting on a train.'

This time, arriving on-board, I didn't get lost. I knew my

way to cabin 414 E Deck on autopilot, threw myself on the bed. It had been a rush. I'd brought a bagful of mail back with me. I could hardly open the door to my flat in Worthing for the accumulated junk mail. Junk is killing the environment.

Now it was time for blue sky thinking. The days ahead were for the passengers, making this the cruise of a lifetime for them, solving everyone's problems. Don't bother about mine. Put them on a back burner.

Passengers were wandering about, mostly lost. Inside the *Countess* was a bewildering place, so many decks, so many corridors, going in all directions. Don't mention starboard and port, aft and stern. It was a wonder anyone ever found the way back to their cabin. It took days to sort out the decks.

I remembered hearing a story about a passenger who had Alzheimer's and was lost on board for several days. His wife was apparently happy to have some time to herself. I don't know if it was true. It sounds true. He was found eating with the crew.

Ahmed, my cabin steward, had already refilled the refrigerator in my cabin with bottles of water. As entertainments director I talk a lot, get a dry throat and drink a lot. Mostly mineral water. Champagne is off limits when your working day stretches into the night hours.

I'm rarely off duty, nor is Dr Samuel Mallory, or Sam as he now insists that I call him. He says it's more streetwise. He hasn't a clue. The man is dishy, dark and Grade A gorgeous. He doesn't need a gimmick. He could be called Horatio Augustus and women would still swoon at his knees. Not me. From now on I'm not the swooning type.

He's in charge of our medical centre. He had a few hours off duty today as well, as passengers came aboard with their luggage and viruses. He may have spent it touring the delights of Southampton. It does have historic spots. Ancient walls and towers, though, search me, I've never spotted many. I did find the West Quay where the Pilgrim Fathers set sail for the Americas in their tiny ship *Mayflower*. In 1620, I think. Quite long ago. They must have been off their rockers.

This was a different cruise to the last one I worked, which had sailed the Caribbean and Mexican Riviera. The winter was on its way out and cruises were now aimed towards shorter holidays in the Mediterranean. All those hot, sultry days on deck and fabulous ports of call. Slosh on the factor thirty-five.

It was going to be three weeks of hard labour. I knew it. I could feel it in my bones. It was no holiday for me even though I loved my few hours ashore and my snatched moments leaning over a rail, watching the tumbling wake, looking for dolphins, enjoying a glorious sunset.

There was this feeling. I had a twitchy feeling. This was going to be no ordinary cruise. But no two cruises were ever the same. Different people did different things. But the problems remained the same.

'Casey? Come aboard safely? No leaping on from a pilot's launch?'

Dr Samuel Mallory was never going to let me forget a previous, somewhat impromptu arrival. The infuriating man stood at my side, a knowing smile on his tanned face, his silvery grey eyes glinting behind his gold-rimmed spectacles.

'Thank you for reminding me, Dr Mallory. As you can see, I am here in one piece and ready to start work. As soon as our entertainers have all arrived, I shall be in my office, signing them in, checking documents, allocating cabins and listening to endless lists of requests. I was going to say demands, but they are not all like Estelle Grayson.'

'Has she left us?'

'Yes, she has a contract on another ship in ten days. Just time to get her stage costumes dry-cleaned. But Joe Dornoch seems to have vanished. How about that? He was a fast runner. He was off the moment we docked. So her dreams of a mini honeymoon seem to have vanished too.'

'Very sad,' said Samuel Mallory. But he didn't sound at all sincere. He thought Joe, our talented lounge pianist, had had a lucky escape from Estelle, a prima-donna, has-been singer. 'Maybe they'll meet again, on another cruise.' He almost sang the phrase.

'That's quite possible. Now, if you'll excuse me, there's a lot to do.'

'No time for a sail-away glass of champagne on deck, then?' he asked. The stewards and stewardesses were already circulating with trays of bubbly. The passengers would soon find out that they were not free. They used to be but times are hard for the shareholders of Conway Blue Line.

'Sorry. Work calls. No doubt you'll soon find a lonely woman passenger, several in fact, only too happy to share their first cruise nerves with our gorgeous doctor.'

'No doubt I shall. My first concern will be to put her worries at rest and give her advice about the Bay of Biscay.'

'May all your concerns be little ones.'

'None of those on board, I hope.'

The *Countess* was a child-free ship. No passengers under sixteen. Not for us crèches and junior clubs and non-stop teenage activities. Not for us early suppers and cabin-sitters and washing machines daily churning out mountains of clean clothes. Or endless treasure hunts and discos and fancy dress parties.

But in every other respect the passengers of the *Countess* were like a small village. We had our share of births, deaths and love affairs. Occasionally a female passenger carrying a baby bump gave us a surprise. And death was always around, and not always among the elderly. Romance was often a bonus among the older passengers. But there were always more women than men, so nothing was guaranteed with the purchase of a ticket.

'This feels so strange,' said a woman passenger standing next to me, holding her glass of champagne. 'It doesn't feel like a ship. She's so steady.'

'It's more like an isolated village, Brigadoon, miles from the nearest land for days at a time,' I said. 'You'll get used to it.' It was then that the crew were stretched, keeping everyone happy, well-fed, fit, comfortable and entertained.

Keeping the passengers entertained was my responsibility. I coordinated arrangements for all the shows, cabarets, lectures, classes and demonstrations. It was non-stop, not only for the passengers but also for the entertainers. I had to keep them in a good humour as well. Like knitting with barbed wire. The odd difficult diva came on board, not mentioning any names. The real stars, even fading ones, were always easy to get along with.

'But the Bay of Biscay may be a little different,' I went on. 'You'll feel some movement of the ship then. The *Countess* has excellent stabilizers but sometimes there's bad weather.'

'I've some pills,' she said. 'I shall take them and come up on deck.'

'Well done. Fresh air always helps and you've come prepared. I'm Casey Jones, your entertainments director. Do come and talk to me, any time.'

'Thank you. I'm Lucinda Ember.'

'Nice to meet you, Mrs Ember.'

A small piece of fuel in a dying fire. Her name gave me an unexpected shiver. I hoped it was not a premonition. I did not want to be intuitive or perceptive. Let me stay sane and ordinary. I've only enough energy for ordinary.

No streamers these days. Forget the black and white films of ships leaving Southampton, festooned with streamers. The council doesn't think they are environmentally friendly. Throw a smile instead.

My deputy arrived. It was a remarkable surprise. I had been given the name of Lesley Williams. But it was Leslie Williams, five foot ten of cool male in slim, belted jeans and open-necked white shirt. I must tell him about jeans. We are not allowed to wear them on duty.

'Am I a surprise?' he asked, as if it often happened. He had a deep voice with an interesting accent. A touch of Cornwall? He was going to be a hit. I knew it already. The ladies would love him. He sounded caring, considerate but somehow vaguely sad. In a flash, I knew we would get on. You know how it is.

'I don't care what sex you are, as long as you are part of this team,' I said. 'We have a lot to do, every day. Have you found your cabin yet?'

'No, I'm still lost.'

'OK if you stay lost for another hour? I've a lot to explain to you.'

'Fire away, boss lady. I'm listening.'

I liked him. He had short brown hair and clear blue eyes. I had not read his documents yet so I knew only a little about him. But funny how you can look at a person and know that you can trust them.

'So do I call you Leslie? Or Les?' Les didn't sound right. A bit like a dodgy car dealer.

'If you don't mind, I prefer Lee. My mother had a fixation on *Gone with the Wind*, and named me after an actor called Leslie Howard who was in the film.'

'He got killed during the war, didn't he?'

'I wouldn't know. Before my time.'

'Then, Lee it is. I'm Casey Jones.'

'So I've heard. And Casey actually stands for K.C?'

'Yes, Katherine Cordelia. You've done your homework.'

We sat down and I took Lee through the routine of the day. He had already worked on another cruise ship as part of the team but this was his first deputy post. He was going to fit like a second glove.

Before I had finished the bells went off and it was muster time for the lifeboat drill. Everyone was supposed to take part, go to their muster stations with their life jackets. Some didn't bother. They stayed in the bars. I was in charge of the Galaxy Lounge area this cruise. Passengers shambled in, dragging their life jackets, half on or half off, straps all over the place, tripping over them. No wonder we had to have a practice.

I went through the drill for putting them on, strapping tight, which bit does what. Don't blow the whistles, please. God help them if we ever had a disaster. No one was really listening. One or two looked anxious-eyed and tested everything that I said. Lee was good, explaining with patience.

We went round, checking straps. Some passengers had their life jackets on back to front. It was Laurel and Hardy without the cinema organ.

It was the best we could do. We had gone through the motions as required by the law. But how many would ever remember? It would be panic stations if we hit an iceberg.

Still, this was a Mediterranean cruise. No icebergs in the Med unless a melting one floated south. So to hell with the life jacket. Put it back in the wardrobe. Let's get ready for dinner. Pass me a black tie, mother.

I stood at the entrance to the Windsor Dining Room, greeting diners as they arrived. What was I wearing? Anyone really interested? I'd thrown myself into a fabulous Schiaparelli dress bought from a vintage shop in south London. Yellow and black stripes, with a tight pleated black bodice. It was amazing, like a bee on legs. But I didn't wear it often, not a favourite. I had to be in the mood and tonight I needed to be memorable. The skirt was long enough to cover kitten-heeled shoes. Break-your-neck heels are for the dancers.

'Hello,' I said. 'I'm Casey Jones. Your entertainments director on the *Countess*. Have a lovely cruise.'

They had no idea who I was or what I did. They pretended they understood. But it didn't matter. They would soon find out as I circulated the decks every day. Word would spread. The right words, I hoped.

'Ah, Miss Jones. We meet again. I expect you've been very busy, getting all your entertainers aboard.'

It was Lucinda Ember. She was wearing a camellia couture dress by Chanel. It was the most beautiful dress I had ever seen. Big, overblown camellias in gold, then more in black, rising to a scooped-out neckline. Long sleeves in black chiffon belled into more gold flowers.

I had to catch my breath. It was stunning. Where had she got it from? How much had it cost? It would have been mind-blowing.

Something about her still gave me the shivers. And that dress. The dress was beautiful but I could not help shuddering. The iconic camellias were somehow depressing, showing a darker side of the famous designer. I would never wear it.

Lucinda Ember was also wearing a lavish Byzantine neck-lace. It was Turkish, but I could not tell whether it was genuine or a reproduction.

'I hope you are coming to the show tonight,' I said. 'It's spectacular.'

'I shall be there,' said Lucinda. 'I don't miss anything.'

It sounded like a threat. But I shook it off. I was becoming paranoid. It was hunger. Breakfast in my Worthing flat had been a stale yogurt needing to be liberated from the refrigerator.

On some evenings I was expected to host one of the tables for eight in the Windsor Dining Room but this wasn't possible tonight. There was too much to do. I hurried to the theatre where the first performance would soon begin. This was for the second sitting passengers who would eat afterwards. It was an upside-down arrangement. The first sitting ate dinner, then saw the show.

Back stage was chaos. I didn't interfere. The shows were choreographed and rehearsed in London. They'd had all after-noon to get used to the size of the stage and the cramped dressing rooms, make costume changes. Now they had to go on stage and smile, smile, smile.

It was my job to MC the spectaculars. Both showings. But I had a feeling that Lee would be able to take my place on some evenings, very soon. The passengers would love him. Susan Brook, my previous deputy, had been a liability on stage. Any stage.

Sometimes I had to remind myself what the current spectacular was called. I had seen so many. Ah yes, the *Showtime Spectacular* tonight. Call that original. But it would be good. The singers could sing and the dancers could dance. And those that couldn't do either wore very few clothes.

After a fanfare, I went on stage with loads of flourish in my yellow bee-striped creation and introduced the evening's entertainment. Then I went off. I had a spare forty-five minutes before I was needed again, to go on stage and orchestrate the applause.

This was when I usually skidded down into the depths of the ship and found the Officers' Mess on F Deck, and grabbed myself a starter or something. I never had time for a full meal.

The Officers' Mess was well hidden among green-painted corridors of offices and stores and passengers' stored luggage. It took a diviner to find it. The mess was well fitted with long tables set with silver cutlery and glasses. But it was self-service from the various hot plates and cold counters.

As I was still feeling cold from Southampton's chill, I went for some parsnip and Stilton soup, followed by a quick, thrown-together Waldorf salad from the salad bar.

The audience had loved the show and the spangled dancers. Their headdresses were bigger than their costumes. I had no trouble in generating the applause.

Then I had less than twenty minutes before I was due back on stage before introducing the second showing, this time for the first sitting passengers, who by now were digesting their enormous meal.

This was what I meant by non-stop work. Sometimes there were problems to sort out backstage, or lighting out front, or sound anywhere. Sometimes I only had time for a cup of coffee.

I was on again. 'Good evening, ladies and gentlemen. Did you enjoy your meal? Wasn't that parsnip and Stilton soup out of this world? We have great chefs on board the *Countess*.'

Dr Samuel Mallory appeared backstage, immaculate as ever, perfectly cut dinner jacket sitting on his broad shoulders. How did he get there? Then I noticed we were one girl dancer short.

'A slight panic attack, a dancer called Maisie,' he said. 'She's OK now. She'll get over it. Probably be able to go on, halfway. The Moulin Rouge number is one of her favourites. She'll probably make that number.'

'I thought you'd come to volunteer as a replacement.'

'The costumes are not my style. I'd need more than a couple of feathers.'

'Have you been busy?' I asked, trying not to think of the feathers.

'A few passengers being seasick before we even passed the Isle of Wight. A couple who forgot their medication. How could you forget to bring your medication? It's incredible. Top of the packing list is medication.'

'It's the cruise magic. The cruise excitement. Don't blame them. Everything is different. Medication is the last thing they think of.'

'It's appalling.'

'Clothes and suntan lotion come first.'

'So where are we going this time?' Dr Mallory sounded quite grumpy. Hadn't he even looked at the itinerary? 'Barcelona, I suppose?'

'Palma first, then Barcelona. Don't you like Barcelona?'

'I had my wallet pinched there, many years ago. Never forgotten it. Not one of my favourite places.'

'It's a wonderful city. You must walk Las Ramblas and capture the magic again. All those living statues and the colourful stalls.'

'I shall sit in a cafe and not move an inch,' he said. 'No shopping.'

'How sad. If I see you, I'll wave.'

'Do that. I may wave back. I may not.'

Barcelona was one of the most vibrant and thriving seaports in the Mediterranean. I couldn't understand how Dr Mallory could ignore it. If he had bad memories, then they had to be erased. Maybe I'd have a go at the process.

Sometime later that evening, when both shows were over and I had sorted out a few problems, there was time to go on deck. My favourite time. I liked to stand by the rails, all alone, and watch the waves rushing by. The sky was always a maze of stars. Moon or no moon, the immense and watchful universe was mesmerizing.

'Miss Jones?'

A voice broke into my thoughts. For a nanosecond, I was annoyed. This was my time, for myself. But I was not paid to have even a nanosecond.

'Hello, Miss Ember.' I'd checked the passenger list, and she was Miss and not Mrs. Passengers always thought we had second sight.

'I'm really sorry to intrude on you. I can see you are enjoying some much-needed time to yourself.' Her voice was fluttering.

'That's all right,' I said, easing myself round to face her. She looked a little pale in the moonlight, fraught and scrawny. As if she had had a fright. But surely not? There was nothing frightening about this elegant ship.

'My cabin,' she began. 'I'm not happy about it.'

Oh dear, a housekeeping problem. She should ask the purser for a cabin change. Nothing to do with me. I am immune to cabin complaints.

'Have you spoken to the purser?'

'Yes, I have. But he is not taking me seriously. I've already told him.'

'What's the matter then?'

Miss Ember seemed reluctant to tell me. She had already been given the brush off by the purser's office. I might be unhelpful.

'I don't really know how to tell you. It's the bathroom,' she said. 'I know you'll laugh at me and I don't want to cause trouble. But I have reported it and no one will believe me.'

'Tell me,' I said, turning off the stars. 'I'll believe you.'

'My bathroom shower is dripping blood,' she said.

So at seven minutes past midnight, I was standing in Miss Ember's bathroom, watching the shower drip blood. It was fresh blood, bright and crimson.

I was not surprised that no one believed her.

# Two

## At Sea

Lucinda Ember was not attention seeking. Her distress was genuine. That's why I went with her to her cabin on A Deck, number 212. It was an outside stateroom with a balcony. Very luxurious. It would cost a lot for single occupancy.

The bathroom was on the right-hand side going into the cabin. Miss Ember went in front of me, and opened the door to the side. She did not look but went over to the glass doors that led to her balcony. She stood there, wringing her hands.

'I don't know what it means,' she said.

Blood was dripping out of the shower head. There was a pool in the bath, shaking slightly with the vibration of the ship. I wanted to wash it away, but realized that it should be left as evidence.

'I'd better get the security officer to come and look at it, and Dr Mallory. He'll want to take samples. Some fault with the shower head, I'm sure. And I'll arrange with the purser to get you moved to another cabin. You won't want to spend the night here.'

'No, maybe I won't. Yet I've just moved in, unpacked and got settled. It's too exhausting to move. But I suppose I had better go.'

I phoned to Richard Norton, the security officer, the nearest we have to a policeman on board. I described the situation briefly.

'Don't touch anything,' he said gruffly. As if I was going to paddle in the stuff like a toddler. I'd obviously disturbed his meal. He was fond of his food. Then I phoned Dr Mallory in the medical centre.

'Blood coming out of the shower? Not exactly a razor cut then, more like a touch of *Sweeney Todd*. It's going to be one of those cruises, I can feel it.'

'No, you can't,' I said. 'You are trying to scare me.'

'Now why should I do that, Casey? You are the most level-headed person I know. Apart from a tendency to miss departures, being taken hostage, and getting shut in cupboards. Quite normal in fact.'

I did not want to be reminded. The cruise to the Mexican Riviera had been eventful. Too eventful. This cruise was going to be different. Plain sailing. Nothing more complicated to solve than finding a few lost bottles of suntan lotion and a couple of library books sliding about on deck.

'Are you coming round? It's cabin 212 A Deck.'

'The posh part. OK. Perhaps the lady would like a sedative? I've a nice line in sleeping pills this cruise.'

'You sound like a shop.'

'I'm a walking chemist's shop. And I've some special offers.' His voice was teasing. I knew what he meant. But I had decided that I didn't want any complications in my life. I had discovered an allergy to commitment.

I made Miss Ember a cup of tea and settled her in the armchair near the window, so that she could watch the sea washing by and the stars twinkling in the night sky. They were soothing. Her face was regaining its colour. She sat carefully, not wanting to damage the camellias sewn on to her stunning dress. I'd have liked to ask her about it, but it was a rule: no personal questions.

She read my thoughts. 'It is a beautiful dress, isn't it?' she said, fingering one of the petals. 'It's Chanel, you know. The camellia was her signature.'

'It is lovely. But difficult to wear without crushing the flowers.'

'I have to be careful how I sit down. She invented the little black dress, you know, something simple and understated. I expect you have one in your wardrobe.'

'Haven't we all?'

Richard Norton arrived first. He was a big, burly man, ex-Marine, in a khaki uniform, different from the crew uniform. He gave me a warm smile in the doorway, hoping to get into my good books. It was wishful thinking. I liked him but I had a suspicion that there was a Mrs Norton tucked away safely somewhere in the Home Counties. Out of sight and out of mind but still ironing his shirts.

'Hello, Casey,' he said. 'What have you got for me this evening? I hope it's nothing more than a bit of rust. Have you called a plumber?'

'I've called a doctor.'

His face fell slightly. Dr Samuel Mallory was unbeatable opposition. Not a man on-board stood a chance with the ladies when the doctor was around.

'Ah well, I suppose Miss Ember is suffering from shock and needs some TLC.'

'She's doing all right,' I said. 'I'll introduce you and then you can look at the luridly leaking shower.'

Richard Norton accomplished both with his usual solid efficiency and made some notes. The shower was still dripping blood. No sign of anything abnormal during the afternoon. Miss Ember only noticed the blood when returning from dinner. So her cabin had been unoccupied during that mealtime. Richard talked to her steward, a rather scared young man called Nicky. He thought he was going to lose his job. They always thought that. Their families depended on the money they sent home.

Samuel Mallory arrived, sat down and talked to Miss Ember. 'What a nasty shock for you,' he said. 'I see Miss Jones has made you a nice cup of tea. I think I'll leave you a sleeping pill, a very mild one, just for tonight. You might have trouble getting to sleep.'

'I think I should like to sleep somewhere else. Miss Jones did say . . .'

'Good idea. I've spoken to the purser and there's an empty cabin that you can move to.'

Sam went into the bathroom and took several samples of the blood in a tube. The dripping was beginning to ease off. He was bemused. He'd never seen blood coming out of a shower before. It was really creepy, like the film *Psycho*. He pulled out the plug and let the blood wash away in a swirling raspberry puddle. There was no point in keeping it. The samples were enough.

He asked Nicky to come and give it a thorough clean with disinfectant.

Miss Ember was not pleased with the cabin that was on offer. It was not up to her current stateroom standard. No balcony. No sofa, no armchair. Twin beds, with the unused

one folded against the wall. The view was the side of a
lifeboat.

'It's only temporary, only for tonight,' I said, hovering. 'You
can move back to your stateroom as soon as it has been given
a complete service and a new shower installed.'

'Haven't you got anything else? A suite? How about the
penthouse suite?'

I shook my head. 'The ship is full,' I said. 'This cabin is
only empty because the couple haven't turned up. Some family
crisis.'

'No, I'm not staying here,' she said, firmly. 'It's too small,
too pokey. And look at the bathroom. It's not like the one I've
just left.'

'But it's a really comfortable cabin. It doesn't have all the
extras that you have paid for. But it's still a nice cabin and
we are only talking about somewhere to sleep for tonight.' It
had been a long day and evening. I was beginning to feel
tired. I'd been on the go since early morning. Miss Ember
still looked as fresh as a, well, camellia. She had to make up
her mind soon.

'I'm really not satisfied with this exchange,' she said. 'That
was blood in my cabin. I am going to complain to the purser.'

'As you wish,' I said. 'But I do have to go and do some-
thing else soon.' This was a lie, a shade of white. Forgive me,
St Peter. There's a limit to my patience at this time of night.
'So if you would please decide.'

'All right, I'll stay here, but arrange immediately for some
of my things to be brought to me.'

'Of course, I will. I'll ask a female steward to bring you
what you want. Perhaps you'd make a list?'

'My toiletries out of the bathroom, nightwear, and some
slacks and a shirt for tomorrow morning. I shall expect my
stateroom to be ready for my return after breakfast.'

'I'm sure that will be possible,' I said, maintaining the charm.
That meant the plumber and Nicky would have to work
overnight. I made a mental note to ask the plumber to put the
old shower into a plastic bag for further examination. I was
beginning to think like a cop.

I also arranged for a small cold supper tray to be delivered
to the new cabin in case Miss Ember was peckish after all the
trauma she had gone through, plus a small complimentary

bottle of brandy. She might prefer that to Dr Mallory's wonder
pill.

When I left Miss Ember she was furiously making notes
on the writing paper supplied in the cabin. She was obviously
composing her letter of complaint to Head Office already.

'Have you settled Miss Ember?' said Samuel Mallory,
catching up with me in the corridor.

'Settled is hardly the right word,' I said.

'What is the right word then?'

'She would say it was dumped. She doesn't like the new
cabin. It's not up to her standards.'

'To be expected. Her posh stateroom is one of the best.
Naturally she doesn't like the temporary cabin too much.'

'It's only for one night.'

'Care for a nightcap and walk on deck? I know you like
the night air to blow away the day's cobwebs.' Sam was remembering the last cruise, when these late walks together became
something of a habit.

'And there's been plenty of those today. The spiders have
been busy,' I agreed. 'But, no thank you. Your job is to keep
our passengers healthy, and charm the female ones. You should
be circulating the bars.'

Sam's eyes hardened for a second, then a gleam of amusement returned. 'As you wish. Medusa has spoken.'

Medusa was a monster from Greek mythology with snakes
in her hair, who could turn anyone who looked at her into
stone. I thought his joke was pretty juvenile. My state of
mental exhaustion prevented me from thinking up a smart
reply.

'And the snakes bite,' I said, turning away. It was the best
I could do.

'Plenty of serum back at the dispensary.'

It was way past one but I did go for a brief deck stroll. I
loved it when the decks were empty but for a few distant crew
swabbing down. Everything was cleaned and polished every
day. The ship must be spotless for the next day's revels.

I leaned over the rail and watched the white-tipped waves
rushing by. The captain had put on a spurt of speed, covering
a good few extra miles during the night. He had a schedule
to keep. The *Countess* always arrived on time.

This was going to be an idyllic Mediterranean cruise, lots

of small islands to explore, and other sophisticated ports of call. The passengers would love it. I would love it. There were even a few places that I hadn't seen before, and that was rare.

Tomorrow I would get to know more of the passengers. Circulate. Try to learn a few names. And no doubt collect a lot of complaints for my trouble.

Richard Norton was at my side. He appeared like a giant out of the shadows. He was six foot three. He was not a great talker, so he stood silent for a few moments.

'I thought I'd find you up here,' he said.

'Blowing away the cobwebs,' I said.

'You ought to know that we have a celebrity on board, travelling incognito with a personal bodyguard.'

'What fun,' I said, immediately interested. 'Male or female celebrity?'

'Incognito, so we don't know. Only the captain has the full details.'

'Maybe it's Madonna?'

'I think she would take over the whole ship. That's her style. No, it's some other celebrity who doesn't want to be recognized.'

'Give us a clue. Royalty, head of state, politician?'

'I told you. I don't know. Perhaps you could keep an eye open? I know how good you are at spotting unusual things,' he said.

'I'll certainly do that,' I said, all tiredness gone. 'Difficult to spot someone who doesn't want to be recognized, but as soon as I know who they are, I'll tell you.'

'You're a brick.'

First I was Medusa and now I was a brick. I was getting my identity confused.

# Three

# At Sea

We would be leaving the Bay of Biscay behind sometime later this morning, passing Cape Finisterre, and heading south along the coast of Portugal. There were fine and clear skies and already the temperature was climbing.

'Good morning, Miss Jones,' said Ahmed, my steward. 'You slept well?'

'Like a log.'

He looked bemused.

'It's a phrase, meaning a sound sleep.'

He nodded, filing it away. 'Like a log. A piece of wood is asleep.'

I took the lift to the Terrace Café where breakfast was served till elevenses took over. I accepted the disinfectant squirt into my hands, rubbed the alcohol together till it vaporized, and took a tray. I had no desire to join the long queue for a full English. My breakfast was always the same: fruit and maybe a croissant if it was a decadent day.

But it was an overflowing bowl of melon slices, chunks of watermelon, grapefruit, prunes, orange slices, pineapple rings, cranberries and raisins. My five-fruits a day, all in one go. I took the tray to an outside table, not put off by the breeze, wanting to be away from people for a few more precious minutes. I could sit and watch the sea.

It would be all hands, feet, arms and faces on deck this morning. The passengers had a lot of activities to choose from, different ways of filling the time between meals – lectures, exercise classes, ballroom dancing, swimming, needlepoint, painting, strolling the shops and art gallery. Or they could simply grab a sun lounger and stretch out to catch a tan. The perfect way to see the world.

Lucinda Ember found me with unerring accuracy as I thought she might. She had that look in her eye. I said goodbye to peace.

'I had a very uncomfortable night,' she began, sitting herself at my table. 'I hardly slept.'

'Oh dear,' I said, spoon aloft, hoping she would notice that I was eating my breakfast. 'What a pity.'

'I expect my stateroom to be ready soon.'

'If you go to the main reception and ask for the purser, you will be able to find out. I'm sure they will have worked through the night to get your stateroom ready for reoccupation.' I knew they had. I'd already checked.

'And I should expect so. Has the doctor found out anything about the blood?'

'I wouldn't know. I'm sure his tests will be very accurate.'

'I'd like to be informed.'

'Of course,' I said, trying to get some pineapple past my lips. 'I'll ask him to let you know.'

'This isn't the end of this matter,' she said, rising to her feet.

'I'm sure it isn't,' I said, maintaining my calm.

'I'm not happy about the way I was treated,' she continued, flinging a long silk scarf over her shoulder. 'I should have had something better than that pokey little cabin.'

'Unfortunately it was all that was available,' I said. I nearly added that perhaps the captain's cabin would have suited her better. We should have asked him to move.

I had a feeling that Miss Ember was going to be a pain in the backside for the whole of the cruise. She had that demanding look about her. But there were other departments on-board all poised and ready to deal with her various complaints. I passed over my responsibility with an inaudible sigh of relief.

One of the new dancers was homesick. She was so unwell that she did not make the morning rehearsal, but was heard sobbing her heart out under a lifeboat. I took her to my office and let her phone home, while she sobbed down the phone for five minutes. Her mother was apparently trying to talk sense into her daughter when Lee Williams came in, sweaty and glowing from an invigorating quoits match on deck. Kristy took one look at him and did a quick retake on the options.

'Well, I'll stay until Palma,' said Kristy, drying her eyes on the hem of her minuscule T-shirt. 'That's all. Then I'm coming straight home. Bye, Mum.'

Lee was making her a mug of coffee. 'That's my girl, the true professional,' he said. 'Do a couple of shows. I bet you look really stunning.'

'Maybe a show or two,' she agreed, nodding.

'I'll be there in the front row,' he promised. 'Throw me a smile.'

He was an asset, parcelled in muscles and a pleasant nature. Kristy wouldn't have stayed on for me. I'd lay bets she'd be on-board for the whole three weeks, dancing her feet off on stage, tanning all day, partying all night. It's what dancers like to do.

I was touring the decks, stopping to talk to passengers, passing the time of day. I recognized a few who had stayed back-to-back. That is, they were doing two cruises without getting off. Saved packing and unpacking.

'You're the entertainments director, aren't you?' said a man in his fifties, tailored in blazer, buttoned-down shirt and slacks. 'Where's the naval lecturer, I want to know?' he blazed.

He was annoyed. He'd probably misread the information in the brochure but he was not going to admit it. An official complaint suited his nature, fed his ego.

'Our naval lecturer is not on this cruise nor is the author on creative writing,' I said. 'We have different lecturers every cruise so that passengers have a variety of topics.'

'I came especially for the naval lectures on Nelson and Trafalgar. I'm an ex-Navy man. Minesweepers.' He had narrow, bad-tempered eyes. I bet the mines had been scared.

'I'm really sorry, but you've missed him.' It would be tact-less to add that the naval lecturer was very good. 'We have lectures on Ancient Rome and Ancient Greece this trip as we are calling into Rome.'

'Historical rubbish,' he said, clearly annoyed with himself. 'I shan't go to those. The brochure clearly said naval.'

It was pointless to argue with him. He knew best. 'Why not try something else? Painting perhaps? You could paint pictures of ships.'

'Nonsense, I don't know one end of a paintbrush from the other.'

We could give him a pot of white paint and a brush.

The *Countess* was like the Forth Bridge, always being painted from bow to stern.

I let him ramble on for a few minutes, getting the spite out of his blood. His name was Commander Frank Trafford (retired), now living in Falmouth, still mad about boats or shipping of any size.

'So you could take over, if we needed support on the bridge?' I said, joking, but he took it seriously.

'Of course I could, anytime. I've commanded bigger ships than this. I'm not going to ruin my health, toasting myself to a crisp on deck. You'll find me in the library.'

Reading maps, I supposed, navigating our course. X marks the spot where the treasure is buried.

There was a good film on tonight in the cinema and I wanted to see it. Johnny Depp in *Pirates of the Caribbean*. Perhaps it would suit Commander Trafford. I didn't know which film it was of the trilogy. I was always missing them at home. I'd watch anything that Johnny Depp was in, even that scary headless rider film, *Sleepy Hollow*.

Mrs Fairweather was travelling back-to-back, which surprised me. I didn't think she would have the money. And she was without her friend this trip, Maria de Leger. Madame de Leger had gone home to write her memoirs entitled *How to Kill Off People Without Getting Caught*. It was a catchy title.

'It's lovely to see you again, Miss Jones,' said Mrs Fairweather. 'You were so kind to me last cruise, when I didn't know anyone. And, of course, Maria has gone as well. I miss her. We became such good friends.'

'Lovely lady,' I said. As long as you didn't upset her, say, by stealing her bicycle during the Dunkirk evacuation. Then she showed a different side to her nature, might harbour a grudge for years. Still, the circumstances had been a little traumatic.

'I hope you have a really peaceful trip,' Mrs Fairweather went on, fanning herself. 'You were rushed off your feet last time. I promise you that I shan't complain about anything.'

I had to laugh. She was a really nice lady. Perhaps there would be a new friend for her. I'd keep my eyes and ears alert.

'You play bridge, don't you? The bridge tutors are looking for experienced players to partner the beginners a few times. You might like to do that.'

'Oh yes, I wouldn't mind at all. Learning to play bridge is hard work. It does help to have a sympathetic partner.'

'There you are, then. A new career.'

We were sailing near enough to the coast of Portugal to see distant hills and cliffs but little else. A seagull fluttered in the wind, undecided whether to stay with us or fly back to land. A glimpse of land was enough to relax the passengers and they were out in full for a deck barbecue at lunch time. There was a selection of curries as well as the usual barbecue fare. The deck barbecues didn't smell as much as the back-garden variety. The fumes were carried away by the breeze.

Dr Mallory sauntered on deck. He was in tennis gear. He'd been at the nets, practising his service. My idea of ball co-ordination was picking them up from the court and stowing them in a pocket.

'Good night's sleep, Casey?'

'Excellent, but not long enough.'

'No dreams of leaking showers?'

'Not a drip.'

'I've done a few tests on the blood samples.'

He could be so irritating. Information had to be dragged out of him. I didn't want to hear that a body had been found under the floorboards of the cabin above. There wasn't much room between decks, only space for wires, water and sluice pipes. A body would have to be dismembered. I shuddered at the thought.

'Don't tell me. Miss Ember will demand to be flown home.'

'It was pig's blood.'

'She'll demand to be flown home.'

Somehow that was even more shocking. It became a deliberate act, not an accident. 'How extraordinary. Was it some joker from the kitchen? Someone with a sick mind?'

'Hardly a joke. Richard is interrogating everyone connected to the butchers' department. Lunch might be a little late.'

It was a joke but he looked concerned. He didn't like the idea either.

'I hope word of this doesn't spread around the ship. We shall have female vapours in every bathroom. They'll be too scared to take a shower in case the phantom pig blood man has paid a call.'

'You have such a neat way with words, Casey. I shall have to deal with the vapours, maintenance with the showers, Norton with the rumours, and you, dear lady, will have to fly out a few extra lecturers. How about relaxation and aromatherapy?'

'Which reminds me, I have to introduce this afternoon's lecturer, Theo Papados, at two p.m. in the lecture theatre. His subject is Ancient Greece, if you are interested, mythology and all that. He's apparently excellent. A man with academic knowledge.'

'It's my favourite subject.'

'Thought it was.'

His gaze was wandering towards the barbecue. There was already a queue. Most men like burgers grilled to a cinder, though our chefs were rather more experienced. Sam eased his weight from one foot to another, as if judging how much empty stomach he had to fill.

'If you don't mind, the carnivore in me calls,' he said. 'Quite loudly.'

'Save me a lettuce.'

I knew I wouldn't have time for any lunch. Theo Papados had brought slides to accompany his lecture and I had to check whether the theatre assistant had set up the equipment. A first lecture was often fraught with a nervous lecturer and an audience that didn't know what to expect. But once the lecturers got into the swing of it I could send Lee to make sure everything was in place.

My Conway Blue Line uniform was fine for making the first introduction, though a bit formal. No time to change. I grabbed a glass of water from a bar, thanking the barman for the ice. He grinned.

'The best Russian vodka, Miss Jones,' he said. He was only kidding.

The curved lecture theatre was already filling up. Passengers came early to get a good seat. It was the same in the Princess Lounge where the nightly spectacular shows were performed. Those stage side seats were at a premium. I've seen handbags at the ready.

The equipment was set up and the slides in place. I showed Theo Papados how to work the machine. He was apparently a lecturer who used notes and stood at the lectern. Our creative writing lecturer on the last cruise had talked from the heart, not a note in sight, roaming the theatre, moving among passengers, getting everyone involved, raising laughs.

Theo Papados was a short man with slicked-back hair, a Greek lecturer from London. He was immaculate in a dark suit and tie, despite the rising temperature. At least the lecture theatre was air-conditioned. I always had to bring a pashmina to watch a film when the theatre transformed into a cinema at night.

He was nervous, even though he was an experienced lecturer. I tried to make him feel at ease as we waited for the seats to fill up. It was going to be a full house.

'We have all been looking forward to your talks,' I said encouragingly. 'It's such a fascinating subject. And of course, we shall be calling at many of the places you'll mention in your talks.'

'Lectures,' he corrected.

'Sorry, yes, of course, lectures.' Big foot, Casey. Both size sixes.

At two p.m. promptly, I went up on to the small stage and introduced Professor Theo Papados, remembering his qualifications at various universities and the books he had published. I briefly mentioned the remit of his lectures.

He was still nervous, adjusting his tie, his cuffs. Very Prince Charles.

'Ladies and Gentlemen, a warm welcome for Professor Theo Papados.' There was a wave of clapping. Our well-fed passengers are a polite lot, as long as they are being entertained.

He adjusted his spectacles and launched into his talk, sorry, lecture. There was no need to worry about him. He knew what he was doing. He was pure circuit professional. I only hoped he would also circulate among our passengers and not shut himself away in his cabin. Our lecturers were expected to talk all day and half the night. We ought to provide free lozenges.

He was talking about the Greek gods Lieto and Zeus and their son, Apollo. Time for me to leave discreetly. I could read up on it later. I slipped out of the back exit.

I wondered about our celebrity, incognito. It obviously wasn't royalty with a capital R. Not even minor royalty. Nor were they political with a small p. Nor a television celebrity or soap star who would have been recognized immediately. An American film star perhaps? Who could it be? Maybe it was a faceless millionaire footballer, who earned more in a week than I earned in a couple of years. Wasn't anyone going to tell me?

The day was going well. Lee Williams and I were working

well as a team. I could see he was an entertainments director in the making. But not quite yet. There were still a few rough edges to file down. I got out my emery board.

My occasional afternoon treat was a cream tea at a table outside the Terrace Café, if I had missed lunch. A warm scone from the oven, a pot of fresh cream, strawberry jam and a cup of Earl Grey. My idea of calorific heaven. Forget the fat content.

I had cream rimmed round my mouth, not caring whether I would get into this evening's couture dress, when Richard Norton appeared by the table, his eyes sweeping over my gourmet feast. He looked a mite envious. He had to watch his weight, even at six foot three.

'What's the matter, Richard?'

'Can you come now?'

'Can't it wait?' I spread jam and cream over the second half of the scone. I was playing for time. 'I need nourishment. No time for lunch.'

'Miss Ember.'

'Oh, no, that lady again. I knew she would be trouble.'

'She's demanding to see you. Half of the purser's office have been trying to reach her but she won't let them in.'

'More pig's blood coming out of the shower?'

'No, she won't say.'

'Is she dying, bleeding to death on the cabin floor?'

'No, I don't think so. Her voice sounds pretty healthy.'

'Then she won't mind if I finish my scone.' I cut off a piece of succulent, cream-topped scone and popped it into his astonished mouth. 'There, that was worth waiting for, wasn't it?'

'Casey, you are usually so caring. I can't believe I'm hearing this flippancy. The last cruise, you were so kind and concerned. I think the world of you.' He was chewing slowly, relishing every taste, as if he was tasting me. He was looking down, devouring me too. The man was rampant hormones encased in a tight uniform. It was a warning sign. I had to be careful.

'And look where it got me,' I said. 'All those dreadful murders. Sometimes I can't sleep, thinking about them.'

'This is different to murder,' he said. 'This is malevolence.'

# Four
# At Sea

Lucinda Ember was hysterical. I could hear her high-pitched voice before I was halfway along A Deck. Nicky, her steward, was hovering outside, thinking again that he was going to lose his job. The stewards live in a state of perpetual panic.

'Don't worry,' I said, earning his eternal gratitude. 'I know it's not your fault. I'm here now. I'll take care of everything.'

I knocked on the door. 'Hello, Miss Ember. It's Casey Jones, remember me? Please let me in.'

The door was flung open. Her face was flushed, her arms flailed, and she swayed on her feet. Even her ruffle-fronted blouse was unbuttoned.

'This cabin is jinxed, I know it is. Come in, come in. Something is horribly wrong and I don't understand what's happening. I'm a passenger, paying top rate for this state-room. Why should anyone have it in for me?'

I didn't understand any of this either, but I took her arm and followed her inside. The sitting area looked neat and tidy. I checked the bathroom and saw that a new shower had been fixed over the bath.

'It's in here, in here,' she gabbled, taking me into the bedroom area. It had a king-sized bed, with blue quilted coverlet. One wall was entirely wardrobe drawers, shelves and hanging space. A door was swinging open, making a very slight noise.

'Look inside,' she cried. 'Look inside.'

So I did.

And wished I hadn't.

It was a very large dead rat, lying on top of a rack of evening shoes, its tail twisted round a gold strap. It looked sacrificial.

Ships often had rats but cruise ships kept them under control. We even had a pest officer on board. He was called immediately. But how could a rat have reached A Deck? If we had any, they were in the nether regions, where neither man nor cat would venture. I didn't know if we had a ship's cat.

'This is very serious, Miss Ember. I will look into it immediately, but the purser needs to be informed. Cabins are not really my responsibility.'

'But you are the only one I trust. You listen to me.'

'Don't worry. Come and sit down. It'll soon be sorted out.'

'I'm not staying here if rats are running round my stateroom. I want another cabin. I want a suite.'

'I think it's dead.'

She shrieked. She was wearing a Karl Lagerfeld ruffle-front blouse and high waisted trousers, and Christian Louboutin boots, nothing exactly picked up from charity shop rails. She was a mystery. Lucinda Ember looked as if she had money to spend, yet my instinct told me that she was trying to rip off Conway Blue Line. It happened sometimes and I had a feeling of apprehension. And it wasn't only her name. I had a fear of fire. Fire on board ship is our worst nightmare.

Passengers often complain about the strangest things. It was a sort of game, them versus us. The majority paid the fare without a single grouse. One lecturer worked it out that mile for mile, it was cheaper than riding on the London Underground system, even with an Oyster card. It was hard to beat that.

But others wanted to take the company to court for every speck of dust, every sleepless night, every bowl of cold soup. They wasted the enjoyment of the cruise thinking up a mountain of minor complaints. They could not wait to get home and switch on the computer and start a new file marked Complaints.

'Why not come on deck while this is sorted out?' I suggested. 'We're passing some lovely scenery. Let's sit on deck and enjoy it.'

'You can't fob me off with lovely scenery,' she wailed, wringing her hands. 'I know my rights.'

I didn't really know what to do with her. We would soon be in Palma and perhaps the thriving capital of Majorca would distract her from rodent problems. No other stateroom was

available for her. We were fully booked. There was no obvious
solution.

I took Miss Ember on deck and ordered Buck's Fizz from
an ever-attentive stewardess. It was a bit early for me but the
drink was welcome, nevertheless. The drinks came with
complimentary bags of nuts. They might be my supper.

'What's happening?' Miss Ember went on. 'Someone has
got it in for me.'

'I don't think so. Surely you don't have any enemies?' I
asked.

She was taken aback for a second. 'No, of course not. I've
no enemies as far as I know. I'm an ordinary citizen.'

'So this is a well-earned holiday?' I probed. No personal
questions was one of the ten commandments. But I needed
to know more about her.

'You can say that again. I'm a teacher. I teach maths. It's
the number one most hated subject on the curriculum. Nobody
pays any attention in class. The pupils talk, text each other,
go to sleep. Yet we all need to know how to add up, subtract,
multiply. It hasn't sunk into the wooden heads of today's
pupils. They think a calculator will do everything. Shop with
a calculator. Buy a house with a calculator. Get a mortgage
with a calculator.'

She had a point. I could understand the frustration.

'And this is your special holiday, a retirement treat perhaps?'

She looked insulted. 'I haven't retired. How old do you
think I am? Cruising is my hobby. I love the sea, ships, seeing
the world.'

She sounded a lot like me. I love the sea, ships, seeing the
world. Except that I worked and she paid. A slight difference
in status.

'I am at a loss to know what we can do for you,' I said.
My Buck's Fizz was of nuclear-strength. Perhaps the barman
thought I needed extra voltage. 'We don't have another stateroom available. We could fly you home from Palma, if you
want to do that. And no doubt Head Office would refund your
fare.'

'No, I don't want to go home,' she said sharply. 'You can't
fob me off with that. I want to see Elba, Corsica and all the
other ports of call.'

'Of course, I quite understand. We'll see what we can do.'

Nothing would appease her, as far as I could see. It was the purser's nightmare. He'd have to sort it out. Find some superior cabin that would suit her. All I could do was calm her down and keep her occupied. She needed a companion, someone who would help her maintain a sense of humour in the situation. Someone like me. But I was not going to volunteer.

'Isn't it a beautiful day?' I tried in cruise-speak.

'As long as you don't have a dead rat in your wardrobe,' she retorted.

I was going off Miss Ember. There was a limit to my sympathy. How could I remove her from my back so that I could get on with my work? I downed the rest of my Buck's Fizz in a slurp. Slurps are good. I even smiled at Miss Ember as I got up.

'Let me go and see what I can do,' I said, lying through my pearlies. 'Maybe one of the officers would move out of his quarters.'

Like the captain.

She didn't know that they had cramped cabins. I'd seen Dr Mallory's and although it was well furnished with wood panelling, he had few comforts and hardly enough room to swing a rat, sorry, a cat. And he had shelves of medical books. It was a bachelor pad.

I escaped to my office. There were a dozen emails to answer. Head Office seemed to think I sat there all day, waiting for incoming mail.

'Oh no,' I said. 'The singer due to join us tomorrow in Palma has become pregnant and won't fly. They are sending out a replacement, an X-Factor contestant called Judy Garland. No, it can't be Judy Garland. Surely no one would dare call themselves after her. She was a real star.' I held my head in despair.

Lee leaned over my computer screen. 'She calls herself Judie Garllund, weirdly different spelling, obviously something her agent has thought up.'

'What a nerve. No one has ever been able to sing like Judy Garland, not even her daughter, Liza Minnelli, and she was pretty good.'

'Perhaps it is her real name,' said Lee, chewing on a biro. It would stain his teeth blue. 'I bet there are dozens of Judy Garlands around this world.'

'But not on this ship.'

I was prepared to dislike her from day one. No one should use the name of an icon, especially a dead icon. I put my head on my desk. Sleep waves were closing my eyes in an iron grip. I could hardly keep them open. I was fighting myself. I blamed the Buck's Fizz.

'Someone didn't get enough sleep,' said Lee with sympathy.

'It was a very late night,' I said. 'Dripping blood, etc.'

'I heard about it.'

'And now it's a dead rat. Nothing is secret on a ship. I'm warning you. Everyone is watching you. Passengers watch the crew. And the crew watch the passengers. No one is immune. You've only got to break a toenail and it's round the ship in half an hour.'

He grinned. 'I'll keep my feet covered.'

'Would you like some time ashore in Palma?' I asked. 'As this is your first trip with us, I don't want you to feel over-worked. I can manage the arrival of Ms Garllund, whatever she calls herself.'

'Thanks,' he said. 'I'd like that.'

I'd been to Palma many times. It was one of my favourite ports of call, but I could give it a miss for once. The great cathedral, Sa Seu, would be there another time, glorious and Gothic, dominating the skyline. If only we knew what life had been like during the building of that superbly sited edifice. I tried to image the stonemasons in the fourteenth century, the bustle of carvers, the wooden scaffolding, the support carpenters, the sprawling village of lowly housing, the pigs, the cattle, the taverns with beer and women, detritus strewn through the narrow streets.

They little knew that their long years of work would become a paying tourist attraction, that living statues would stand immobile in the burning sun, a hundred cameras at the ready. It had once been built to the glory of God, now it was a shrine to the glory of commerce. Now you had to pay to view the glory of God.

'Good,' I said. 'The forecast is fine with clear skies. You'll enjoy it.'

I was getting this strangled feeling. I could not pin it down to anything – indigestion, homesickness, loneliness. Yet all these maladies existed. Everyone thought I was so cool and calm and yet inside I could be a turmoil of emotions. Sometimes I couldn't untwist the turmoil or find any answer waiting there. Things were never the same, no promises kept. Memories drifted and faded, recalling the fun of childhood. A childhood long gone, enduring four older brothers and care-free river days. I could steer a raft at four.

It was as if someone had altered the scenery overnight and every day was a new beginning. I had to struggle to find myself as an adult.

'Casey? Are you all right?'

Our Dr Mallory was now kitted out, full dress uniform, to sit at his table of eight, first sitting, order wine, talk to the lonesome, chat up the winsome, make everyone feel at ease and laugh. He had those special glittery eyes. Some passengers invented slight indispositions in order to bathe in those eyes. It was forgivable. I had never seen a man with such laser eyes. I wondered if he was born with them, used them to good effect at nursery school, comprehensive, university, accident and emergency.

'Ah, Sam,' I said, using his streetwise name. 'Have you come to save me from catastrophe?'

'Are you expecting something to happen?' He looked mildly concerned. 'Shall I take your pulse?'

'I can feel it in the air,' I said.

'Too much Buck's Fizz,' he said.

'Not funny,' I said. 'Dripping blood, dead rats, what next? What do you suggest, Dr Mallory?'

I needed more than this from him. Samuel Mallory had been my saviour during the last cruise. I expected some sort of rapport now, not that I was looking for anything more, anything romantic, anything permanent.

All I wanted was support. Pretty mundane and ordinary.

'I suggest you go dancing with your new deputy, the neatly built Lee Williams,' he said mildly. 'He looks the perfect partner for midnight strolls on deck and late-night heart-to-hearts.'

This was a new and distant Dr Mallory. He puzzled me. Was he a mite jealous? He was giving me the brush off in the politest way, as if all the traumas of the last cruise had never happened. If that's how he wanted it, then I would go along with whatever he wanted, try to forget how kind and caring he had been. Perhaps I had imagined the whole scenario.

'Sure,' I said. 'I'll take your advice.'

Soon we would be approaching the end of the Ancient World. It's where the Atlantic Ocean meets the Mediterranean Sea and medieval sailors thought the sea ended. In the early morning we would round Cape St Vincent and sail southwards towards the Strait of Gibraltar, heading towards Palma.

Sam went to eat at his table and I went to introduce the next spectacular show, *Me and My Girl*. It was a good show with great songs, and it was no hardship to sing its virtues. My dress was a Pucci turquoise silk with a silver belt. Very classy. Very expensive. I tried to forget how much it cost.

I did my usual circulation between shows, including catching a few mouthfuls at my table in the Windsor Dining Room. The food was out of this world. Officers were expected to host tables for at least a few meals. Passengers understood that we also had to work. It was a juggling act. There was always so much that needed checking. Quiz nights, ballroom dancing, disco, the casino, films, cabaret acts as well as the spectacular. No wonder passengers got worn out and caught up with their sleep on deck. I'd always watch a late film. Maybe I was born during a matinee at our local, the Dome. My mother would never admit it.

The cruise was going well, apart from the leaky shower and a stray rat. It couldn't last. I still had this uncanny feeling of distrust. Some passengers died on a cruise. It was one of the hazards. They came on-board, elderly and frail, and maybe it was a good way to go, after a lovely day at sea and a wonderful meal.

Dr Mallory passed me in a corridor but he didn't stop and talk. He merely nodded and moved on. This was not like him at all. It gutted me. What had I done to deserve this freeze-out?

Then he turned round. 'Nice dress,' he said, and walked on.

What did he think I was? A clothes hanger?

I was up on deck, taking my customary late night stroll, alone. The dark blue sea was rushing by as the captain made up a few miles overnight. The night sea and the night sky were magical. All those stars, twinkling away in a vast hemisphere of black velvet. Could they see us? What did they think of us?

I felt a difference in the vibration of the ship. The *Countess* and I were as one sometimes. She was slowing down. I could feel the sluggishness. I heard bells ringing, not the emergency count, but something different.

Then I knew what it was. Dead Slow Ahead.

For some reason, in the middle of the night, we were coming to a halt in the middle of the ocean. This huge ship was slowing down and coming to a complete halt. I kept back, well out of the way, as crew and officers began to gather starboard.

Something was happening. It wouldn't be in the ship's newspaper because I had already sent it to press. What did they expect me to do? Sub all night?

The great ship shuddered, still riding the waves, but not moving. I heard one of the lifeboats being winched down. It made a lot of noise, despite being well oiled and in perfect condition.

There were voices but I couldn't make out any of the words. I saw some figures clambering aboard, blankets being thrown over them. Then I saw a very small rowing boat being winched up on a hoist. It looked as if it was on its last legs, wood rotten, gaping holes, no oars. Had we made a flamboyant rescue? Saved some souls from the depths. Hallelujah.

I could smell their fear. The figures were exhausted, being helped to stand, being rubbed, given drinks.

Dr Mallory was on deck now, medical bag at the ready. The survivors were immediately hustled below decks. The lifeboat was winched back to its moorings. Crew were washing it down. The rowing boat had disappeared. Was I dreaming? In minutes it was as if nothing had happened.

Nobody noticed me in the shadows.

But I had seen it. I had been there. It had happened. I'd find out about it tomorrow.

# Five

# Palma

Everyone clammed up. I couldn't get a word of sense out of Richard Norton or Dr Mallory. They denied knowing anything, put on blank faces, and walked away. But I knew I was not wrong. I had been there. I saw it happening.

None of my friends among the crew admitted anything. 'You must have imagined it,' they said.

The passengers were unaware that anything unusual had occurred. They didn't know that we now had extra passengers. Names unknown, nationalities unknown. This plus our incognito celebrity made me very nervous. Call it intuition, call it imagination, call it sitting through too many films. We didn't want shutterbugs on the dockside at every port, filming shots for the tabloids.

Label it what you will, something wasn't right. I had been the only witness but I kept quiet about where I had been hovering. If things were that tight, I didn't want to be in the firing line. I would find out in my own good time. I always did, didn't I?

We had passed south of Isla Formentera and Ibiza and made our approach to the harbour of Palma by eight. We were fast alongside by nine.

I had once spent a delightful day on the nudist beach on Formentera. I walked for miles before there was a solitary patch for my beach towel. The sturdy Germans without even a thong did alarm me at first, but I got used to it. I mean, after you've seen one . . .

The water had been idyllic, clear, clean and blue. I swam topless but no one saw me. I was well past the lighthouse. No one had the energy to walk that far in the heat. I made it back to the quayside and the waiting tenders in good time. The sun was sizzling and my skin was not for burning.

'Didn't I hear a lifeboat being winched down in the night?' I asked Richard Norton again, in passing. 'Man overboard, was it? Did one of the crew slip on his mop?'

He shook his head. 'Your imagination, Casey, is what's overboard. You were dreaming.'

'One of the lifeboats is decidedly damp this morning.'

'Dew, my dear. Dew.'

I'd never heard of dew on board ship. Dew was a land thing, wasn't it? I knew that frost was frozen dew. But I didn't press the point.

Mrs Fairweather waved to me from a deckchair placed against the rails on the promenade deck. She had a pile of books beside her from the ship's library, and a tapestry holdall from which a pair of knitting needles were protruding.

'Miss Jones, don't tell me if you think I am being an old busybody, but I understand a poor lady travelling on her own has found a mouse in her cabin. How awful. One simply can't imagine a mouse running about on the *Countess*. Everything is always so spic and span.'

I didn't tell her that it wasn't a mouse. 'It is a clean ship,' I said. 'Spotlessly clean. Every inch is washed, vacuumed, polished or dusted every day.'

'I know. There's always someone around, working with a duster.'

'And through the night.'

'Then it must have been a joke,' she went on. 'But not a very nice one.'

'In very poor taste,' I agreed.

'I hear the poor lady is thinking of flying home from Palma,' Mrs Fairweather went on. How news travels. 'What a shame when we have such a wonderful cruise ahead of us, all those interesting islands. Full of history.'

'We don't have another spare cabin that we can move her to. The accommodation is fully booked.' That underground grapevine spread news faster than I could report it to Head Office. The passengers had probably spotted the celebrity by now and were laying bets on when he/she would come out of the closet.

'Might I make a suggestion? As I am also on my own, I should be very willing to share my cabin. There's a second bed folded against the wall which could easily be put into use. I have few clothes and there's plenty of hanging space for more.'

Some people are saints and Mrs Fairweather was one of them. She had a standard cabin with twin beds, one folded away as she said. Rather like mine in size. It was spacious enough for one, but pretty cramped for two.

'You really are very kind,' I said. 'Perhaps you should meet Miss Ember first and see how well you get on. Shall I organize some coffee for you, in the Galaxy Lounge in half an hour? If she decides to leave, the flight from Palma is not till the early evening.'

'Good idea,' said Mrs Fairweather, closing her book. 'She might think I'm a boring old fuddy-duddy.'

And Mrs Fairweather might not like the acerbic maths teacher. Lucinda Ember could be quite ferocious.

I hurried away to organize the rendezvous and some refreshments. The new cabaret artiste, Miss Judie Garllund, was due any time now, and I wanted to be around when she arrived. I had not met her before and knew little about her, apart from a brief CV and a touched-up photograph which her agent had sent.

She was wreathed in a halo of blonde hair in the photo, so it was difficult to tell what she really looked like. Sharply pencilled eyebrows and large glossy lips overshadowed her other features. At least she was not trying to look like the legendary Judy. She was any age, from eighteen to thirty five. I hoped she could sing.

Our agent in Palma always met new entertainers at the airport and laid on transport. Not my problem. Miss Garllund was due to have a twin cabin similar to the one used by Miss Ember the previous night. The steward would have serviced it ready for her arrival. I ordered some flowers from the florist. She didn't merit flowers but it saved them from a premature watery grave.

Lucinda Ember was bemused by the invitation to have coffee with Mrs Fairweather. She was in the middle of packing, having decided to go home and have her ticket price refunded. She was also hoping for token compensation, after enduring the trauma of rat and pig's blood.

'Why should I have coffee with someone I don't know?' she said, rolling up some gossamer stockings. 'I've enough to do. Could you send someone to help me pack?'

'Mrs Fairweather thought it would be nice for you to have a break before you leave the ship. In the Galaxy Lounge, then, in half an hour? I'll see if there is a stewardess who can give you a hand.'

'All right. I'll have coffee with this Mrs Fairbrother. Is she paying?'

'It's complimentary, Miss Ember. Mrs Fairweather is a very pleasant lady.'

'Isn't she going ashore?'

'Perhaps she's going ashore this afternoon. Some passengers like an afternoon stroll, especially if they have been to Palma before.'

This was eye-swivelling time. I'd had enough of Miss Ember. Still smiling, I managed to dislocate myself from her steely gaze and escape. The coffee was laid on in the Galaxy Lounge with a plate of nibbles. The pastry chef was very good at bite-size nibbles. I could have eaten the lot.

I introduced the ladies to each other. They were direct opposites. One warm and motherly. The other like a dragon drained of blood. I didn't hold out much hope of a rapport. They wouldn't have anything in common.

Miss Judie Garllund arrived with enough luggage to clothe the entire dance troupe. Someone had steered her to my office and she stood there, obviously ill at ease, pacing the floor. There was not much room to pace.

'I didn't want to come,' she said, dabbing at her forehead. 'My agent booked me on this cruise without getting my consent. I don't like flying. I don't like the sea. My cabaret act is pure theatre.'

I said nothing about the option to refuse to fly. Didn't she read the small print? She could have got herself out of flying with some convincing medical condition.

'How awful for you,' I said, going into overdrive. 'And we have been so excited about having you on-board. The passengers have talked of nothing else for days. It is a privilege to have you with us.'

Where did I learn this drivel? It came out of my mouth, streams of verbosity, till Judie Garllund began to relax and think the booking wasn't so bad after all. I ordered Buck's Fizz and it arrived double-quick. The barmen must have recognized an emergency call. I ate all the fruit garnish.

'You'll be surprised when you see the theatre in the Princess Lounge. It's big enough for spectacular shows and yet intimate enough for cabaret acts.' I even amazed myself. 'Passengers sit in armchairs with tables for their drinks. It's like a classy nightclub.'

'I'd like to see it,' she said, sipping her drink.

'You'll have a passenger-standard cabin and I'll arrange for you to eat in the Windsor Dining Room. Passengers always enjoy having a star at their table. It adds a lot to their enjoyment of the cruise.'

She was relaxing more and more by the minute. She was not unlike her photograph, with a halo of frizzled out fair hair, drawn-on black eyebrows and lots of lip gloss. Add a glamorous dress and some great songs, and she would pass.

'We have an excellent stage crew and I'll be able to arrange rehearsal time for you,' I went on. I was going to be there, at the back of the theatre, listening to every note. 'I'm sure you are going to enjoy your time on board the *Countess*.'

I used the word *enjoy* three times in the last minute. I needed a thesaurus.

'I'm still going home from Gibraltar. I don't fancy the Bay.'

'Of course. Your return flight is booked.'

Judie was looking a little less taut after her second glass of Buck's Fizz. It was also doing me a lot of good. Champagne on an empty stomach was euphoric. Had I had time for breakfast? It was a long time ago.

I phoned for a steward to take Judie and her mountain of luggage to her cabin. I was not sure if I could walk. We arranged to meet after lunch in the Princess Lounge. This would give her time to settle in and me time for essential eating. There was no time for me to go ashore, although I would have liked to visit the beautiful cathedral. The souls of all those stonemasons crushed me. How many had died in the building? Imagine falling from the high wooden scaffolding with no angel wings to catch you.

I went out on deck, needing air. The view of the sprawling port was magnificent, lines of huge ships, so many masts of gin palaces and millionaires' yachts. Halyards rattled and snapped like a chorus. How come all these people had so much money? And I worked my guts off to pay the mortgage on a small flat in Worthing? One day I'd have some furniture.

But the sun was dazzling, catching on white hotels and cascades of flowers from balconies. My bad humour vanished into the sea. It was my personal sunrise. The whole picture was beautiful. And I was here, not drenched on a windswept deck in some north-easterly storm.

'Ah, is it our popular Miss Casey Jones? And how are you? I don't seem to have seen you for days. The Bay was a bit brisk so I was busy.'

It was Samuel Mallory, looking cool and immaculate in black jeans and a white T-shirt, ready to go ashore, panama hat in hand. It was his off-duty look. The wind was teasing his dark hair but it was unable to disturb his granite stare.

'It is me,' I said. 'I haven't changed. I look the same as the last cruise.'

'But you've changed.'

'How? My hair is the same colour. I haven't put on weight or lost height. Maybe the loss of sleep has added a few wrinkles. But I am the same person.'

'No, you're not, Casey. You are not the same person. Remember the wonderful day we had together in the Azores? All that laughter? Where has that sweet and carefree young woman gone?'

I didn't know. It hurt to think of that day. It had been magic. We had been lost in another world, feeling so close, linked together as if life was soon to end.

'I'm sorry, Sam,' I said, using the shortened name he liked. 'But cruising is work. And that is what we are here to do. I keep passengers happy. You keep passengers healthy. We have something in common, but that's all.'

Dr Mallory hit the railing, hard fisted. He was staring ashore, into the distance. I could see a small tick in his cheek flicking. He was deep in serious thought.

'Don't be stupid, Casey. Get this into your head. Nothing was happening last cruise. I like wandering around with you. There are a couple of hours left in Palma before we sail. Let's walk around the town, breathe in the Balearics, relive their history. Casey, do yourself a favour, come down to earth for a few hours.'

I could not resist him. Miss Garllund could chill out by herself. So I missed her rehearsal.

I went as I was, in my blue Conway skirt and crisp white shirt uniform. No time to change. No time to eat, but Sam bought me a melon and strawberry smoothie with a straw from a harbour side stall. It was nectar. Sometime later we shared a crisp salad sandwich, thick with leaves and sliced tomatoes. We walked and talked, remembering other winds and other suns.

'Will you go around sometimes with me on this cruise, nothing special, simply keeping me company?' he asked. 'Save me from the marauding mob of sex-starved matrons?'

'You flatter yourself. I don't want to intrude on your social life.'

'I need rescuing, Casey. It should be in your job description. Any crew member in need of self-preservation should be allowed to call on your services.'

'You can take good care of yourself. Get the radio operator to phone you every half hour with an urgent cabin call.'

'Ingenious, Miss Jones, but I think I'd soon run out of patients. I'll always remember those hours in the Azores. You were so different then,' he said, with a sad shake of his head. 'It was very special.'

I fell apart when he said that. I still didn't know what to do. But we walked, occasionally brushing hands, along the front of Palma, like people who had all the time in the world before them, who had nothing to decide, who had nothing difficult ahead.

But the tour coaches were returning and work reared its demanding head, as people spilled out on to the dockside. Sam went to deal with any injuries. I had everything else. The tannoy blasted out the names of passengers who were not yet on board, or whose cruise cards had not registered. They needed rounding up. But many did not hear their names. The tannoy system did not reach every nook of every deck, despite what admin believed.

The sun was going down and a foreign coolness swept the decks. The theatre group had been rehearsing all afternoon while everyone was ashore. Tonight's show was ready to go. The girl dancers were exfoliating, shaving and eating lettuce, their hair in jumbo rollers. Don't ask me what the male dancers were doing. Probably the same.

It was time to change. Lee Williams was one of the last on board. He'd been swimming, walking, sightseeing, shopping, had a great time.

'I'm sorry if I'm a little late,' he said, breezing into the office.

'You can do the bingo and the quiz tonight to make up for being late.'

'My favourites,' he grinned.

'That's what I thought.'

The *Countess* was letting go her lines and backing slowly off the berth. Once clear, she swung the stern to starboard and headed out through the breakwaters. She then set course towards Barcelona, passing the western coast of Mallorca in the falling darkness.

There was time for a little circulating as first sitting passengers went into the Windsor Dining Room. I was wearing my favourite Amanda Wakeley dress for the twentieth time. It was a sleeveless, mushroom-shaded chiffon, full length with crystals on the curving neckline. The colour complemented the blonde streak in my dark hair and the dress was so cool to wear.

I'd forgotten all about the departure of Miss Ember, the purser's department having made the flight arrangements. So I was more than surprised to see Lucinda Ember and Mrs Fairweather arriving at the dining room entrance together. They seemed to be talking quite pleasantly, but parted to sit at their different tables, either end of the room.

I was full of curiosity and made a devious detour towards the large table where Mrs Fairweather was sitting. She caught sight of me and waved me over.

'My dear, I have to thank you. It's all worked out perfectly. Lucinda is not leaving the ship after all. She's happy to stay on for the cruise, although she will still apply for compensation when she gets home. It was a dreadful experience for the poor lady.'

'That's good,' I said. 'So Miss Ember was pleased with your offer and is going to share your cabin?'

Mrs Fairweather's faded blue eyes sparkled. 'No, it's better than that. I'm going to move into her stateroom. It's on A Deck, you know. I was born in the country and I'm not afraid of a mouse or two. She says she's got masses of room and a balcony. Won't that be lovely? I've never had a balcony before. There's a king-sized bed which they can unzip and divide into separate beds, so that's no trouble. It's all worked out beautifully.'

For the time being. The odds on it lasting did not seem too hot and I didn't want Mrs Fairweather to be upset about anything. I would feel responsible if anything happened to her.

Fingers crossed for Mrs Fairweather. Everything else crossed for myself.

# Six

# Barcelona

Once in the turning basin, the *Countess* swung short round bow to starboard before thrusting sideways to the berth. It was a tricky manoeuvre. Passengers hung over the rails for their first glimpse of the great city, church spires and tall buildings receding into the distance. The onion-topped spires of the still unfinished Sagrada Familia dominated the skyline.

Most of them thought it was like parking a car. Forty-five thousand tons of steel like parking a car? Need a good lock on the wheel.

A little shopping time along the colourful boulevard, Las Ramblas, would be therapeutic, if Lee could hold the fort in the office. But I was doubtful. Miss Garllund was proving an odd sort, one minute cooperative and the next a feral cannon. She didn't like the colour of the lighting. She didn't like the timing. She wanted to change the days when she was scheduled for shows. The schedule was practically hewn in stone, everyone knew that. Only a monumental disaster would alter the rota of show spectaculars and individual artistes.

I saw Miss Ember and Mrs Fairweather taking the first shuttle bus into the heart of the town. Chalk and cheese, but I wasn't sure who was which. It was good to see that they were on speaking terms. Their first night had passed amicably, it seemed. Grapevine reported that they had gone to the quiz night and collected the second prize.

Lee was already in the office. He looked up from his desk. 'Miss Garllund has called three times. She will only speak to you.'

'Fine. I'll speak to her when she calls the fourth time. Do you know what it's about?'

'It was fairly garbled. She needs a set built or something.'

'A set built? What does she think we are? A construction firm?'

I switched on the computer and ran through my emails. All the usual spam. I deleted the rubbish. Why did these people think I was in the market for buying Viagra and anatomy extensions? I did not need a personal loan nor had I applied for a job with an international bank.

'She wants a Juliet balcony.'

'Then she'd better find a Romeo to build it for her.'

'Tut, tut, Miss Jones,' Lee teased. 'Where's that sweet nature of yours?'

'I left it in bed, where I should be now.'

'Your fault for getting up so darned early.'

'I prefer to do my mile run before the promenade deck gets clogged up with passengers. I like them, of course, but they walk in rows. It turns any exercise into an obstacle course.'

I switched off my mobile and shot out to the lift. There might be time for a quick breakfast in the Terrace Café before having to deal with set building. The queue was not too bad. Barcelona was a regular port of call and many had been there before. A walk along Las Ramblas and a leisurely coffee at a street cafe would suit them. They didn't have to hurry, could take their time.

The organized tours were enticing but they meant an early start. I'd have liked to see the jagged mountains of Montserrat or take a boat trip along the Tossa de Mar's beautiful coastline. One day perhaps, as a passenger, and subject to weather conditions. One coach trip recently spent four hours stranded in fog. Being marooned on a coach, looking out of a window at cloud was not much fun. At least they got their money back and complimentary wine at dinner.

There was a free table on deck, so I took my bowl of fresh fruit outside. The view was inspiring. Sometimes I thought I ought to live in Spain, eat oranges and mangoes, teach English, become a tour guide, write historical romances. The warmth and the relaxed atmosphere suited me.

'May I join you? For a moment of mooching?'

Dr Mallory had a tray full of carbohydrates and fats. He had a crew-necked jersey on as if it was cold.

'That's a very unhealthy breakfast,' I said.

'It's called fuel,' he said, spearing a delicious-looking hash brown and popping it into his mouth. 'Your body doesn't get any fuel, that's why you are underweight for your height.'

'My weight is my own business,' I said, spearing a slice of melon with similar enjoyment.

'It'll be my business when you collapse from malnutrition. Only don't do it in port. The paperwork is horrendous. So, are you going ashore today?'

'I was going to but doesn't look like it now. We have a new cabaret singer aboard, Ms Judie Garllund, who wants a Juliet balcony.'

'Not, *the* . . .? I'd build her anything. Does she want a yellow brick road?'

'With difficulty,' I said. 'That one's been dead many years.'

'True.' Sam's eyes twinkled over his spectacles. 'A momentary mistake on my part, on hearing such a famous name. She was a real star.'

'Are you going to tell me about the unscheduled passengers who came aboard at midnight with a small beaten-up rowing boat? I recognized the blast for dead slow ahead. We came to a stop to pick them up.'

'Some unscheduled who? Where did you get this rigmarole from? I don't know what you are talking about.'

The Berlin Wall again. He was not going to tell me anything.

I was still hungry, but I was not going to succumb to a croissant in front of this annoying man. Biscuits were stockpiled in my cabin as Ahmed also didn't think I ate enough. But biscuits did nothing for me. I fed them to the seagulls. They weren't fussy if they were past their sell-by date.

'Give me a ring if you're going ashore,' he said, nonchalantly, folding mushrooms into a rasher of bacon as if he was operating. 'We could have a coffee.'

'I might need counselling by then. Juliet balcony to fix.'

'I could do that, too. The counselling, I mean.'

Our gorgeous doctor was a poppet as well as being far too handsome for his own good. But I didn't want him in my life. I didn't want anyone. I was a cool cat who roamed the roofs on her own. Isn't that a line from some film?

Miss Juliet minus a balcony was waiting in my office before I had even wiped the juice off my mouth. She was frocked up in mauve taffeta and black tights, despite the rising temperature.

'You take your time,' she said, tapping my desk.

I could see I was in for trouble. I put on my most soothing face. 'Sit down, Miss Garllund and let's sort this out. I understand you want a balcony?'

'Yes, a Juliet balcony, for one of my songs.'

'A whole balcony for one song?'

'Yes.'

'You do understand that this is a ship?' I could get the sack for this. At Head Office, it's called insolence. 'We don't carry an excess of wood or ironwork, or a crew of set-builders. Barcelona probably doesn't have an IKEA store where we could buy a kit.'

'This song requires an extra dimension.'

'Perhaps you could sing a different song?'

Her halo of frizzled fair hair began to wobble. She was beginning to lose her composure. Oh dear, I'd wondered if this could be the foreseen trouble, and now I was seeing real trouble, charging straight ahead for me like the headless killer in *Sleepy Hollow*. It would have been interesting, if it hadn't been so frightening.

No Johnny Depp on horseback to rescue me. More's the pity.

'I won't be treated like this,' she said in a shrill voice. 'I have my show, which people have loved all over the world. They expect this song. It's my signature tune.'

What signature tune? Pardon me, I'd never heard of it.

'Would a rope balcony do?' We could do rope. Plenty of rope aboard.

No, apparently rope would not do. Miss Garllund ranted for a full five minutes till we were both exhausted. I'd have built her the Taj Mahal by then to get her out of my office. Lee put a coffee in front of me.

'I'll see what I can do,' I said, defeated.

'I want it by my first rehearsal,' she said, flouncing out.

Lee looked at me with sympathy and admiration.

'White flag time,' I said, gulping the coffee. It went down like a flush of champagne. But the effervescence didn't last long. My taste buds shrivelled. 'This is awful coffee,' I added.

'Sorry. The machine is on the blink.'

'Get it fixed.' I immediately regretted those abrupt words. 'I mean, will you please phone maintenance and get them to fix it.'

'No problem. I knew what you meant.'

This easy-going Lee was on my wavelength. It was a relief and I sent him a grin of thanks.

'By the way, that dead rat,' he said.

'So you know about the rat too.'

'Everyone knows about the rat. I think it had been dead for several days. It therefore follows that someone kept it in a refrigerator.'

I shuddered. The thought put me off eating anything that had been anywhere near refrigeration.

'Have you told Richard Norton this possibility?' I was not one for stealing other people's bright ideas. 'Give him a ring.'

'OK. I'll add private investigator to my CV.'

'You do that. I'm just about to add set-builder.'

The Juliet balcony was impossible. We were not geared up for sudden artistic demands. Scenery was always minimal. Spectaculars had the odd pair of substantial pot plants, or archway, or backcloth. Drama should be in the imagination. I doubted if I could persuade Miss Garllund to sing on an imaginary balcony.

I was still thinking about what I had witnessed on deck. Where were these extra passengers now? Were they mingling with the passengers or were they under guard? And what were they doing, out in the Atlantic Ocean, in something the size of a seaside dingy?

'So when are you going to tell me about these extra passengers we've taken on board?' I asked Richard Norton, catching up with him on deck. He pretended not to understand.

'Extra passengers? What on earth are you talking about?'

'They came aboard in the middle of the night.'

'Tut-tut. You've been dreaming again.'

Richard was toweringly tall, and his stride was difficult to keep up with. He didn't stop walking, trying to shake me off like an irritating kitten that was clinging to his heels. This was not like Richard, though of course I had given him the push off last cruise. Some men harbour a grievance for months.

'Someone has got to tell me,' I said, clutching his sleeve and stopping at the same time. He was brought to a sudden halt. 'What happened?'

He turned abruptly. 'Don't do that.'

'Don't do what? Try to have a civilized conversation with

you? Try to get some information? How can I do my job if
I don't know what's going on? Passengers stop me and ask
things. Do you want me to look like a proper moron?'

He looked a little taken aback by my onslaught. We were
supposed to work as a team. I was not all couture dresses and
vintage gowns.

'I didn't know you were interested,' he said.

Pathetic. He plummeted in my esteem. Take off the uniform
and what have you got? A quivering, overweight, fleshy mass
rejected from the services. This was harsh, I knew, but then
I'd had a battering that morning. I was not in the mood to be
gentle or forgiving. Or fair.

'So how about coming clean? I'm not asking for anything
that's confidential. OK, I know we have a celebrity aboard, travelling incognito, for as long as it takes everyone to suss out who
it is. But what about the survivors who were picked up out of
the water in the middle of the night? Is that all hush-hush, too?'

'I don't know what you are talking about,' Richard said
stiffly. 'Nothing happened in the middle of the night. You are
overwrought.'

I took him off my Christmas card list. It was the least I
could do. I was not putting myself at risk for him again. I'd
had enough of this prevarication.

'Don't ring me when you want a favour,' I said, steaming.
'I'll run my team and you run yours, if that's the way you
want it. Of course, we are a lot brighter so we'll get there
before you have put even one foot out of bed.'

I hurried off to find the stage crew before I really lost my
cool. If Judie wanted a balcony, then perhaps they'd fix her
up something round the funnel and she could sing her number
from up there. It would be different.

But I didn't get as far as finding anyone from the stage
crew. There was a crowd of passengers clustered round the
shop window of the Bond Street salon which was always
closed when the ship was in port. Surely the fashion model
was not that exciting? They had some nice sports gear and
evening clothes, but definitely mature cruise styles.

'Miss Jones. Can you do something about this?' Professor
Theo Papados, the lecturer, turned to me. I wondered why he
wasn't on shore. Lecturers usually liked to wander around,
picking up information. 'It's not funny.'

I pushed my way through the crowd, wondering why I had to sort out everything. For a moment I couldn't see what was causing the disturbance. The model was wearing vintage Chanel, that wonderful stylized black and gold camellia dress, similar to the one Miss Ember had been wearing two evenings ago. Similar? But it had to be the same dress, down to the last detail. Chanel would not have made two gowns exactly the same. This was Miss Ember's own dress, on the model, in the shop window.

But what made it really scary was that a blown-up photograph of Miss Ember's face was pasted over the model's oblique features. It was a grotesque parody.

'Just a joke, I'm sure,' I said quickly. 'I'll get the manager to remove it.'

If I could find Derek Ripon, the manager of the shop. He'd probably gone ashore by now. It was a day off for him and his staff, unless there was major stocktaking to do.

But it wasn't only the dress or the photograph that were causing consternation among the passengers. I followed their downward gaze. The model was standing in a pool of blood, her pointy toes dripping.

Shop models don't normally bleed. They are without soul or arteries.

# Seven

# Barcelona

It was move quickly time. Priority: move the evidence. Priority: photograph the evidence. Priority: return evidence before it was missed. All at the same time. I wasn't sure why I needed the gruesome model photographed. Perhaps because I thought no one would believe me.

Professor Papados was still standing there, apparently mesmerized. Maybe it reminded him of some Greek myth.

'Professor Papados,' I said. 'Could you do me a favour? Do you have a digital camera? Could you take a photo of this shop window, now, as it is with the model?'

'I can do better,' he said, coming to life. 'I have a mobile phone which takes photographs. The days of the Brownie are over.'

'And you can get a print from the mobile?'

'Of course. If you'll let me use a computer. It'll be in your hands by tomorrow,' he promised. He seemed quite pleased to be doing something. Most of our lecturers mixed well. Perhaps he was shy and was now thawing.

'Thank you. I'm really grateful.'

The Professor went into Lord Snowdon mode and was taking photos from all angles. Memo to self: do not make fun of Professor Papados, ever again. He was a good egg, or some dish similar.

I found a member of staff who could open up the shop which was a miracle. We put up window drapes and removed the offending model. It was definitely Miss Ember's dress. It was still wearing her perfume and some of the flowers were crushed where she had sat on them, The bodice and waist had been pinned back so that it fitted the size zero figure of the model.

I examined the dress carefully and was pleased to find there was no damage, no cuts or splodges of blood. After all, it was vintage. It ought to be in a fashion museum.

Before the cleaner came to wipe the floor, I scooped up a sample of the blood into a screw-top jar lifted from the beauty counter. They always had empty ones on display. The head of the model came off and I put the head in a carrier bag. Please, nobody trip me up and have hysterics, start screaming, bring security running. If security could run.

Another investigation for the ship's doctor.

'More blood?' he would say, raising those dark eyebrows. 'Really, Casey, this is becoming obsessive.'

But first, the Juliet balcony. The stage carpenters were not enthusiastic. They agreed to provide a low platform from stock, which Judie could stand on. They also had a plywood lattice archway from an old show which would frame the singer. But build a balcony?

'Can't be done, Miss Jones. Not enough time. No spare timber,' they said, as if they were being asked to build a house.

'It hasn't got to be substantial,' I said. 'It's only for a song. How about ropes, garlanded with flowers? Would she know the difference if they were well disguised?'

They agreed to ropes and flowers. I would have to buy them several rounds. Ropes and flowers were thirsty work.

My few hours ashore were slipping further away. I wouldn't even have time to dash to the nearest market. I love open-air markets, all the fascinating sights and smells. My souvenirs were always bought from ramshackle stalls, made locally. I'm a market groupie.

'Miss Jones. You're still on-board?' Samuel Mallory was obviously about to go ashore. He was in those sharp black jeans again, white T-shirt, Armani jacket. Señoritas of all ages would swoon at his feet. He was irresistible. I couldn't vouch for the señoras. Draw a black lace mantilla.

'Busy morning,' I said. 'Sorry, more blood for you.'

He read the label on the jar. 'Lancome Hydra Zen, Neurocalm. How interesting. Is this a new species?'

'It's a sample of blood.'

'Another shower?'

'Shop window.'

'And what have you got in that carrier bag which you have clutched to your bosom?'

'It's a head.'

He nodded sagely. 'I thought it was. Do you want me to take that from you as well? I'll put it somewhere for safe-keeping. You don't look too happy, carrying it around.'

'I need to think about what to do with it,' I said vaguely.

'I understand. Heads are always a problem. Especially un-attached heads.'

'Don't laugh at me. It's a headache.'

'Unattached heads are always a headache.'

He was laughing at me now, quite openly. I went to walk away, get on with my work, but he caught my arm firmly. 'I prescribe a walk on shore, Casey. Get your feet on dry land, take five. Doctor's orders.'

'Sounds good.'

'How about a walk on Roman remains? We could walk the line of the walls, gates, ramparts and temples? Look at a few chunks of stone?'

'You know I would love that, but I don't have enough time. You can't even tempt me with the Shoe Museum or the Chocolate Museum.'

'Pity. I fancy the Chocolate Museum.'

So that's how I came to be walking along the wide sea promenade of Barcelona, skirting the squares, the statues, the grand monuments to every explorer who had ever left those shores. I only had time to grab a hat, sunglasses, crew card and some money from my cabin. It was going to be a short visit, but Sam was right. A break would refresh me. Get my thoughts straight.

He was an easy companion, talking trivia, anything except heads and blood. He was amused by the Juliet balcony, made several suggestions, all totally useless, but fun. His imagin-ation let rip. 'How about a rocking balcony made from a hammock?'

'I'll run it past her.'

'One of the passengers this morning asked me if I was qualified,' he said.

I hid a smile. We get a lot of funny remarks. A passenger once asked me who was steering the ship when the captain was at his cocktail party. 'So, what did you say?'

'I said I was practising.'

We broke into silly giggles. I had to sit on a wall to stop

myself falling down. I waved my hat in front of my face to create a breeze. It was getting hot. The sun was like a furnace. There were going to be a few red faces this evening.

'Have you time for a quick coffee before I walk you back to the ship?' said Sam.

'Yes, a quick one. But I can walk myself back. She's over there.' The white upper decks of the *Countess* were visible among all the other ships in the harbour. I only had to point myself in the right direction.

We sat at a small street cafe, under a striped shade, watching the world pass by, drinking big cups of good coffee. A small plate of snacks appeared, mouthfuls of sweet and spicy things, some made of honey and coconut. Some tiny brown birds, species unknown, hopped about on the pavement for crumbs. Their wing feathers flapped, gathering in cooler air.

I found myself telling Samuel about the new style of window dressing in the Bond Street salon. He didn't interrupt until I had finished. He looked thoughtful.

'It appears that someone has it in for Miss Ember,' he said. 'I wonder who it can be and why. She seems a reasonable lady.'

'She's not the easiest person to get on with. Although our amiable Mrs Fairweather seems to be coping. They were still talking this morning.'

'Mrs Fairweather could get on with a boa constrictor. She sees the best in everyone. She thinks you're wonderful.'

I nearly choked on my coffee. 'Well, I am wonderful,' I agreed, dabbing my mouth. 'Most of the time.'

'So this is the blood that you want me to test. I stored it in a refrigerator in my surgery while you fetched your hat. I also took a quick peek at the head in case it needed to go into the currently empty morgue. I'll get it photographed for you and let you have it back.'

'Thank you,' I said, humbly. 'I don't know what to make of it.'

'Has the dress been returned to Miss Ember's stateroom?'

'Yes, I didn't think there was any point in keeping it. No clues or anything. It isn't as if a crime was committed and we needed forensic tests for debris or hairs.'

My forensics were a bit elementary. I knew they could

discover amazing things, but from vintage material? It would be loaded with years of trace elements.

'Will her steward be in trouble?'

'Yes, I think so. I've arranged for the head steward, Karim, to replace Nicky with someone else, just for this cruise. It seemed sensible. Let it all calm down. It probably wasn't his fault. Nicky couldn't be expected to guard the stateroom night and day.'

'But Miss Ember would expect it. She'll expect the earth, moon and skies now,' said Sam. 'She'll demand the royal touch.'

'Do you think she needs to be told? Couldn't we keep it from her? She hasn't returned to the ship yet and all the evidence has been removed. There are only the photographs taken by the good professor.'

'Although it might be easier, I doubt if the captain or the purser would approve of such a devious plan. I should imagine that she has already been offered a considerable refund on her fare. And wasn't she offered a flight home? What else can they do?'

'I know,' I said, suddenly. The next step in the compensation chain came to me in a flash. 'They'll offer her another cruise, in lieu, completely free, with pounds to spend on board.'

'Wow, nice one. I'd put up with a few dead rats for one of those.'

'Are you thinking what I'm thinking?'

But Dr Mallory would not be drawn. He got up and stretched languidly. 'Time to go shopping. I need a new panama hat. Perhaps Adolfo Dominguez will have one in my price range. See you back on board, Casey. Don't get lost. You go in that direction, remember, no detours round street markets.'

He tipped his current hat and set off towards the shopping district. He'd done his good turn for the day. St Peter had written it down in his notebook. Another gold star for the doctor's record. They'd reserved his white feather sofa.

I retraced my steps, not looking forward to various imminent interviews. First a report to the purser, then maybe the captain would want to see me. Would I have to tell Miss Ember? On the plus side, there was thanking the professor for the photographs he had so graciously taken, and informing our star that she had the Juliet balcony that she yearned for.

In all, a busy day. Thank goodness for the oasis of calm ashore. I was back on an even keel.

The light on my computer was blinking frantically. I had emails from practically everyone on board ship, including security. It was like Facebook. I saw the purser first, then the manager of the Bond Street salon, Derek Ripon (he was known as Rip-off behind his back), and Captain Nicolas. I managed shocked, efficient, protective, traumatized, helpful and mystified, all at the same time. Quite a feat.

They couldn't blame me for anything. Only assess the way I handled the situation. Nine out of ten for handling, apparently, said the captain. Mr Ripon was annoyed that I had taken the model's head. I waffled on about tracing the photograph, the sort of glue or Sellotape being important evidence.

'Well done, Miss Casey. Not easy for you, I'm sure. You coped very well in the circumstances,' said Captain Nicolas. 'Would you be prepared to tell Miss Ember? I shall understand if you would prefer not to. In which case, the security officer will do it.'

'I think it would be better coming from a uniformed officer,' I murmured, opting out. Cowardly, Casey. I was allowed this one, I reckoned.

'Quite right. I'll call Richard Norton.'

'I'll be on hand, of course,' I added. If she started throwing things at him, I'd be there to catch.

'Yes, that would be appropriate,' he said, closing the interview.

Passengers were returning from the day ashore and all the trips. The ship was starting to hum again, busy and vibrant, the security machines working overtime as they screened purchases and cruise cards. Everyone seemed to be in a good humour. They'd had a lovely day and were looking forward to a shower, a drink, a gourmet meal and a show. In any order.

All the pre-departure checks were made and the *Countess* was ready to sail. No one had been left behind. Passengers were blissfully unaware of the hectic behind-the-scenes activity. Lines were let go and the thrusters were used to move the ship off the tight berth. Once clear, we steamed out towards the northern breakwaters, passing small and large shipping, passengers waving to anyone who cared to wave back.

I left a message for Richard Norton, asking him to let me

know when he was going to see Miss Ember. Meanwhile I
had to get ready for the evening's mad rush round the shows.
It would have to be a simple, understated outfit. I did not want
to look overdressed for the interview with Miss Ember.

My grey silk with black beading was understated. I added
a silver belt and plain silver slippers for running about in. No
time for careful hair styling. I gave it a quick brush, then tied
it back with a silver ribbon and let it fall around in general
disorder.

It was an Abba show this evening. I did the introduction
on stage and then fled to the first sitting where I had time to
host my table for ten minutes. They were a pleasant group,
pleased to see me, telling me about their various busy days.
Time for a starter. Spinach and ricotta tortellini in cream and
mushroom sauce sounded good. My taste buds nearly fainted
with joy. There was barely time to gobble the fillet of bream
with lemon mayonnaise, and I was almost too full. But not
too full for a generous half glass of wine.

'I'm sorry,' I said, finishing the glass. 'I have to go. Maybe
one evening I'll manage a whole meal with you.'

'Don't worry, Casey. We get to eat your share of the sweets.'
They meant the petit fours served at the end of dinner.

On my way to the back entrance of the Princess Lounge
theatre, I noticed a phalanx of stewards keeping everyone
away from one of the side bars. Something was going on. I
peered in the glass windows and recognized the broad shoulders in an immaculate dinner jacket. It was Dr Mallory.

He was on his knees, working on someone on the floor of
the bar. He was using a portable defibrillator to restore a heartbeat. A shirt had been opened and I caught sight of a hairy
chest, but not the face. Dr Mallory was working ceaselessly,
as if his patient was coming and going. I could see the sweat
on his forehead as he tried to maintain a heartbeat.

It must have been ten minutes that I stood there, helping
to keep inquisitive people away. The brightly lit graph was
now showing a flat green running line on the screen. His
patient had gone.

I heard Sam's voice, dispirited and low, noting the time of
death. He had worked so hard and lost. He packed up the
defibrillator and closed the lid, then got up from his knees
and wiped a hand wearily across his forehead.

'What was it?' I said at the doorway, stopping him as he made to leave. For a moment, my face didn't register. He looked shattered.

'Cardiac arrest. He had a dicey heart. There was a chest scar where he'd had open-heart surgery. Probably a mitral valve problem.'

'Do we know who it is?' I asked.

'One of yours,' he said. 'Your Greek lecturer, Professor Theo Papados, I believe. Nice chap.'

# Eight

## Toulon

It was a shock. My few meetings with Theo Papados had always been pleasant if a little tepid. He had been a reticent man as academics often are. Now he was dead. It didn't seem fair, to be wiped out like that, so fast and undignified on the floor of a bar. Perhaps he knew he was living on borrowed time.

Then it hit me. Practicalities. I'd have to get another lecturer flown out. The passengers needed their daily dose of culture. Head Office would find someone. They had lists of contacts. Did I have time to email them straight away?

Then it hit me again. Where was his mobile phone? The one with the photos of the tampered model? I actually needed them. Although most people believed me, some photographic evidence would not go amiss.

Derek Ripon was already making irritated noises. I had a nasty feeling that he thought I had planted the dress and the blood to discredit him. Tell me how, O Master of the Shop Keys? He had once refused me a staff discount, but I hadn't taken it to heart. Rejection was part of life. I was used to it.

I sent the email. I did the shows. Passengers started to ask questions. The ship's grapevine was in overdrive. Miss Ember was predictably still upset, but what could we do? We couldn't upgrade her to the penthouse suite. It was occupied by a very pleasant couple from Manchester. She began writing a furious letter while Mrs Fairweather made consoling cups of tea.

'But you still have the dress, Lucinda,' she said. 'It's only been in a shop window. And there's no damage to it. In fact, your lovely dress has become quite famous.'

Thus spoke the voice of common sense.

The professor's mobile phone was nowhere. I made

enquiries all evening without seeming too indiscreet or insensitive. No one had seen it. His steward searched Professor Papados's cabin for me, after I implied that the doctor needed the phone. But it was not there. Nor was it anywhere in the bar where he had collapsed. It had disappeared.

It seemed a year but was only hours before I caught up with Dr Mallory. He seemed quieter than usual, less flamboyant. His face was drawn. The loss of a patient had affected him and there had been a stream of passengers returning from the trip ashore with minor injuries. They wanted their money's worth, draining his energy with lengthy descriptions of other slight indispositions.

'Hey, Dr Mallory,' I said. 'You look in need of some tender loving care. I know of a good doctor.'

'Lead me in his direction,' he said. 'Or a pretty girl would do. Have you got one as pretty as you?' A glimmer of amusement returned to his eyes. He had relaxed for a few seconds, knowing his flippant remark would annoy me.

I brushed my escaping hair out of my eyes. If he wanted to flirt, he could have flirting. 'Now let me see, yes, I can do tender. A soothing flannel to the neck, cool drinks, soft music. Loving care, even better, hot water bottle, lullaby, tucking you up in bed.'

'I like the sound of the tucking up,' he said. 'When could you start?'

'As soon as I have Professor Papados's mobile phone.' I regretted saying it the moment the words were out of my mouth. The amusement faded from his eyes. 'I'm so sorry,' I went on. 'I saw how hard you tried to save him. I was there, watching from the other side of the bar window.'

'It should have worked,' he said. 'He had a good chance. I thought I was in there winning, then suddenly it all went wrong and I don't know why. I can't explain what happened.'

'And you don't know why?'

He was staring out of the window as if going over it again and again in his mind. He was tapping his brain for clues.

'No, Casey. It should have worked. I was clearly winning. I have a friend back at Guy's, a cardiac consultant. He might be able to tell me. All the odds were in Theo Papados's favour. Then suddenly it changed. As if something else kicked in.'

I didn't really understand what he was talking about, but I

was ready to listen to whatever he wanted to say. At the same time I was guiding him toward to the Terrace Café where the midnight buffet was in full swing. It was not gourmet food but a selection of sandwiches, pizzas, soup, cakes, ice cream. If you are starving at midnight, cold apple pie can look good.

I took a tray and filled two bowls with broccoli and Stilton soup, put a couple of rolls on a plate, and went over to a window seat. I guessed he hadn't eaten. The night was black outside, the sea rolling by endless and soundless.

We sat down and he nodded his thanks towards the soup. He'd had nothing substantial since our coffee under the balconies of Barcelona. This soup was a favourite of mine. I even made it when I was home at my flat in Worthing. A sudden pang of homesickness caught me. My home and all my things were special to me. It even had a distant view of the changing sea. I collected shells from the beach, blue glass, crystal bits and pieces. I loved the sharp edge of real cut crystal.

'Have you met Miss Jones?' he began to sing under his breath, as he dipped in his soup spoon. 'You're a girl who understands, I'm a man who must be free.'

I sang through the next few lines for him. 'And all at once, I own the earth and sky.' I took a pause. 'I know you are man who must be free, Sam.'

'But you've been so cool lately,' he said, breaking up the roll and dunking it in the soup. 'I wondered what I had done wrong.'

'Nothing. You haven't done anything wrong. It's me over-reacting. I was reading too much into a friendship by mistake, of course. Friendship is all I want. Nothing more complicated.'

'Sure,' he said. 'I understand. Just friendship. It suits me.'
'Good.'

'As long as we have a few special moments together.' He winked.

His words took me by surprise. Sam was a smoothie. He knew what to say, how to say it and when. The fact that he was finishing up my soup did not come into it. He was hungry and his appetite had returned. He needed his strength for tomorrow's patients. Tomorrow was an unknown factor.

'That was below the belt,' I said.

'I'm a doctor, remember. I'm allowed to go there.'

Tiredness made it impossible for me to flip back a smart reply. So I let him win on points. We went on deck for the shortest of walks. The wind was getting up. It was a north-easterly course towards Toulon. My hair was blowing all over the place and I had lost the ribbon. I wished I had a pashmina round my shoulders.

Sir Galahad wasn't feeling the cold and didn't offer his jacket. I used his body as a wind shield. It meant dodging about around him which Sam thought was a new kind of dance. 'Like it, like it,' he said. 'It could catch on.'

He walked me back to my cabin on E Deck and left me with the briefest kiss brushing my right cheek. It was like the wing of a butterfly.

'Sleep well, Casey. Sweet dreams. Hope they are all about me, in a better mood.'

'I'll let you know.'

I was out like a light, as soon as my head touched the pillow. I don't remember my dreams but they were not frightening. Some time in the night I was aware of noises along the corridor but I was too far gone to never-never land to wake up and wonder about them.

Maybe it was cleaners. Maybe it was repairs. But there was certainly some activity which was noisier than usual. At night, the ship was full of vibration, creaks and shudders, even on the most modern of vessels.

Maybe it was Juliet's balcony being constructed. Judie Garllund was intruding into my dreams. She had that much influence on my life. It was unacceptable. I wanted my dreams to myself.

The next port of call was Toulon. It was new to me, a large military port on the south coast of France. I wasn't bothered if I went ashore or not. It wouldn't be very interesting. Armoury and guns. Lee could go and look at warships.

But I changed my mind rapidly on first sight of the harbour as the pilot eased us into a tight berth. We were all fast port side to the quay by a minute after 8 o'clock. It was a delightful place, sunlight already streaming on to a harbour lined with cafes and pastel-washed houses. A marina was bobbing with yachts and fishing boats. There was a lovely French feel about it, leisurely and less bustling than Barcelona.

Judie Garllund pounced on me before I had even finished my mile on deck. She was flushed from hurrying after me.

'I don't call this service,' she said. 'You running around the deck before my set is ready for me. I expected to rehearse all morning.'

'Have you checked with Trevor, the stage manager? There may be another activity in the theatre this morning. Sometimes the crew have a fire drill.'

'I should have thought my rehearsal takes precedence over any fake fire drill.'

'It might not be a fake fire,' I said.

She looked stunned for a second. 'I don't believe you. Perhaps when you have sorted your priorities, you'll meet me in the Princess Lounge theatre. There may be a few other things I need.'

'Is your real name Frances Ethel Gumm?' I asked.

'No, of course not. What a ridiculous thing to say,' she said, with a flounce. She hadn't a clue what I meant. So much for being a genuine Judy Garland fan.

My lazy deck-side breakfast was not to be. I rushed through a lukewarm shower and hotter coffee in my cabin, put on the Conway Blue Line uniform skirt, shirt and scarf. Very formal. The hat would have been going a touch too far.

'What's all this? A meeting that I haven't been invited to,' said Dr Mallory, passing me in a corridor. He was also moving at a quick trot, bag in hand.

'I am about to face the wrath of Juliet on her balcony.'

'No blood, please.'

'I may push her off it.'

'That's allowed.'

My spirits surged, like a firework let loose. A few light exchanges and he made the morning sunny. Careful, Casey, this is dangerous ground for your size sixes.

Judie wasn't there, but her balcony was. I thought the carpenters had done a terrific job. It was only a foot off the stage but then this is not the Globe Theatre. They had looped garlands of flowers across the front, and above was a latticed arch. Lit properly, it would look good. Good enough for one song.

Trevor appeared beside me, a growth of stubble on his chin, bags under his eyes. He looked tired. Heavy night, perhaps.

'Is the wicked witch of Oz coming in?' he asked.

'Very soon.'

'Then I'm disappearing fast. I had her breathing evil spells down my neck all yesterday and although I am partial to buxom blondes, this one gives me the creeps.'

'Have I got to deal with her on my own?'

'That's what you're paid for, Casey.'

Perhaps he wasn't partial to tall brunettes with a blonde streak either. We had always got on pretty well, but were not exactly buddy-buddies. He was efficient and I was efficient. We recognized each other's efficiency. And that was the limit.

I caught glimpses of Toulon harbour through the windows. It was enticing me with thoughts of a glass of cassis at a harbour-side cafe or a bowl of delicious bouillabaisse, my all time favourite fish soup.

Richard Norton, the security officer, strolled into the lounge. He was also in uniform. No time ashore for him either.

'I thought I'd find you here,' he said.

Great detective work, I thought. Watch out, Sherlock Holmes.

'Hi, Richard,' I said, bright and breezy. 'How can I help?'

'I hear you've been making enquiries about Professor Papados's mobile phone. Is there a reason for this?'

Now, my residual feelings of affection for Richard Norton had evaporated once I realized he was keeping quiet about a Mrs Norton under lock and key somewhere in the suburbs. But I wasn't going to hamper his enquiries about anything he might be investigating. I'd come clean.

I took him over to one of the cosy tables for two that were perfect for night-time romancing. Dust was dancing in the air. But this was eight thirty in the morning, stark daylight, not a drink in sight.

'Professor Papados took some photographs on his mobile, which I asked him to do. He didn't have time to get them to me. I don't know if he even had time to get them printed. But I would like to have them.'

'Photographs of what?'

This man was seriously slow. He was an ex-Marine. Perhaps he got an extra hard bump on the head in some muddy manoeuvre.

'The model in the Bond Street shop window. The model

who was wearing Miss Ember's Chanel gown. The model whose feet were dripping with blood.'

I spelled it out to him.

Richard heaved a sigh of relief. 'It's not very serious then, is it? I mean, it doesn't matter whether we get these photos or not. It was just a prank.'

'Quite a nasty prank. Those photos might hold a clue as to who did it.'

'I don't think so. I think we can call off the search for the mobile,' he grinned as if in a Western movie. He got up. 'I'll leave you to deal with your entertainers while I do the serious stuff.' He went out, laughing. Not sympathetic, at all.

I wandered up and down the tiers of the theatre, wasting my time waiting for Judie Garllund. I had better things to do. My computer was bulking up with emails. They all had to be dealt with before I could go ashore.

Now, I am all for artistes being dead serious about their work, and I had dealt with some divas in my time. But this woman was in a class of her own. I think she thought she was Judy Garland. A reincarnation, perhaps? I had not heard her sing *The Trolley Song* or *Somewhere Over the Rainbow*. I'd not heard her sing at all. It was becoming a worry.

Judie Garllund arrived, bursting through the doors with an armful of music. She was geared up in a floral dress with fishnet stockings and a big straw hat. Her face was fully made-up – false lashes, hair extensions – for a rehearsal?

'Where are the musicians?' she said, not even acknowledging my presence. I said nothing, went down the carpeted stairs, taking my time, wondering what would happen next, and sat myself in a comfy armchair.

'Did you arrange for the band to be here, this morning, at . . .?' I looked at my watch. I'd been growing nails for such an occasion. 'Nine twenty a.m.?'

She looked blank. 'I beg your pardon?'

'Your musicians. Did you ask them to rehearse with you this morning? It is normal procedure to make your own arrangements for extra rehearsals. Of course, they may be ashore by now. Toulon is a really pretty port to explore.'

She began foot-tapping and pacing. 'No one told me that. You said nothing about making my own arrangements.'

'You didn't tell me you were having an extra rehearsal this morning. You've had your scheduled rehearsal time. There's your Juliet balcony, as requested. I hope it suits you.'

She didn't even look at it. She was looking anywhere but at the balcony. It was absurd behaviour. Her music fell to the floor and I went down to help her pick the sheets up. I glanced at some of the titles. They seemed an odd ball collection, not a show with a theme.

'So what exactly do you call your show?' I asked. 'Does it have a theme?'

'It's called *Judie Garllund and Songs*,' she said.

'Very snappy,' I said. 'We have you down as *Judie Garllund and Movie Greats* in the ship's newspaper. At least, that's what Head Office told us to put. Do you remember giving them your programme?'

I was beginning to tire of this pantomime. I was here. She'd got her balcony. I could leave now and get on with the morning's schedule. Suddenly she launched herself at me, banging at my face with her fists.

'This is all your fault,' she shrieked. 'You're trying to make me look a fool. I won't have it. I want to see your superior.'

I managed to dodge her blows. 'You're looking at my superior,' I said. 'I am in charge. I'm not trying to make you look a fool. You're doing that very well by yourself.'

She hit me again. Her nails were sharp. This was becoming a cruise awash with blood. At least now it was my own blood dripping down my face. I tasted it on my lips. It had a melon flavour.

# Nine
# Toulon

'Hell hath no fury like a Juliet scorned,' said Dr Mallory, dabbing at my scratches. 'My nurse should really be doing this but she's a little squeamish about theatrical fights. It must be hereditary.'

'It wasn't a fight. I never touched her.'

'Don't worry. There are reliable witnesses. She went for you, although we don't know what you said. It might have been provocative.'

'It was completely unprovoked.'

'Perhaps it's the way you look, so cool and confident, in your uniform. Whereas she is the opposite. You know, shapeless, useless and a mess. Do you know where she went?'

'I've no idea. Trevor dragged her off me and at first I couldn't see because of the blood in my eyes. Perhaps she's gone ashore.'

Dr Mallory attached a butterfly strip to the cut on my forehead. 'There, you can hardly see any difference. The grazes will soon heal. No make-up for a couple of days.'

'I look awful,' I said, regarding my new face in a mirror. 'Swollen, red and bruised.'

'More for the grapevine to speculate over at drinks time.'

'I am beginning to think that providing topics for gossip is my main role on this ship,' I said, pulling a streaky fringe of hair down over the cut. It bounced back. I needed some mousse or gel. 'What about that blood on the model's foot? Have you had time to test it?'

'Sorry, I haven't done it yet.'

'Do you have a stock of blood donor's sachets in your surgery? Have you checked them?'

'Now, there's a thought. No, I haven't, but it's next on my

list. I'd assumed that the person putting the dress on the model had a nose bleed.'

'I think it's more sinister than that.' I was feeling low and depressed.

Dr Mallory patted my hand in an irritatingly paternal way. 'You concentrate on your gorgeous stage shows and leave all the sleuthing to me. As you know, it's become a fixation with me, solving all the problems you create.'

'Now that's not fair. I don't create the problems. They seem to land on my plate.' But those eyes were twinkling and I knew he didn't mean it. He was taking a rise out of me to see if I would respond.

'That's my girl,' he said, getting up to clear the debris off his surgical tray. 'That's sparked you up a bit. I don't like seeing you look so down, especially when the beautiful harbour of Toulon is still on our doorstep. Isn't it a lovely place?'

The medical centre was well equipped with its own dispensary, microscopic equipment, X-ray and treatment room, two bedded wards for passengers and separate accommodation for crew. There was an emergency room with ECG equipment, oxygen, ventilators and sea rescue outfits. The second sister was also a trained midwife, which could be useful. We had several passengers with baby bumps. Further down the spotless white corridor and discreetly out of sight was the operating theatre, and further still, tucked away, the morgue.

'Thank you for doing my face,' I said.

'Anytime, but not too often,' he said.

I took a lunchtime break to walk round the harbour. It was bathed in sunshine and the streets were cheerful and elegant. I walked further into town and at every street corner was a cafe with people outside enjoying a liquid lunch. It was getting hot and I saw a young woman cooling her legs in a circular fountain, her black, strappy dress hitched up to her thighs. She smiled at me. I was almost tempted to join her. A breeze blew some of the water in my direction. The spray flew like diamond droplets through the air.

I sat in the shade under the Three Dolphins fountain for a few moments before retracing my steps and going back to the *Countess*. I couldn't really spare any longer. Work still awaited me. There might be an email about a new lecturer to replace poor Professor Papados. I also wanted to know about the arrangements for his body. He might have a wife or family who would want a funeral in his home-town. There were several options.

Head Office had not wasted any time. They had a possible replacement but could not confirm it until the following day. We now had several consecutive ports of call so there was no urgency. There are no lectures on port days. A breathing space.

But I still had to deal with the volatile Miss Judie Garllund. There was no question of bringing a charge against her, despite the viciousness of her attack on me. I was not badly hurt, having dodged most of the blows, due to my dance training and her inaccuracy. But her whereabouts was my responsibility. We couldn't have her causing mayhem in the dining room, throwing forks about or thumping people with wine coolers.

I decided to have the purser confine her to her cabin for the time being. It seemed safer. We would postpone her show until she had calmed down or showed some remorse. A letter of apology would go a long way.

But Madame had taken herself off to her cabin, locked herself in, and was only answering the door to room service. I hoped she enjoyed the in-house movies. They ran the same film endlessly until the morning change of programme.

Miss Ember phoned. She wanted her Chanel dress dry-cleaned but did not trust the on-ship cleaners. 'They wouldn't know what to do with a dress as special as mine,' she said. 'Will you take it ashore at St Tropez tomorrow and find some specialist shop? They must have one with all those stars living around there. People like Posh and Becks wouldn't take their clothes to any old dry-cleaners.'

I doubted if they even bothered with dry-cleaning. They probably bought new. Now this was a dilemma. It was not part of my duties as entertainments director to run shore errands for passengers. I was there to make sure they were entertained and happily occupied. But I could see her point of view.

St Tropez was not a docking port. It meant climbing in and out of a tender on a possibly choppy sea, and it might be a problem carrying a heavy dress. Miss Ember didn't want to spend the day ashore looking for a specialist dry-cleaners. I could find out an address from our port agent. They always knew everything.

I couldn't understand why she wanted it cleaned. No one had worn it, only a polystyrene dummy. The thought of someone even touching her vintage dress must be giving her the wobbles.

'All right,' I said, stifling a sigh. 'I hope I shall have time. I'll get the one hour service.'

'And the company will pick up the bill?'

'Of course.'

Then it twigged. The cost would be expensive. One less bill for when she got home. She'd probably throw in a few extras to have cleaned at the same time.

And she did. She added a long evening skirt and a pashmina that she said had touched the dead rat in the wardrobe.

'I couldn't possibly wear them again after having touched a rat,' she shivered as she handed over the clothes. 'You don't mind, do you, Casey?'

Did I mind? What could I say?

Watching the *Countess* leave Toulon was an exercise in brilliant seamanship. She was tight against the quay, port side, with hardly any room to manoeuvre. She could not back off the berth because the curving stone quay was too close for comfort. Instead, inch by inch, the captain eased the stern away till it was clear of the stone wall, swung the ship bow to port, then reversed diagonally out of the harbour mouth.

This was real seamanship, easing the huge ship away with a gentle and delicate touch, as if she was a mere feather on the water. I wanted to applaud.

Once the *Countess* was clear of the harbour, she could steam forward and set course towards St Tropez. It was a beautiful evening with a light scattering of cloud and a moderate south-easterly wind. As I watched Toulon growing smaller and fainter, I hoped that another time, perhaps, I would be able to go ashore without a bashed-up face, and really explore its delights.

I wondered if the young woman in the strappy dress was still bathing her legs in the fountain, or was she by now meeting her boyfriend at one of cafes? Were they holding hands, gazing into each other's eyes?

We saw, watched and observed so many people in other countries, if only for a moment, whose lives went on after we had gone. We were transient, yet sometimes we were affected by what we saw. The carefree attitude of that young woman had touched me. I wanted to be free like her.

I once rescued a puppy, nose stuck down a roadside hole, on a Greek island. The more it panicked and scrabbled about, the deeper it got stuck. I dug it out with a plastic spoon and fork begged from a nearby cafe. I found its mother chained to a nearby tree, without water. The rescue task continued with hunting for a plastic food container and filling it with water. It took all afternoon. I only just made it back to the ship and my work as deputy entertainments director on that line. Even then, back in the early years, I cut it fine, returning to the ship. Time I learned. A case of arrested development.

Mrs Fairweather returned late to the ship, but without Miss Ember. I met her struggling through the reception area. She was laden with shopping.

'Wonderful day,' she said, struggling with her bags. 'Lovely shops. Such pretty things. I've got a lot of grandchildren.' I took some of her bags as she tried to get into the lift and find the deck button at the same time.

'So Toulon is the tops?'

'Yes, I really like it. A very pretty place.'

'And Miss Ember? Is she back on board?'

'Yes, Lucinda came back hours ago. The heat was too much for her. She said she had to look for something she had lost.'

'The purser's office has all the lost property. She should ask them.'

'I'll tell her. I don't know what she has lost.' The lift reached A Deck and Mrs Fairweather staggered out with her shopping. 'Thank you so much, my dear. I can manage from here. Have you done something to your face? You look a bit different.' She was so diplomatic.

'Just a tiny accident,' I said. 'Walked into a door.'

'You should be more careful.'

It wasn't far to the Terrace Café so I took the opportunity of a quick cup of coffee and a calorific eclair. Cruel that something so light and delicious could be lethal.

Lee met me and his face lit up. 'Glad you are all right,' he said. 'I heard about the fracas. Thought you might be wounded beyond recognition. Would you like me to do both the evening shows?'

'Now that would be really helpful, since our resident doctor has barred make-up and I can't go on stage without a few dabs of concealer.'

'All you ever need is mascara,' said Lee, soothing my ego instantly. What a lovely man. 'Why not take it easy for the evening?'

'Shall I do your quiz night? Is that a fair swap?'

Lee looked relieved. 'That would be great. We have some competitive teams and I was in danger of being lynched last night because of a decision I made on an answer.'

The quiz was always popular and some of our passengers were pub quiz regulars and knew practically everything, from geography to sport and back again. It would make a change – I could host my dinner table without rushing away and dress smart casual.

I laughed. 'I won't make any controversial decisions but agree with the majority. It'll be fun. Thanks a lot, Lee.'

Smart casual was a pair of white linen trousers, a silk camisole top in pale turquoise and a shimmer jacket. All from M & S, their spring collection. Flat sandals with a butterfly bow. My feet were grateful to be spared heels.

Everyone was politely curious. My face was the main topic of conversation at the table till the starter courses arrived. What everyone was having was discussed and compared for taste, appearance and acceptability. It was always the way. Everyone wanted to try the other dishes, like a panel game. My starter was crumbled avocado topped with shrimps in a pine nut sauce. The rest of the meal was a gastronomic haze.

The upstairs bridge bar was packed with teams ready to pit their wits against each other. Some were quiz addicts. Some were volunteers or press-ganged to make up numbers. Most teams were six strong.

I knew I was going to enjoy this. I had all the answers.

'For our new quiz-comers, let me explain briefly the elements of this quiz,' I said, seating myself at the centre table with all the questions neatly stacked in front of me. They were produced for the company by an expert quiz master for each cruise.

'There are eight sections – general knowledge, movies, geography, history, music, television and sport. And the very popular faces section. Each section carries a maximum of five points, with the exception of music and faces which are worth ten each. So the total number of points is fifty. First prize is this excellent bottle of champagne. Second and third prizes are bottles of wine.'

The audience cheered, already happy and well-fed after a good meal with wine. They had pens and answer papers at the ready, drinks on the table, brains unzipped and ready to go.

'General knowledge, first question,' I announced in the hush. 'Who won the Nobel Prize for Literature this week?'

I liked doing the quiz, especially when I had the answers in front of me. I even managed to work the CD player for the snatches of music, which was a first for me. CDs usually came apart in my hands. 'We want the title or the band,' I said. I didn't know any of them. Not my era.

Then I handed out the sheet of ten celebrity faces. One sheet to each team. The celebrities were from all walks of life. Pop, politics, TV, films, theatre, finance and of course, royal families from around the world. Some of the photos were taken a long time ago and that's when it became difficult. Queen Elizabeth, as a little girl, standing by her dolls house, was one of them. The buxom girlie tabloid celebrities all looked the same to me. I could do this section, had a stab, some guesswork. Got nine of them right.

I collected in the answer sheets and put on some music while I retired to a nearby side room to mark them. There was a swift advance to the bar to top up drinks.

'Don't be too long, Casey,' some wag called out. 'We can't wait forever for that champagne.'

'Just give us the bottle now,' jeered another team leader.

In the quiet little room I began marking the answer sheets. They were a clever bunch. Outside the dark sea was rushing by, and through the glass I could see stars shooting about all over the place.

My spine froze with fear. Someone was staring at me through the glass. It was no more than a glimpse of a shape. It could have been a man or a woman.

# Ten

# St Tropez

Passengers thought they would be bumping into movie stars and celebrities on every street corner of St Tropez . . . Brad Pitt, Angelina Jolie, Sienna Miller, Robbie Williams and Geri Halliwell. But they were going to be disappointed. The stars kept away from this crowded, noisy, traffic-throttled French harbour town and departed to their villas along the coast or hidden in the hills.

The narrow streets were crowded with tourists and locals. It was almost impossible to walk on the pavements. Powerful, fume-belching motorbikes and scooters roared round the harbour road, scattering pedestrians. The harbour was packed with a clutter of rattling masts, huge white luxury yachts and floating gin palaces.

I knew what it was like. I'd been there before. If I didn't have Miss Ember's dry-cleaning, I would not have gone ashore. The *Countess* was too big to come into port and was anchored half a mile out at sea, north-west of the harbour. The wind was variable, force two.

There was a continuous tender service taking passengers from ship to shore, but it was not an easy manoeuvre for crew or passengers. The *Countess* was besieged, port and starboard, by flotillas of noisy motor boats and speedboats coming out to stare at us and take photographs. They created a huge swell and the landing platform, hung and secured to the side of the ship, was rocking and banging. It made stepping on to the tender a scary work of art.

Burly crew members, used to timing the step aboard, helped passengers make that step across an ever-changing swirling gap of choppy sea. The elderly and the lame were game for the leap but not agile enough. Many of them gave up and decided to spend the day on board, rather than be fished out of the water.

Several of the tenders stood guard at sea, trying to dissuade the pesky speedboats from approaching the ship, but the local sightseers didn't realize or care how dangerous they were making it for everyone else. They zoomed in close, taking photographs, creating choppy waves which splashed into the tenders.

'Can't the captain do something about this?' said Commander Trafford as he waited to go ashore. 'He should phone the coastguards. Get them to do something about all these dratted speedboats.'

I waited until the queue had diminished and went carefully down the swaying steps to the landing platform. I was clutching Miss Ember's precious dress. It would be curtains for my salary if I dropped it in the water though it was probably insured.

Two crewmen took my arms and timed my step on to the tender. I only just made it as the tender rocked away.

'Thanks,' I called out, shaken but not stirred.

The oppressive heat hit me immediately as I stepped ashore. A burning sun was high in the sky. St Tropez was a hot and heaving mass of people. My map was useless. Some of the narrow cobblestoned streets were not named or had names hidden by advertisements. Once picturesque fishermen's cottages had been vandalized into arty boutiques selling overpriced clothes and souvenirs. It was shops, shops, shops everywhere. Shops and cafes and amusement arcades. The old St Tropez had vanished along with its dusky pink and ochre houses.

It was a scandal. St Tropez had once been such a delightful harbour.

Occupation number one was jumping out of the way of taxis and scooters racing round the roads and pavements. They didn't hesitate to mount the pavement and career through pedestrians if something was coming the other way. It was a walking nightmare. And I was suffocatingly hot, cotton trousers clinging to my skin. I longed for a swishy skirt, for air round my legs.

The sooner I found this dry-cleaners, the better. It was at the back of the old town and I was glad to rid myself of the bulky dress bag. The assistant did not seem in awe of the vintage

Chanel, but slung it on to a hanger and pushed it along a rail with a flick of her long hair. So they got a lot of Chanel.

I paid for the vastly expensive one hour service for all three items and decided to kill time by walking round the big open-air morning market. Some of the stalls had shades. It was becoming unbearably hot in the crowd. The market was the usual mixture of cheap clothes, food and souvenirs. I gave up looking at displays of local cheeses and smoked meats and found a nearby cafe.

My money had run out. I only had enough euros left for an iced lemonade. It was delicious and cooling. Soon I was sucking broken ice and cupping the coldly dewed glass in my hands. Time ticked away in the irritatingly slow way it does, when it knows it's being watched.

I spotted passengers combing through clothes on a Moorish style stall. They had a rail of long, loose cotton Arab kaftans which men or women could wear. My cotton trousers and T-shirt were longing for some air swishing round my legs.

In an hour, the vague assistant had said. I went back to the dry-cleaners on the dot of twelve. I wasn't going to risk them closing for a long lunch and endless Mediterranean siesta. The assistant took my receipt and stared at it for a long time as if it was foreign.

'*Pardonnez-moi, madame,*' she said, 'but zee dress has already been collected.'

'That's not possible. I'm here now and this is the receipt. Please look again. It's a Chanel dress, black and gold, not easily mistaken, and a black chiffon evening skirt and a pashmina.'

She tossed her long glossy hair and went behind the serving area, into the back of the shop. She was gone so long I thought she had emigrated. She returned, carrying the skirt and the pashmina in carrier bags.

'Here you are,' she said.

'But where is the dress, the black and gold dress?'

'The dress was collected some time ago. You take skirt and pashmina.'

'But who collected them? Who was it? They didn't have the receipt. I have the receipt.'

She shrugged her slender shoulders and regarded her nails. '*Je ne sais pas.* I did not see them. I was getting cappuccinos.'

It was like talking to a shop dummy.

'I'd like to see the manager,' I fumed. 'Would you please fetch him?'

'The manager has gone for zee day. He will not be back till tomorrow.'

'Is there anyone else here?'

'Only zee valet.'

'Valet?'

'He does zee cleaning.'

So that's what they call them these days. They valet the garments. I was getting mildly homicidal. My expression did not betray how much. No wild-eyed bull in a cleaning shop.

'Perhaps I could talk to him.'

'Perhaps . . .' She went out back again. She was like one of those changing figures on a Swiss clock. And she took as long. A young man came out, wearing cut-off jeans and tight black T-shirt. He smelled of chemicals, the stuff they use to dry-clean. He was bronzed, very handsome.

No wonder the girl took such a long time. He was time-consuming material.

He grinned at me, all sparkling white teeth. 'Zee black and gold dress, *oui*?' he said in a fetching accent. 'You wants zee dress?'

'Yes, please. I want the dress. Here is the receipt.'

'Zee dress 'as gone,' he said like a magician, flicking his hands. '*C'est tout. Voila.*'

I was losing my patience with this pair. 'I should like to search for it myself. May I have a look round? You may have overlooked it.'

'Izz not allowed,' said the girl. ''Ealth and safety.'

'I'm not going to blow up the place. Please describe whoever came in and collected the dress. You have given the dress to someone who did not have a receipt. That must be wrong.' I was speaking very slowly and clearly in order not to explode with annoyance.

'I was not 'ere,' she said.

'Nor was I,' said the young man.

'It was zee manager,' they said together.

I could visualize terrible repercussions if I returned without the dress or a very good explanation.

'Please write this down on a sheet of your headed stationery and explain that the dress has been collected by someone else and at what time it was collected.' I said it all even more slowly and clearly.

It still threw them. They did not understand headed stationery. They didn't have any. They only had receipts. I made them write it down on a couple of receipts and sign and date it. By now, they were giggling together, so God knows what they were writing. It was not in English. I wished I had an instrument of torture. They deserved the stocks at least.

I put the receipts in my shoulder bag. I'd had enough of this charade. I wanted to be gone.

'Money, please,' said the girl.

'Money? What for?' I suddenly thought they were going to charge me for the brief statement they had written.

'For the skirt and the pashmina.'

My lemonade coolness had completely evaporated by now. 'I have already told you a million times, I have a receipt,' I nearly yelled. 'This is the receipt. Look at it. I have already paid. The one and only receipt for dress, skirt and pashmina.' I waved it around. 'You gave it to me yourself when I paid the cost, to you, in euros. Remember?'

'I was not 'ere,' she said.

'Of course, you were out getting cappuccinos,' I said nastily. 'The receipt wrote itself. If you came down to earth for five minutes and did your job instead of snogging with Adonis here, somewhere out back, you might remember.'

'My name's Pierre,' he said with a shrug, sending the girl a seductive look. She melted, wishing I'd get lost.

Their English was better than they made out.

Everyone wanted to return to the ship at the same time. There was a thirty-five minute wait in the broiling heat. As a crew member, I had to let passengers go before me, even if I needed to get back to my work. There was little shade and the water-less and hatless were sitting on any wall or rock or rail. Some began arguing with the officer in charge of each tender.

'Can't you take a few more?'

'Look, I was here before that woman.'

'She's waltzed up to the front of the queue.'

At least they were letting the wheelchairs on first. There was some civilized behaviour.

'Ruined St Tropez, haven't they?' said an elderly couple turning to me. 'Turned it into a playground.'

'At least they rebuilt the old town in the original style, after the bombing,' I said, taking a long drink of water. I offered them an unopened bottle but they said they had plenty.

'It was badly bombed in the war, wasn't it?' they spoke in alternate sentences. 'Must have been a pretty place once. It was that Brigitte Bardot film that started it all, wasn't it? With a bit of luck, we'll get on this launch.'

We did. Once on board, I heard from the officer at the helm the reason for the long delay on shore.

'A bit of an accident,' he said, deftly steering the tender away from the quayside. It was bliss to feel the cooler air, though the speedboats were racing alongside us like a swarm of locusts. The swell was splashing into the cabin.

'Not serious, I hope.'

'It was as choppy as hell. The wash around the landing platform was making it pretty tricky. People were standing up as they always do, wanting to be the first off. The tender tossed on a big wave and half a dozen passengers fell over. One woman fell awkwardly and broke her leg. Another broke her wrist, and a lot had nasty cuts and bruises.'

'How awful,' I said. 'A broken leg? What a way to end a holiday.'

'We couldn't get the woman with the broken leg off the tender or up the gangway, so Dr Mallory took her back to St Tropez and arranged for her admittance to a local hospital.'

'I suppose she'll be flown home, poor woman.'

'It's those bloody speedboats,' the officer said, under his breath. 'They ought to be prosecuted. I'd mow them down. They've no idea how dangerous it can be.'

They were still buzzing round the *Countess* like a swarm of idiots when our tender reached the ship. We were tossing and rolling on the swell. It felt very unsafe.

'Don't stand up until I say so,' the officer said loudly to the passengers. He was nervous, trying to look calm.

Fortunately, there were no more accidents. Our transfers were orderly, if a bit daunting. I put my faith in the crewmen and their firm grip on my arms to see me safely across the gap. Unfortunately, it also reminded me of the last cruise when I missed the ship and had to step aboard from the pilot's launch. Half the passengers had been leaning over the rails watching my undignified arrival.

I said goodbye to the nice couple and hurried to my office. Lee looked up from his chaotic desk. I don't know how he managed to work so efficiently when his desk was like a tip.

'What's happened?' he asked.

'I don't know how I'm going to handle this,' I said. I poured myself some coffee and sat down. 'I've lost the dress.'

'Cripes. How did that happen?'

I was grateful that Lee didn't immediately assume it was my carelessness. He offered me a biscuit which I nibbled. It was cardboard. I don't like biscuits.

'I don't really know. When I went back to the dry-cleaners, someone had already collected it. The two youngsters in the shop were besotted with each other and useless. I've got the skirt and the pashmina and a written explanation from the assistant, but I don't reckon Miss Ember is going to take it quietly.'

'Perhaps it was Mrs Fairweather?'

'I'm pinning my hopes on the good lady. But somehow I've got to find out without letting on that I haven't collected it.'

Lee stood up and straightened his shirt. 'How about I go and chat? I'll ask her if she enjoyed her day ashore. Maybe she picked up the dress for her friend.'

'Would you? Thanks. That's one way of doing it. I'd be very grateful.' I sank back into my chair.

'I'll see if she's watching the tenders from the rail. I understand that coming aboard is hardly a bundle of fun, but as a spectator event it beats the greasy pole.'

'You could say that.'

Lee finished his coffee and went out. I couldn't hold my breath though I wanted to. My training said that holding one's breath was dangerous.

It was late before Dr Mallory surfaced from the health centre. He looked worn out and had not bothered to change. He went straight to the Galaxy Lounge bar and ordered a brandy and soda. He needed it.

'Busy evening?' I said.

'Come and sit with me, Casey. A white wine for the lady,' he added to the barman. He turned to me. 'You could say so.

We've got a full house. So many people got hurt getting on or getting off those damned tenders. It was a disaster.'

'It was those speedboats, dozens of them. They created a huge swell. It was impossible to keep the tenders steady.'

'I know. And one poor lady is spending the night in St Tropez Hospital, before being flown home tomorrow. And I've got every bed full of injuries. It's like an epidemic. I'm dead beat.'

'Too tired for a walk?'

He swallowed the rest of his brandy and took my arm. 'Never too tired for a walk with you, angel face. I can manage one quick circuit of the promenade deck. I need the exercise and fresh air.'

He wasn't talking much as we traversed the empty deck. The daytime chairs were stacked up and fastened down. Debris had been cleared away. Decks washed down. Everything was ready for the next day.

'Night, Casey,' he said, opening one of many heavy glass doors. 'I must go and check on my patients. No sleep for the permanently wicked.'

'The lady who broke her leg. Do I know her?'

'Haven't you heard? It was that nice lady with the funny nickname. Weather forecast or something.'

My heart did a jump. I knew exactly who it was.

# Eleven
# Monte Carlo

Everyone was hoping that the next port of call would not be a disappointment. We were heading for the Côte d'Azur, the glamorous coast of the French Riviera, and those magical places, Cannes, Nice and Monte Carlo. They were all within a short distance of each other and I'd been there several times. A coach ride in any direction had you gawping at the palatial pastel-washed houses of the rich and famous.

Mrs Fairweather's accident was already fading from passengers' minds, but not from mine. It was bad luck to happen to such a nice lady.

I'd rung the ship's agent at St Tropez to enquire after Mrs Fairweather.

'The lady is comfortable in a private hospital, receiving the best of care,' he said. 'We shall be flying her home tomorrow by air ambulance. It is all arranged.'

'That's good. Please give her my love and best wishes.'

'Of course, Miss Jones.'

'And can you send her some flowers and charge them to me?'

'No problem.'

I tried not to think of the other problem. Miss Ember would be on her own again. The crew were starting to call her Dismember Ember which was a little on the cruel side. It would be encrypted to DE by next week.

I couldn't think of anyone kind enough to share with her. And I wasn't going to volunteer. Perish the thought. I gave the dry-cleaning package to her new steward and scuttled away, if a tallish person like me can scuttle.

There was no roaring mistral today so disembarking from the tenders was a tranquil operation, though there were some nervous women.

'Nothing to worry about. Trust the crew,' I said, standing at the head of the gangway steps. 'Let them time it for you and step across when they say so.'

'It's not as bad as yesterday, is it?'

'Nowhere near. No swell at all. Calm as a duck pond.'

It was also only a short distance to the quayside where the red, yellow and pink stucco houses climbed the steep streets and alleyways up the hills. There were small and friendly cafes lining the quayside where it would be a pleasure to sit and watch the harbour activities.

Richard Norton walked briskly up to me. He had his official face on. A man on a mission.

'A word, Miss Jones.'

'Certainly, Mr Norton,' I said. 'Which word would you like? A word sounds serious.'

'It is serious,' he said, drawing me aside out of hearing of the curious few. He ducked his head from a low-hung beam. 'We have a shoplifter aboard. Items are disappearing from the Bond Street salon. I need your help.'

'Are you sure? Passengers sometimes forget to pay and go back later with their cruise card. It happens.'

This was a no-money ship. All purchases and bar transactions went on a computerized account and were paid for at the end of the cruise. Passengers signed for every transaction. It was foolproof.

'I wish it was as simple as that,' said Richard. 'I've had the manager, that damned Derek Ripon, on my back for two days. They've lost clothes – small things like scarves and tights – some fake jewellery that was on display, cosmetics and creams and stuff. Last night a bottle of expensive perfume vanished off a shelf. Some fancy name. Dior's Poison, I think.'

'Why does he think it's the same person? It could be six different people.'

'Gut instinct, he says. Quoted his years in the retail trade. He doesn't really know, of course. These people like to think they know.'

'Proof would be better.'

'I've asked his staff to report any suspicious behaviour, loitering and so on.'

'Perhaps a professional shoplifter doesn't loiter. Maybe they are in and out in the flash and they wouldn't even be noticed.'

'Will you keep an eye open?'

'Sure. What for? Someone wearing lots of scarves, fake jewellery and smelling to high heaven?'

'Please take this seriously, Casey. We can't have a shoplifter on board the *Countess*. It's bad for our image.' He cleared his throat. 'Are you going ashore? Are you going to visit some of your posh friends?'

Oh dear, our towering security officer was having a fit of the grumps. He had clearly not forgiven me for my current coolness but I was not interested in any on-board romance with a hormonal husband on the loose. It was a pity he felt he had to take it out on me every time we met. If he was trying to worm his way back into my affections, he was going about it the wrong way.

'The Grimaldi family keep phoning and saying we must catch up, but I'm not sure if I'll have time. There's shopping to do, as always.'

'What it is to be so popular,' he said. Sarcasm didn't become six foot three of rejected manhood either. He shrugged and made to turn away.

'Why don't you go to see the village of Eze,' I said, trying to smooth over the broken glass of his fragile ego. 'Apparently it's a spectacular village, hanging right over the sea – a sheer drop, medieval buildings, magnificent views. And no traffic allowed inside which seems a seriously sensible policy.'

'Sounds perfect.' He was interested, despite his resentment. 'A village for pedestrians only.'

'If I get a car to the outskirts, would you like to visit the village? A short visit, a walk around, nothing heavy.' He was melting like a sorbet in the sun.

Richard had shrunk to small boy stature, was asking for a treat. I didn't want to encourage him. If I gave him an inch, he'd take five and a half yards. But I did want to see the village. Hardly ethical. My curiosity was threatening to overtake good sense.

'Sure, I'll give you a buzz. It's a time factor. Busy, you know.'

'OK. Phone if you want to go ashore. You know my number.' That's how it was left. I wasn't lying. I did have a lot to do.

Lee had asked if he could go ashore here. He'd never seen

Monte Carlo and had volunteered to escort an excursion. Crew were always welcome as extra headcounters. All the excursions employed a local guide who were the walking guide books. They were OK as long as you didn't ask any awkward questions.

'You'll enjoy Monte Carlo, rising from the sea, a whole town perched on a huge rock, everything dramatic. There's the fairy-tale palace, home of the Rainiers, full of priceless furniture and magnificent frescoes,' I said. 'You must go to the Grand Casino. It's fabulous. Go and lose a few euros for me. And don't forget to look at the ceiling of the Salon Rose.'

'A ceiling. Why?'

'It's famed for the naked nymphs smoking cigarillos.'

'Am I old enough for all this decadence?' he asked, grinning.

'It's fun spotting the celebrities. I saw Sam Neill, the actor, the last time I was here.'

'I won't have time or energy for all this,' he said, shaking his head. 'Naked women, film stars, and royal palaces. I'd better take plenty of water.'

'Please be back early. It's the fabulous Judie Garllund this evening and I'm getting this uneasy feeling.'

Judie Garllund was due on stage for her solo spot tonight. She was heralded in the ship's newspaper as a rising star, singing songs from shows. That's how she finally stipulated the blurb should run, though I did point out that it didn't say much.

'Can't we jazz it up a bit?' I'd asked on the phone a few days back. It was the only way I could contact her. She never seemed to be around anywhere, only in her cabin.

'I don't need to be jazzed up,' she said.

'How about "Straight from the London stage" or "Television's newest star"?'

'I don't want any of that tabloid baloney,' she said in a muffled voice as if she was eating a bun. The cafe and the dining room were awash with food and yet she was eating in her cabin. I looked at my watch. This was between meals.

'All right,' I said, capitulating. 'Perhaps when you give your second show, we'll think up something a little more snazzy.'

There was a gulp and a choking cough the other end of the line. 'I have to do a s–second show?'

'Didn't you read your contract? Two solo shows and a couple of odd spots in spectaculars. It's not exactly a lot of work.'

There was no reply. I think she had fainted.

Now I had to check that she was fully recovered from her earlier indisposition and ready to go on stage this evening. It was like having a root canal. Although I have dealt with dozens of tricky situations, it's not something I enjoy.

Courage Casey, I said to myself. She's only a rather nervous singer. She got her Juliet balcony, didn't she? So she should be grateful to me and full of welcoming smiles. I'd even forgiven her for the nails on my face.

There were no welcoming smiles. I knocked on her cabin door several times. Her steward was hovering with his trolley load of clean towels.

'Have you seen Miss Garllund?'

'No, I have not seen Miss Garllund,' he said helpfully.

'When did you last see her?'

He shrugged his shoulders. 'Yesterday, perhaps.'

Yesterday? It would be my luck if she was lying on the floor after taking an overdose of ten mg Valium, washed down with neat brandy. I hoped Dr Mallory was on-board. But he would still be busy from yesterday's shoal of casualties.

'Would you please unlock the door?' I asked. 'I am worried that Miss Garllund may be ill and in need of a doctor.'

'Yes, of course, Miss Jones.'

Doctor was the magic word. All the crew adored Dr Mallory. He treated them for nothing and with as much care as if they were the wealthiest passenger aboard in an expensive suite with a balcony and a butler.

The cabin was in chaos. There was stuff everywhere. Music scores lying open on the floor, clothes on the rumpled bed, the bathroom a clutter of cosmetics and screwed-up tissues. Half-eaten food lay on plates, with open bottles of fizzy drinks.

'I am coming to do the cabin now,' said the steward, half-heartedly.

'A bit of a mess,' I said. I always kept my cabin neat. The stewards were not employed to clear up personal debris.

'Very messy,' he agreed.

'Is it always like this?'

He sighed with resignation. 'It is always like this.'

I gathered up the clothes and put them on a chair, so that he could at least make the bed. There were a couple of T-shirts with the Conway Blue Line logo. She'd bought herself some souvenirs.

The music scores were of quite old shows. Singers usually brought sheet music, not whole scores which are heavy to carry around. The *Sound of Music, Oklahoma, Annie Get Your Gun*? Not exactly inspiring. I couldn't imagine Annie Oakley singing from Juliet's balcony. I hadn't seen any of her rehearsals but it was time I found out exactly what she was singing. When and if I could find her.

'Miss Garllund has gone ashore,' I was told at the gangway. They checked on the computer where cruise cards were swiped. 'Yes, she has gone ashore today.'

A fine sweat broke out on my forehead. This was unheard of behaviour. Most entertainers stayed on-board if they had a solo spot that evening. They wanted to relax, rehearse, conserve their strength, wash their hair, check all the last-minute details.

But all thoughts of the extraordinary straying vocalist vanished in the next few minutes. There was the most almighty row going on near the end of the line waiting to board the tender. The voices were loud and angry. It was a husband and wife, or partners, or whatever their current battle status. But they were going at each other, hammer and curling tongs.

'It's your own fault. I told you to pack them. Why blame it on me that you haven't got them? You're always blaming me. I already wait on you hand and foot, why should I do any more? It's your own stupid fault.' The woman's face was flushed, her voice rising like a force ten gale. The man beside her was tight-mouthed, tight-fisted. They were both in their fifties, well dressed, preserved in Botox and Dewars.

'You fat-faced, stupid old cow. I can't rely on you for anything. Nothing to do all day except play bridge with your crow-faced cronies and microwave a few Tesco dinners. You can't even be bothered to cook these days, not even a boiled egg. All I asked you to do was check my case, my packing. It wasn't much to ask. You'd got all day.'

'Do this, do that, ordering me about like an unpaid servant. That's all I ever hear from you,' she spat at him, eyes narrowed and glinting. I noticed she was wearing a lot of unsuitable shimmering mauve eye shadow. 'Orders, orders, orders.'

'Who's paying for this cruise, I ask you? Who has worked hard all year to pay for this?'

'Oh, don't give me that crap. All this crap talk about hard work. Your hardest work is under your secretary's desk.'

There was a gasp and stunned silence among the other passengers in line for the tenders, and then a few embarrassed titters. I'd heard enough. This was getting vicious and below anyone's belt. Not exactly my job but it was not my style to walk away from disruption of any kind. I wasn't called Cacoethes Casey for nothing. Not many people called me that.  Not many people know what it means.

'Hello,' I said calmly. 'I'm Casey Jones. Would you mind coming with me? There's a quiet room off here where we could talk.'

They were highly agitated, moron faces set in fury, eyes like daggers. They looked as if they would refuse, both determined to carry on their row in public, as if it was cathartic. The woman wasn't ageing well, looked old and bitter, carrying a magisterial bosom which gravity was defying. I wasn't happy about leaving either of them.

'I may be able to help,' I said, a right little agony aunt in the making. 'It'll only take a few minutes and then you can go ashore on the next tender. Monte Carlo is such an interesting place. You'll enjoy your visit.'

It was pat, like a tour guide. Any minute now I'd be showing them on to a coach and counting heads.

'This bloody man is impossible,' the woman shouted. 'I can't do anything right. God knows why I'm here on this bloody ship.'

'You've said it,' he grunted. 'Get off if you don't like it. The sooner you pack the better. Why don't you jump overboard? Bloody big splash. I'd be glad to get rid of you. Suit me.'

'This way please,' I said, insisting that they follow me. 'I don't know your names. Is it Mr and Mrs . . .?'

'Belcher,' he said. 'Mr and Mrs Greg Belcher. Not for much longer, I hope. I'm up to here with this woman. I'm going straight to my lawyer as soon as we get home.'

'And good riddance to you,' said Mrs Belcher. 'The sooner

you piss off, the better. Then I can get on with my life without you cluttering up the house with dirty pants and smelly socks.'

'You won't get the house,' he roared. 'I'll make sure of that.'

'Oh yes, I will. Ten years' hard labour won't count for nothing.'

'I didn't want to come on this bloody cruise in the first place,' he grumbled.

'Oh no, you'd rather play golf, day in, day out, propping up the nineteenth hole with your cronies. Some handicap, you've got. Your main handicap is too many pints and whiskey chasers.'

Quite a few of the passengers were distinctly uncomfortable by now. I needed to move Mr and Mrs Belcher before they came to blows.

'Would you mind coming with me?' I tried again, more firmly. 'This way, please. There's a room at the side where you can continue your argument in private.'

'It's none of your business, young woman,' the woman spat at me. 'Keep out of it. Leave us alone. Go away. Clear off.'

It was a small inside room, no window, where we took passengers who had brought aboard something illegal or not allowed. Sometimes purchases had to be searched. One passenger tried to smuggle aboard a monkey from Gibraltar. The unfortunate animal gave away his own presence. A zipped holdall that jabbered was not a normal souvenir.

'You can't treat me like this,' said Mrs Belcher, bosom heaving, clearly on the point of losing control. 'I won't have it.'

'What are you trying to do with us?' Mr Belcher spluttered. 'I won't stand being hustled about like this by a nobody.'

'It's merely a small room where you may feel more comfortable. I could bring you some coffee while you wait for the next tender. One has unfortunately just left.'

Somehow the nobody got the reluctant couple into the interview room. It was more like an office with a desk and filing cabinet. Mrs Belcher went straight to the filing cabinet and started drumming her fingers on the top.

'Whatever you've forgotten to pack you'll be able to buy in Monte Carlo,' I said. 'There are wonderful shops. They stock everything.'

'That'll suit her,' said Mr Belcher, glaring. 'Dora was born with a credit card in her mouth.'

'I'll get you some coffee,' I said, escaping. I thought they both needed it. I needed it.

I hurried to the nearest bar and got a stewardess to bring a tray with a pot of coffee to the room. The Belchers were sitting in stony silence. I was going to leave them to sort it out, hoping they wouldn't hurl the coffee at each other.

'You'll really enjoy Monte Carlo,' I said cheerfully, ignoring the ice forming into glacial peaks.

'Really?' Dora Belcher was determined not to give an inch. 'I won't enjoy anything with this bastard,' she snarled.

I was about to suggest that maybe it would be a good idea if they went their separate ways for the day, giving both of them a chance to cool down, when my mobile phone rang.

'Excuse me,' I said, going outside.

'Casey? Can you come to the medical centre?' It was Dr Mallory's soothing voice. 'There's something you ought to see.'

I'd look at anything to get away from the brawling Belchers. 'OK,' I said. 'I'll be with you in a few minutes. I'm with two passengers at the moment.'

The Belchers were calming down. Mrs Belcher was pouring out some coffee. She didn't pour one for her husband. No more waiting on him hand and foot. For a moment I felt sorry for her. It's no fun when your looks start to go and I could see that once she had been an attractive woman.

'Now you enjoy your coffee,' I said. 'Then go ashore on the next tender. Monte Carlo is really worth a visit.'

Afterwards I wished I hadn't gone to the medical centre. Maybe I'd been hypnotized by that lovely deep voice or the thought of drowning myself in those light grey eyes, so full of amusement.

Whatever it was about Sam that always worked its magic on me, it wasn't there today.

# Twelve
# Monte Carlo

S amuel had completed some preliminary tests on blood samples taken from the body of Theo Papados. He'd not had time before with the rush of casualties from St Tropez.

'There are traces of some foreign substance in the blood,' he said, clearly not happy with his findings. 'It's not something I can identify, working with this basic equipment. I'd need a laboratory. I've a friend at Guy's who may be able to help out. Maybe it's the reason why the professor so suddenly died. Whatever this substance is, it kicked in and that was the end of our lecturer.'

'It's all Greek to me.' The graphs on the screen meant nothing.

'Not funny, Casey. Not one of your best.'

'Sorry, it wasn't meant to be a joke. I'm a fraction shattered, off balance. I've been dealing with a married couple almost coming to blows in public.'

'The Belchers?'

This was a surprise. My eyebrows shot up. Had I missed a warning notice in the ship's newspaper under the flash line 'Port Hazards'?

'Mrs Belcher came aboard with a black eye,' he said, scrolling through notes on his computer screen. 'Mrs Dora Belcher, aged 53, from Kensington. She said she walked into a door. The door being an upright Mr Belcher in my opinion.'

'She was wearing a lot of make-up, now you mention it, probably to cover the bruising. They both have pretty volatile tempers. Perhaps they need watching.'

'Monitoring. We don't want any domestic violence on board. So how is our songbird, the legendary Judie Garllund? I've seen her quite a few times in the last couple of days. She is suffering from a variety of ailments including palpitations, sore throat, headaches, nausea and dizziness.'

'Sounds like stage fright to me.'

'Exactly what I thought. I recommended deep breathing, relaxation, plenty of sleep and more exercise. But I doubt if she was even listening.'

'She certainly wasn't listening when I advised against going ashore when she has her solo spot evening. Her cruise card has been swiped and she has gone ashore. Perhaps taking your suggestion to get more exercise. I hope she remembers to turn round and come back on-board in good time.'

'You're looking tired,' said Samuel. For a moment his eyes changed, were warm and concerned, his voice less formal. 'A lot of problems?'

'Only minor, nothing major. I could say the same about you.'

'Shall we swop jobs?'

'Done. Show me how to use the blood pressure sleeve.'

His appearance was, as always, pristinely smart and immaculate. Not a spot on his whites. His eyes were shadowed and there was a slump to those broad shoulders, but he was still absolutely, unavoidably delicious.

'Nothing that a few hours of sleep won't cure,' he said. 'We could both do with a nap. Care to join me? I know where there is a discreet couch, at present unoccupied.'

'The operating table?'

'Casey, please. I wouldn't be so unromantic.' He was amused.

'Yes, you would, especially when it concerns me. Anything would do for good old, hard-working, uncomplaining K.C. Jones.'

'You really know how to hurt me,' he said, returning the slides to a refrigerated compartment. 'I shall remind you tonight when we are having a celebration drink in the bar.'

'This is new. What will we be celebrating?'

'We'll be celebrating Miss Garllund's miraculous last-minute recovery from stage fright and her exciting performance on stage. Standing ovation, repeat encores. A star is born.'

'If pigs could fly.'

Passengers were beginning to return to the ship. Where had the day gone? Time had flown by on fluffy wings to a melancholy five o'clock. And I had meant to get so much done. I kept out of Miss Ember's way. She was the purser's problem now. But I had not reckoned on her perseverance. There she was, making straight for me, all floating scarves and big hat, her stiletto heels making pointy marks on the decking.

'Miss Jones,' she said, barring my way. She had been ashore and was laden with posh shopping bags, all glossy labels. 'Have you got my Chanel dress?'

'Er, no.'

'Did you take it to the dry-cleaners in St Tropez?'

'Oh, yes.'

'Did you pick it up with the skirt and the pashmina?'

'No.' I was still sticking to the truth. Miraculous in the circumstances.

'Then where is it?'

'I don't exactly know.' The patron saint of trapped truth was definitely on my side. I'd light a candle.

'I suppose that stupid Mrs Fairweather dropped it in the sea when she fell over. It would be exactly like her. I've never met such a clumsy woman.'

'No one saw her drop anything,' I said, coming to the poor injured lady's rescue with sincerity. 'No one knows if she even collected it. Perhaps it was someone else.'

'She probably still has the dress. Will you check that she is not taking it back to England with her when she flies home? I know she liked the dress. You could tell by the way she looked at it and kept making remarks about the perfect sewing.'

'Of course, I'll check,' I said, not intending to do anything of the sort. This was rubbish. I was no snooper. The whole thing was becoming a farce. I half expected men to come flying out of nearby cabins in their M & S boxer shorts, chased by irate wives waving hair dryers.

'I'll do what I can,' I said, continuing the charade.

'I'm relying on you,' she said. 'That dress is evidence.'

I was not sure how a dress could be evidence. It was not damaged. The rat hadn't gnawed at the hem nor had the shop model stuck her false nails into the camellias.

'Of course, Miss Ember, now if you'll excuse me?' I escaped on a false errand before she could raise the question of a cabin companion. Perhaps one of the stewardesses might be persuaded to do a spot of disaster-sitting for overtime pay.

Our songbird had not yet reappeared. I was beginning to feel one per cent worried. At this rate, the count could rise rapidly. It was not the first time that a diva had caused trouble but no one had ever missed a show. The opportunity to sing was always too tempting. Some producer might be in the audience, on holiday, but still looking for talent for his new show. There might be a rep from a record company out to spot a new star, waving a million-pound contract.

The last tenders were arriving back, full to the gunwales with tired passengers, still chattering away. It had been a good trip, making a day of it in Monaco after a drive along the coastal road to the Middle Corniche. I never got to the medieval village of Eze and never phoned Richard. Some had preferred the old town of Nice then a walk along the elegant Promenade de la Croisette in Cannes. On a clear day you could see the Alps. No one was grumbling.

'Who is it tonight?' I heard a woman say.

'It's that Judy Garland.'

'I thought she was dead.'

'No, she can't be. Not if she's singing here tonight.'

I was getting twinges of apprehension and alarm. Judie was cutting it fine. Soon all the ship's tenders would be stowed and the *Countess* would be ready to proceed to sea. When the last tender was back, she would weigh anchor and back off the anchorage, setting a north-easterly track towards Santa Margherita.

The last tender returned and tied up. There was no sign of Judie, unless I'd missed her. I half expected to see a fast-moving motor boat speeding out to the ship, a female at the helm waving frantically. But there was nothing.

I checked her cabin again and security. Her cruise card had not been swiped back.

I went to see the dance captain of our troupe of lovelies. Dawn Charmans was a gorgeously lithe and slim girl with muscles of steel. She ruled her girls with firm discipline plus a healthy dose of East End humour.

'Wotcha Case,' she said. She always called me Case. 'Wot's up? You don't look a bundle of fun tonight. Dishy doctor stood you up?'

'Miss Judie Garllund,' I began. 'I think she's done a runner.'

'The new singer? Not surprised. You should have copped

her rehearsal. Bloody disaster, excuse my French. Talk about amateur. I don't reckon she'd ever sung in anything bigger than a church hall out in the sticks. Did some female impersonations, Streisand, Winehouse, Piaf, but they all sounded the same. I'm surprised Simon Cowell didn't send her home twenty seconds after she opened her mouth, if she really did audition for *The X Factor*, which I just can't believe.'

My face fell. My worst nightmare and it was my fault. I should have checked earlier. All this stuff about a Juliet balcony had distracted me. If somehow she had got past all our reference checks at Head Office and was an amateur, not an *X-Factor* contestant, then no wonder she was nervous and hiding out in a cafe on shore.

'There's going to be a big zero nothing on tonight,' I said morosely. 'I suppose it's too much to ask if you have a reserve dance show up your sleeve? If you are wearing a sleeve, that is.'

Dawn was busy inspecting her stuck-on talons. They were a quarter of an inch long, all sparkly with stars. 'It just so happens, Case,' she began, all mysterious. 'I have been incubating a smashing idea for the last few days. So, along the lines of the Simon Cowell show . . .'

'*The X Factor*?'

'Yes. We could do a skit on it. Our boys and girls could do solo turns, like auditions, some form a group, singing for survival, and we'd have our judges giving their opinions, and the audience could vote on them to stay or be sent home. They'd love it. Except they could hardly go home. Bit of a swim.' It was a good pitch.

'Would it work?' I asked dubiously.

'My lot can all sing to a degree, some better than others. And they'd be great at the screaming and crying buckets.' Dawn was looking really hopeful. She'd been cooking this idea for more like weeks. This was her big chance. 'I'd introduce everybody, you know, be the lady compère, the host.'

'Well . . .'

'Audience participation,' she added.

'Do you need to rehearse it?'

'It won't be rehearsed. It'll be impromptu, like it was for real. You could be one of the judges,' she said, thinking this was a big carrot to dangle.

It wasn't a carrot but I could see it as a form of control over the performances. The show might need a steady hand.

'And our dreamboat doctor, of course. If he's free, not operating on anybody. We've gotta have a bit of male glamour on the judges' table.'

She didn't count me as glamour apparently.

'What about the security officer, Richard Norton? He's very solid and down to earth,' I suggested, warming to the idea. There was no other solution unless Judie arrived on deck, having chartered a helicopter. 'And perhaps a passenger? Have we anyone aboard with show business experience?'

'I'll try and find out. We'll start the show with one of our stock ensemble numbers and end it with another. That won't be any trouble. I'd better get a move on, whip up some volunteers. So, is it OK, Case?'

'I think it'll have to be. I can hardly show a film in the Princess Lounge. No screen. We need a judges' table at the front and four chairs. Trevor can arrange that. We also need a good strap name. We can't use *The X Factor*. We'd get sued.'

'How about The XYZ Factor since we don't know what we're doing?'

'Perfect.'

She gave me a big grin. 'Don't worry, Case. It'll be a riot.'

That was the last thing I wanted.

There wasn't much time to organize the new show. Announcements were made over the tannoy. I needed a stunningly glamorous dress if I was to be on the judges' table. I wasn't going to have Samuel outshine me. I wore my ruched red satin from Topshop with cross-over back straps and tantalizing plunging neckline. It was an event dress. There was no time to do more than clip my hair up in a tumble.

Dawn Charmans found a retired theatre owner called William Owen. He didn't mind missing his supper in exchange for champagne in the top deck grill later, with some of the lovelies. He had kind, twinkly eyes and was obviously delighted to be able to air his professional knowledge.

Samuel Mallory arrived at the very last moment, looking devastating. He'd had an extra after six shave. Those eyes threw me completely off balance. I had sparks coming out of my fingertips.

'That's some dress,' he whispered, sliding into the seat beside me. 'But you have forgotten to do up the front.'

'It is done up,' I said. 'Careful, the mikes are on.'

'Clothes are your armour, they're hiding your insecurities,' he added.

'They reflect my identity and self-worth,' I said.

It was a great show, considering it had been thrown together at the last minute. One of the young male dancers had a strong voice and was a potential winner. Nervous Kristy, the new chorus dancer, sang a soulful *If My Friends Could See Me Now* which was pretty good. Richard made lots of sensible, obvious remarks. Mr Owen's comments and criticisms were spot-on. Dr Mallory was amusing and controversial, trying to do a vague impersonation of Simon Cowell's laid-back style. I was . . . well, I was the usual honest me. Smile, Casey.

The audience loved it. They hissed and booed and clapped. Dawn Charmans looked stunning, having poured herself into a glittery silver dress.

'Don't forget to vote,' she announced at the end of the show. 'Voting slips at the door. Every vote counts.'

There was a break between the dinner sittings while the audience changed and the performers had a chance to chat and relax. I went to get some coffee. Maybe we'd join the lovelies for supper in the grill.

'Sorry about this afternoon,' I said to Richard. 'There simply wasn't time.'

'Quite understand,' he said stiffly. 'Perhaps another port in the Med.'

'Absolutely.'

We had assembled for the second showing of The XYZ Factor when Dr Mallory received a call on his mobile phone. He took it, standing some distance away from the judges' table. His face gave away nothing. He switched it off and went to talk to Richard Norton, but Richard was already answering his phone. His face was one of horror.

'Oh my God,' he said. He hung up and turned to me. 'Gotta go,' he said. He was striding up the side aisle and out of the Princess Lounge before I could speak to him.

'What's happened?' I said to Samuel as he came over to me, my hand over the table microphone. His face gave nothing away.

'Sorry, Casey,' he said. 'I've been called away. Emergency. Give my apologies to Dawn. You'll have to find two other judges.'

I had no idea what was going on but it must be serious if both Richard Norton and Dr Mallory had been summoned. I made some sort of announcement and a faded but still pretty middle-aged woman from the audience volunteered to be a judge. Mr Owen's twinkly eyes twinkled even more when she sat beside him.

'I used to be on the stage,' she confided to me. 'But a long time ago.'

'Surely not that long ago, m'dear,' he said.

Trevor, the stage manager, leaped into the breach, glad for once to be up front and not invisible behind the scenes. He was wearing black jeans and a T-shirt which were perfectly suitable. He'd certainly had enough stage experience and a fund of recycled jokes which he trotted out. The second showing of The XYZ Factor was up and running.

Afterwards, I hung about, talking to the audience, while the votes were counted. I saw Lee hurrying towards me. He looked grim, running his hands through his hair.

I turned to him. 'Lee? Tell me. What's happened?'

'They've found a woman,' he gulped. 'With her head bashed in. A crater the size of an egg cup.'

'Do they know who it is?'

'It's a passenger called Dora Belcher.'

# Thirteen
# At Sea

S o the news travelled. We might as well have announced it over the tannoy. The passengers knew more than I did. And what they didn't know, they made up. Thus rumours take hold.

I assumed that Mrs Belcher had been found in her cabin but I was wrong. She had been found in the interview room where I had taken the couple that morning. That shook me. I was questioned about the incident by the captain, the security officer and Dr Mallory. It was as if they thought I'd done it. I felt like a suspect.

'Don't be upset,' said Samuel, later in the Galaxy Lounge bar. He'd bought me a brandy and soda. This was getting to be a habit. 'It's routine procedure. Mrs Belcher wasn't killed in the interview room. She was killed elsewhere, sometime after five o'clock, after the tenders were stowed and we were heading for sea. She was moved somehow and dumped in the interview room.'

'How do you know?'

'No blood in the interview room. She'd stopped bleeding.'

'I keep thinking I could have prevented it,' I wailed. 'If I'd done something more.'

Samuel shook his head. 'How could you? What could you have done? You can't wave your magic wand and declare people's personalities changed for the better. They argued constantly according to the passengers in the cabins either side of theirs. We know Mrs Belcher came aboard with a black eye.'

'Are you assuming that Mr Belcher hit his wife with something?'

'He's denying it. He says he was in a bar, drinking, most of the evening. The barman confirms it and the cruise card bar purchases tally with the time. The perfect alibi. It looks like classic domestic violence but maybe it's not. He does seem very upset. A Bafta performance, if he killed her.'

'Looks like we've got a murderer on board.'

'Hmmm, unless the villain swam back to shore.'

'Do we know what was used to kill her?'

'Not yet. Richard Norton has found nothing in their cabin with any traces of blood. We need one of those infra red instruments that pick up tiny smudges that the eye can't see. Or there's a Luminol spray which shows up blood stains by making them fluorescent.'

'Blood can be washed off.'

'There are always traces left, if not to the human eye, then to a microscope. Murderers are often caught that way. Confront them with the path of sprayed blood in certain rooms or on walls and they confess.'

'You think this is murder, then?' I shivered. The destruction of life was never easy to accept. I knew I would not be able to sleep tonight. The thought would be with me all night. We had a monster walking among us.

'She hardly tripped and fell on a blunt instrument by herself. It had to be something hard enough to fracture her skull, something like a brick or a rock.'

'No bricks or rocks on board ship.'

'It wasn't something like a bottle or piece of wood. There was no residue or fragments in the wound. We've got to find the murder weapon. Cheer up, Casey. Don't look so glum. You can't take the blame for this one.'

'I'm not glum. I'm upset.'

'Of course, I'm sorry,' he said swiftly. 'Murder is always a shock. A & E had its quota on a Saturday night when the pubs closed.'

Dawn Charmans was on a high after her hugely successful show, The XYZ Factor. She was drinking champagne like water, seeing herself stepping into Sharon Osbourne's shoes on television. The dresses wouldn't fit.

Judie was still missing. No one had seen her. We'd left her behind in port. She'd have to get herself home.

I suggested that Dawn might like to do it again in place of Judie's second solo show, with members of the crew as the entrants and with judges panel from the passenger list as before.

Kirsty, the young dancer who won the event was also on a high, but on sparkling mineral water.

'I hear the captain has a good singing voice,' I said.

'Good heavens, no Case, please don't ask the captain to take part.' Dawn was aghast. She was always a little in awe of our captain.

'Only joking. I haven't been anywhere near his bathroom.'

'I'd give your dishy doctor some personal voice coaching any day.'

'Not my dishy doctor. Half the female crew are setting traps for him and all of the female passengers.'

'But he only has eyes for you,' Dawn said, with a grin.

'He needs new lenses.'

Scotland Yard were going to fly someone out to the *Countess*. Richard Norton was none too pleased, but it was maritime law and he had to put up with it. The detective would be joining the ship at the next port of call, Santa Margherita on the Italian Riviera.

I didn't sleep. I was too wired up to sleep, couldn't even close my eyes. A walk on the decks might have cleared my head. But I was even afraid of shadows.

The passengers were a more resilient lot, getting on with the serious business of planning their day between meals. The sober faces of the evening before had been replaced the next morning with their normal British good humour. Some even made bad jokes about this being a murder mystery cruise, and Miss Marple would soon be joining the crew.

But minute by minute, those on deck became aware of something different happening. They could not quite pinpoint what was changing. It made them uneasy. They could feel the *Countess* slowing down, if it is possible to put the brakes on forty-five thousand tons of ship like an emergency stop. Tattered shreds of conversation became confused and apprehensive.

Dead Slow Ahead. I recognized the signal blasts though the passengers didn't. I thought about the figures I'd seen bundled aboard at midnight. That mystery had never been solved. It was still tapping on my mind.

Crew were alerted. Some passengers panicked. They thought the engines had broken down and they would be doomed to days on end floating about mid-ocean, running out of food, running short of water. Strict rations and no shopping. Maybe there would be complimentary booze.

'Don't worry,' I said to a couple of nervous women. 'We are only slowing down. There must be a good reason. The captain knows what he's doing.'

'Nothing wrong, we hope?'

The good reason was floating, adrift, portside. It was a small yacht, about fourteen feet long, bobbing on the waves, a broken mast dragging in the water. It looked deserted and battered.

A rubber dingy was being lowered from the promenade deck with two crewmen in life jackets. They had long poles and grappling hooks. There was quite an audience of passengers craning over the rails, camcorders recording every moment of the rescue drama. It was all good stuff for winter evenings when having the neighbours in to see their holiday snaps. Doris and George, who went to Weston-super-Mare and stayed in a caravan, would be impressed.

Dr Mallory strolled on deck, a bottle of water in hand. He'd found time for some sleep and it showed. No more panda eyes half open behind his glasses.

'Trim little craft,' he said. 'My dad used to have one like that.'

'So you still know how to handle a boat?'

'She was called *Tipperary Lady*. I remember navigating by the stars at night. All comes in handy. Stitching a torn sail is not unlike stitching up a wound.'

'How are your patients?'

'Recovering, I'm happy to say. A couple are returning to shipboard life today, wearing plaster casts courtesy of Conway Blue Line. I never charge for the plaster.'

'But you charge for everything else.'

'Naturally, and they get the best service.'

The crewmen had hauled the yacht alongside, made it fast, and were clambering aboard. One went into the tiny stern cabin. He came out again pretty fast. He signalled something to the officer who was in charge of the operation. It was difficult to make out what was going on. I felt a tremor of alarm.

'I don't like the look of this,' said Samuel. 'I think I may be wanted. See you later, Casey.' He disappeared inside, taking the lift down.

The crewman was being sick over the side. Camcorders were hastily switched off or panned to a more salubrious view of the *Countess*, her clean white lines glistening. The sun was visiting each deck in turn. She was rocking gently on the swell, her engines now on a low throb. The captain didn't like bringing her to a complete halt, mid-sea. He was a man with a mission – to get sixteen hundred paying passengers to a dozen ports of call on time and home again to Southampton. If he could do it, so could the railways.

Now we were a lifeboat rescue service in action. It was a rule of the sea. If any craft in distress needed help, no matter how big or luxurious you were, you stopped and offered help. Everyone understood, or nearly everyone.

'Can't stand all this hanging about, doing nothing,' said one disgruntled man, looking at his watch. 'Can't they get a move on?'

I curbed my tongue. Careful, Casey. It was not my job to argue with anyone. It would only cause aggro. Better to walk away and leave him creating bile in his stomach. He would have indigestion after lunch. I hoped.

Our intrepid doctor was climbing down a rope ladder slung down the side of the ship, holding on with one hand. Very Tarzan, without the leotard. He had his emergency bag in the other hand. It wasn't for the nauseated crewman. He clambered into the rocking dingy and then went across on to the broken yacht. After speaking briefly to the crewmen, he ducked down into the stern cabin.

He didn't stay long, and was on his phone immediately. There was a flurry of activity. I could guess what they were going to do. They were going to haul the yacht aboard, probably on to the lower stern deck, the area normally reserved for crew members at leisure.

But we were in Italian water. The captain would have to inform the Italian authorities. They'd be swarming on-board tomorrow. The passengers might even be delayed going ashore. There was always that possibility. Red tape often strangled a routine procedure.

'Isn't this exciting,' someone said. 'I've never seen a rescue before.'

Not exactly exciting for whoever or whatever was in the stern cabin. And hardly a rescue if we were too late.

I didn't want to know.

\*   \*   \*

Richard Norton was in a state. He didn't like the idea of a Scotland Yard detective intruding on his patch. So he became his own worst enemy, smoke coming out of his ears, annoying everyone with officious demands and orders. He put crime scene tape round the interview room and Mr Belcher's cabin which upset a lot of people. Mr Belcher was moved to the empty cabin that Lucinda Ember had turned down.

'It's only temporary,' Richard blustered. 'We've got to dust for fingerprint evidence.'

With what, I wondered. We didn't carry fingerprinting equipment. He'd seen too many films.

Then Richard insisted on taking extra statements from everyone. He made me give another one about their row that morning and what happened when I ushered the couple into the interview room.

'So what happened then?'

'Nothing happened,' I said. I'd already told him about six times. 'They just went on yelling at each other. I went away and got them some coffee.'

'What happened while you were away?'

'How on earth should I know? I wasn't there.'

'Did Mr Belcher threaten Mrs Belcher at any time?'

'No.'

'Are you sure?'

'I said no, didn't I? I wouldn't have said no, if I hadn't been sure. Look, I've already been through all this with you, Richard. I've got a lot to do.'

'I'll get your statement typed up and you can sign it,' he said heavily, the woes of the entire universe balanced on his shoulders. 'I may need to see you again, clear up a few points.'

'Mind your blood pressure,' I said, leaving. 'I can see it climbing.'

The doctor was next in line for interrogation. Samuel raised his dark eyebrows. 'Am I in for the water torture?' he asked.

'It's worse than that,' I said. 'He's pulling out toenails.'

'Oh dear, I'm rather fond of my toenails. They've been with me for a long time.'

'Taboo subjects. Don't mention Scotland Yard, CID or the Italian police. Those words are a red rag. He doesn't like interference.'

'Thanks for the warning.'

'Are you going to tell me what you found in the cabin of the yacht?' I asked.

'No,' said Samuel firmly. 'It's not for your delicate ears.'

The yacht had been winched up on to the stern deck, made fast and covered in a tarpaulin. It was out of bounds to everyone, waiting for the Italian police to take charge. They were on their way to join us.

As usual, rumours were circulating. They ranged from deposed royalty to aliens. One hypersensitive passenger was now insisting that she had seen lights on the deck, dancing about. She was teased about little green men from then onwards. Her nickname became E.T.

'Dr Mallory, if you please,' said Richard Norton, coming to the door of his office. 'I haven't got all day.'

'Neither have I,' said the doctor, briskly. 'Make it quick, Dick.'

Richard Norton hated being called Dick.

It was a soporific day with a blue sky that stretched forever, and a light breeze that merely ruffled a few tendrils and cooled warm skin. Everyone was on deck, except for the bridge players who had barricaded themselves into their room and were locked in combat. They had put chairs against the doors, tired of people who used it as a short cut to the Princess Lounge bar. It was against all regulations but it was difficult to argue with them.

'I could get some notices printed for you to hang on the door,' I suggested. 'How about "GAME IN PROGRESS"?'

'We've tried that. It didn't work. People still traipse through, being chatty and noisy. It ruins our concentration and we're sick of it.'

I left the bridge fanatics to work out their own salvation. Another Berlin wall wasn't the answer.

A couple of hours later the bridge players were not so chirpy. Some comic had jammed a key into the locks of both doors and neither would open. It was another hour before I managed to get a carpenter to come and take the doors off their hinges and let the clearly distressed players rush out for the nearest loos.

They never barricaded themselves in again, merely erected a wall of icy coolness and disdain towards anyone who dared to walk through while they were playing. They froze them out.

# Fourteen
# Santa Margherita

This delightful seaside resort was one of the prettiest on the Eastern Riviera, with its busy waterfront, sweeping bay and clear water for swimming. There was a charming town with pastel-washed houses and hotels with shuttered windows and cascades of flowers from every balcony.

The shops were small and colourful, not a supermarket in sight. The bars were frequented by the locals which is always a good sign. A green oasis of grass, statues, palm trees and wooden benches separated the town traffic from the harbourside, and here lovers met, women gossiped and men smoked their pipes.

'It's all so pleasant and normal,' I said to Lee. 'This huge cruise ship is anchored a mile off their scenic coast and they barely glance at it. They don't bother about selling cheap stuff to the passengers, or plying taxis everywhere, or drumming up business.'

'It's the laid-back, relaxed Italian style of doing everything tomorrow.'

'Do you want to go ashore?'

'Yes, I do, but I realize it's really your turn, especially after yesterday. You need a break. I've been ashore the last three ports.'

'And today I have to stay aboard in case I'm needed for questioning. But if you could come back early, I might catch a free hour later on.'

'OK. I'll do that. Back by lunch time. Thanks, Case.'

Another one calling me Case. It was catching.

As if they hadn't had enough of cruising, many of the passengers were taking a boat trip up the scenic coast to Portofino, for a walking tour of this camera-perfect little village. Or perhaps they were going to see the church where the remains of St George (the dragon slaying one) were supposed to be buried. Or perhaps it was for the Italian wine and hot focaccia served on the boat trip. I hoped they realized there was a lot of uphill walking involved.

Both contingents of police arrived at the same time. It was somewhat confusing at first, but the Italians were slim and dark-haired in dapper uniforms, whereas Detective Chief Inspector Bruce Everton was big, blue-eyed and very Scotland Yard. His hair might be fair if he grew it longer. He'd had the shortest crew cut possible which meant his ears stuck out. But he had what I call a good face for a man, especially a policeman. Not handsome but manly and well proportioned.

Captain Nicolas came out on deck to greet the Italians and DCI Everton. The DCI arrived on one of our tenders, low-key and unobtrusive. The Italians came in their own police launch, cutting fast through the waves, the launch rearing like a warhorse, slapping the water.

'Welcome aboard the *Countess Georgina*,' said the captain. 'I wish it were a social occasion and not so sad and serious. Perhaps you'd like some coffee before you begin your enquiries? I'll then introduce you to members of my crew, my security officer, Richard Norton, and Dr Samuel Mallory.'

Bruce Everton was already shedding his jacket. 'Nobody told me it would be this hot. It was raining when I left Heathrow.'

He was wearing a crisp white shirt that had lost its crispness on the flight. His tie was a club tie, striped. Bowling or rowing, I guessed. I wasn't needed yet. They would call me.

Lucinda Ember waylaid me again on my way to the office. She was wearing an extravagant sort of frock, pleated mauve chiffon with big sleeves, which would have looked perfect on a twenty-year-old. I stood my ground, rallying forces to deal with whatever grievance she'd thought up for today.

'Have you got my dress back?' She went straight for the jugular.

'No, I haven't.' Always stick to the truth. It paid.

'What have you found out about it?'

'Nothing.'

'Well, you're not doing your job properly, Miss Jones. I think a letter to Captain Nicolas about your inefficiency is due,' she went on.

'As you please, Miss Ember.' I knew Captain Nicolas well enough to hope that he would simply file it in some inaccessible place, like the top of a wardrobe. Maybe he'd make the occasional jokey remark in passing. 'Lost any Dior dresses lately, Miss Jones?'

I could sense that Miss Ember was already composing her letter. 'I'm sorry we were not able to find you another companion after Mrs Fairweather broke her leg. But we'll keep looking.'

'Don't bother,' she said huffily. 'I'm not sure I want a companion. I paid good money for single occupancy of my stateroom and I certainly didn't expect to have to share. In fact, I think the company should refund me for those days that Mrs Fairweather occupied half my stateroom. That woman never stopped talking.'

Her audacity had me speechless. We'd been trying to help her with a companion. For a moment I was nonplussed.

Then a tiny bell sounded a tinkling alarm in my head. It was a sort of sixth or seventh sense. It occurred to me that Miss Ember was up to something. Possibly the company would offer her a free cruise in compensation for the blood in the shower and the rat in the wardrobe. They were always generous. But we couldn't accept responsibility for the appearance of her dress in the shop window, nor its current disappearance.

And Mrs Fairweather's company had been a sympathetic move to help Miss Ember through any residual nerves from both shattering experiences. I was beginning to wonder if they were that shattered.

I didn't think for one moment that Mrs Fairweather had taken a shine to the Chanel dress and gone off with it, alongside the trauma of a broken leg. It was a ridiculous idea.

I was saved from further interrogation by Miss Ember by my phone ringing. I moved away for some privacy. It was Richard Norton, stiffly asking me to attend his office.

'Attend?' I asked innocently. 'How lovely. Is it a party? Shall I bring a bottle?'

'Detective Chief Inspector Everton would like a word with you,' he went on. 'Take you through your statement.'

'Which one? I've given you dozens.' Cut it out, Casey. No need to be stroppy with the man. Richard was under stress, his nose severely out of joint. The Yard had sent one of their senior officers, at least in rank if not in age. 'I'll be there in five minutes.'

I liked the DCI immediately. He was sitting on the edge of Richard's desk and had loosened his tie. He was drinking iced coffee which they make very well on-board. He got off the desk and came towards me, holding out his hand.

'Miss Jones, thank you for coming. I hope I haven't taken you away from something more important.'

He was tall, over six feet. I'd cross a road with him any day. He was taller than Samuel but not as tall as Richard. Athletic build. He obviously worked out at some police gym. His eyes were a clear, light blue with a fan of crinkles, as if he laughed a lot. Perhaps laughter was the only way he could deal with the horrors that confronted him every day.

'No, not at all,' I murmured, sitting down. I wished I'd tidied my hair before coming. I knew it was all over the place. I looked like an upended mop.

'I've read all your statements so there's no need to take you through them again.' He shot up in my esteem. 'But there are a few further questions.'

I nodded. 'Shoot,' I said. But I wished I hadn't said shoot, wrong word.

'Did you see Mr and Mrs Belcher go ashore in a tender?'

'No, I didn't. I had other things to do.'

'And you left them together in the interview room?'

'Yes, to cool down. There was coffee for them.'

'Was the interview room locked during the day?'

'I don't think so. There's nothing in it. A desk, a few chairs. But the purser will be able to tell you that.'

'Did you notice anyone going into the interview room during the day?'

'No. I didn't go anywhere near it.'

'Had you noticed any suspicious behaviour of any kind during the day?'

Where did I start? I had the most suspicious mind of anyone on-board. I was a female Sherlock Holmes (call me Sherrie H), piecing things together, spotting irregularities, wondering why this and that was happening. This was not the time, nor the place to tell him.

'Well, a few things but nothing that's especially relevant,' I said.

'That's all for the moment, Miss Jones. Thank you.'

I got up to leave. It had been easy. No gruelling interrogation. 'Just one more thing, Miss Jones,' he said, sipping his iced coffee. 'Did you go ashore at the last port of call?'

It was that last question. The one that mattered. That detective on telly in the shabby raincoat, Colombo, always had a last question. The barbed one with the poisoned dart.

Did I go ashore? For a second, I couldn't remember. I couldn't even remember where we had been, which port, or what I did that day. So much had happened since then. It was all a blur.

I shook my head. 'No, I don't think I went ashore. It was St Tropez, wasn't it? Yes, I went ashore there. No, sorry, it was Villefranche. I'm a day out. That's it . . . Monaco and Monte Carlo. No, I'm sure I didn't go ashore. Positive. It was a busy day.' I sounded flustered. I was annoyed with myself for using sure and ashore in the same sentence. It sounded like a weak joke.

DCI Everton was writing something down. 'Thank you, that's all, Miss Jones. Please let me know when you can remember exactly your whereabouts and activities that day. Perhaps you could let me have a list.'

I went outside, grateful for some fresh air. I leaned over a rail and watched the tenders plying their continuous service between the ship and the quayside. Santa Margherita was one of my favourite places. I could easily spend a month here, in a small hotel, having a lazy time, exploring all the picturesque villages nearby, eating at local cafes.

That last question was meant to pin me down. There's always one last question that tricks the villain into saying something he didn't mean to say. The DCI was checking up on me. Surely I wasn't a suspect?

But I could be. I was the only witness as to what happened in the interview room in the morning. Mr Belcher might have threatened that they were going to report me for interfering in a domestic matter, for publicly humiliating them in front of other passengers. If they had threatened to report me, it gave me a motive of sorts.

I tried to dredge up any other fragments of a motive. If Miss Ember was found brutally murdered, I'd certainly be top of the suspect list. I'd probably give the murderer an alibi.

Derek Ripon was the next one to waylay me. It was a day of entrapments, ambushes, accosting. Pass me Harry Potter's invisible cloak.

'I suppose now we've got a murder, no one is interested in petty crime,' he said bitterly. 'I'm still losing stuff out of Bond Street.'

'Oh dear,' I said, clucking with heartfelt sympathy, playing cute.

'Yesterday it was a silver bangle off a display. We had chained it to the stand but the thief took the stand as well.'

'Missing: one stand. Missing: one chain,' I said, pretending to write it down like a copper on the beat.

'You're not taking this seriously,' said Derek Ripon. He was so thin, he could go through an ajar door sideways. He prided himself on never eating any of our sumptuous food. He lived on rice cakes and Ryvitas. 'That bracelet was priced at £175. It was elaborately engraved, very pretty.'

'And worth every penny, I'm sure,' I said. 'Well, you'll soon find out who has taken it. The passenger list is thinning. Three women and one man down, only a thousand or so suspects left.'

'I don't think that kind of flippant talk, Miss Jones, is exactly helpful. It doesn't suit you,' he said stiffly.

'Sorry, it's the only way I can stop myself from screaming the place down and tearing my hair out.'

I must have looked fierce and wild-eyed, because Derek Ripon backed off quickly, muttering something about talking to me another time when I was in a better mood. Not if I could help it. I thought I knew every nook and cranny on the *Countess* but there was nowhere I could hide. I desperately wanted to hide.

'Like a nice, quick jab?' said Dr Mallory, appearing at my side like a good genie. 'I've got something that would put you out for twenty-four hours. It's guaranteed painless with the sweetest of sweet dreams. Pay me a twenty, and I'll make it Brad Pitt.'

'Give it to me quick. I'm stressed out. That DCI thinks I'm a suspect. He wanted to know where I was every minute of the day Mrs Belcher was murdered, whether I went ashore or not. I couldn't remember. I can't remember anything.'

'Don't worry, Casey. Everyone is a suspect. We all are.

Practically everyone had the opportunity but who had both the opportunity and a motive? That's the crucial question. Who had a motive?'

'It wasn't me.' I sounded about five years old, accused of stealing a packet of Smarties from Woolworths. Samuel put his arm round me in a purely bedside manner. But it was comforting and as always, he smelt so refreshingly nice.

'I need to hide somewhere,' I went on. This didn't sound like me. 'People keep finding me. The wrong kind of people. It's very alarming.'

'I know a single cabin, top deck, rarely used. You wouldn't be disturbed. Rather heavy reading on bookshelves. Nice bathroom.'

I knew where he meant. I had been there once before, to use the bathroom. Not exactly a romantic rendezvous. A very urgent call which I could not ignore.

'I'll remember that when I need to hide.'

'Take it easy, Casey,' he said, patting my arm. 'No heavy lifting.'

I went ashore, much later. Hardly time to look at the Basilica of St Margaret of Antioch, the fondant pink and yellow church in the square, or at the numerous paintings for sale outside in the Piazza Caprera. The church had huge, double height steel doors. There was hot air coming out of grids in the pavement.

I found two hotels where I would like to stay, right on the front. The Helios and the Metropole. And there was the Trattoria Da Pezzi where I would eat, with a photo outside of the beaming chef. It was a rural restaurant with counters of delicious fresh fish, marble tables, wooden chairs, bar stools of cane. I would eat huge bowls of pasta and grow fat. Italians like big women. I like Italians. Well, some of them.

The lightness and brightness of the place washed over me and my spirits lifted. It was what I needed. Dr Mallory often said I had a chip on my shoulder. But here it was barely noticeable.

# Fifteen
## At Sea

The Italian maritime police took the yacht away and the body of the man found aboard. That much I learned though I have little Italian and they were not disposed to chat about the find. They had a list of missing lone yachtsman and apparently he fitted a description. He'd been missing for over a week.

Though from what I gathered, there was not a lot of him left to identify. He'd died in the cabin, open to the elements and the mercy of seagulls. It made me feel quite sick. Apparently seagulls are partial to a touch of necro-snacking, a source close to the enquiry told me. And to think I saved them my uneaten rolls.

The DCI had spent the day interviewing people and he'd been closeted with Samuel for a long time. I kept out of his way. We passed once on deck and he nodded, possibly not remembering my name.

He reminded me of someone but then I'd met so many hundreds of people since I started working cruise lines. I'd need a megabyte computer instead of a brain to remember them all.

Lee was MC for this evening's shows. He was somewhat nervous but not showing it too much. He looked smooth in a well-cut dinner jacket, white shirt and bow tie. I noticed that the black trousers were not an exact match. It's difficult to match blacks. He'd put the outfit together from separates. I wondered if this meant anything.

'Someone stole my trousers,' he said, volunteering what I wanted to know. 'I was pressing them in the ironing room. Went to my cabin to fetch a damp cloth and when I got back, they'd gone. I couldn't believe it. I was only away half a minute.'

'No one will notice. It's my eagle eyes. That's funny, about them being stolen. We've got a light-fingered shopper on-board too. Someone who forgets to pay. I hope your trousers turn up. Perhaps a passenger took them by mistake and will discover they are the wrong pair when they try to fasten the waist.'

Lee was slimly built. He grinned. 'I've lost weight despite all the lovely food. I never seem to have time to eat.'

'And you'll have even less tonight. Watch the time carefully. It's easy to miss that final curtain of each show. You get distracted and the time flies.'

'I don't intend to leave backstage for a second. I'll hang around in some dim corner till it's time to go on again. It's too risky. But I could still get distracted, all those lovely dancers in their skimpy costumes.'

I nodded. 'You'll be on the ball backstage. Break a leg.'

'Not literally, I hope.'

I left Lee rehearsing his introduction. The show tonight had an Italian theme – films, shows and a snatch of opera. The dancers' costumes were fantastic. Lee would have to keep his mind on his words with all the girls running from their dressing rooms in their flimsies.

I joined my table of eight at the first sitting for dinner. It was the second time there had been an extended space in my timetable to join them. They gave me a warm welcome, indicating that I should share the wine that they had ordered. There were two jolly married couples from the Midlands, an elderly lady with her companion, and a woman of about fifty on her own. She didn't say much, smiled rarely. Her name was Mrs Hilary Miles.

As I hadn't wanted to out-dress the ladies, I was wearing a black silk trouser suit and flat silver sandals. It was cool, casual and comfortable.

It was another meal fit for the gods. It was a miracle that the kitchens produced food of this standard, day after day, in kitchens down in the depths. And everything served with such flair, like an artist's creation. Swirls of this sauce and that, an edible decoration, a carrot or radish carved into a fancy shape, a sprig of dill, a tiny morsel of shaped pastry. It seemed a sin to plunge a fork into such artistry.

This table was a nice crowd and I was glad I had joined them. They were amused by some of my stories of past cruises, but I was careful not to tread on any toes or monopolize the conversation.

'We get asked such funny questions. One passenger asked

me if the crew slept on board, and another wanted to know if an outside cabin was outside the ship.'

There was general laughter. Mrs Miles said little. I tried to draw her into the table talk.

'Which port of call have you enjoyed the most so far?' I asked her.

'I never go ashore,' she said.

'Never?' This was surprising. Wheelchair-users sometimes stayed on board or a very frail passenger. But Mrs Miles was neither. She looked a fit and healthy fifty-year-old, despite a certain pallor to her face. Perhaps she didn't go out on deck either.

'I don't like foreign countries,' she said flatly.

'Some of them are really interesting,' I said. 'Conway always choose ports that are stimulating or historical. Or simply pictur-esque. Some of the scenery is outstanding.' I wanted to say that she didn't know what she was missing, but it might have been misconstrued. 'We shall have to put together a special tour that you simply can't resist. In Rome perhaps,' I suggested.

'Don't bother,' she said, turning her attention to the roast duck, and signalling that the conversation was at an end.

The two couples had never been to Elba but had looked up its history on Google. The talk degenerated into a discussion of Napoleon's life and habits and we became a table convulsed with laughter. Even the elderly lady contributed a few risqué remarks which astonished her companion.

'Mildred, dear,' she reprimanded, stiffly.

'Don't Mildred dear, me,' said the elderly lady, laughing. 'I've lived even if you haven't. But never mind, there's still time for you, even if it's running out for me.'

The companion maintained her huffy attitude, refusing to be amused by anything. I wondered how long she had been with Mildred. When the meal ended, a waiter came by with a silver-headed stick and handed it to Mildred, helping her out of the chair. She was very stiff and lame.

'Arthritis,' she said, smiling at me. 'Damned nuisance. Thank you for making it a lovely meal, Miss Jones. I haven't laughed so much for years.'

'My pleasure,' I said. 'I've enjoyed your company, all of you.'

I smiled round the table to include everyone, but Mrs Miles had already gone.

\*     \*     \*

'Evening off?' Sam asked, putting on a funny Jack Warner voice. Jack used to say 'Evening All' in some long-ago television programme called *The Blue Lamp*. It became a catch phrase, but I didn't remember the show. I wondered how Sam knew it. Perhaps he liked re-runs and repeats.

'DVDs of old television shows,' he said, reading my mind as usual. 'I used to watch them when I was on night duty and it was quiet.'

'I expect you really liked Muffin the Mule.'

'And Sooty. I loved Sooty. One of my favourites.'

'Bill and Ben?'

'Terrific. But I shan't attempt an impersonation. Funny looks from the passengers,' he said, with a grin. 'Your deputy was good tonight. I caught the end of the show for five minutes. He went down well with the ladies. Very smooth.'

'Then you have some competition at last. You won't have it all your own way, collecting a blonde harem on every cruise. I didn't check on his delivery. I thought it might put him off if he saw me hovering in the aisles. There was no need anyway. I had every confidence in his ability,' I said.

'You can talk, Miss Jones,' said Sam. 'You're collecting admirers by the dozen this cruise. There's poor rejected Richard Norton who nearly falls over his own flat feet every time he sees you. The new DCI is totally smitten, said he'd never met anyone so charming. And young Lee, despite being a wow with the ladies, is your devoted slave. He'd polish your boots if you asked him to.'

'What rubbish,' I said, feeling a blush colouring my cheeks. 'You do talk absolute nonsense, Dr Mallory. Hardly a suitable bedside manner.'

'It's my in-bed manner,' he said in a loud whisper, which made my blush deepen. He was teasing me, as he always did, those light grey eyes twinkling. I hoped no one heard.

'So how is DCI Bruce Everton getting on with his enquiries? He's not going to tell me,' I said. 'But you can tell me, seeing how we are such buddies.'

'Strangely, I am not supposed to tell anyone. We are all suspects, including me and you. But of course we all know that you wouldn't have smashed an ashtray down on Mrs Belcher's head. Your aim is rotten. You would have missed. I've seen you playing deck quoits.'

'So it was an ashtray?'

'One of those heavy crystal ones, the old type, rarely seen around the ship these days. One of the bright stewardesses noticed it had traces of blood. Soon the ship will be non-smoking from bow to stern. But not yet, passengers are still allowed to smoke in certain areas since we are in waters outside UK regulations.'

'Was the ashtray from the Belchers' cabin?'

'No. It was from the Galaxy Lounge. Someone nicked it, later wiped it clean – but not very well – and put it back. The barman noticed that it had no cigarette ends in it and was suspicious. The ashtrays in the bars fill up quickly. He asked a stewardess if she'd emptied it.'

'Did you ever smoke?'

'In my student days, those little cigars, until I did an autopsy on the lungs of a smoker. Black as tar. That put me right off. And you?'

'I was caught smoking at a bus stop. Aged eleven, wearing my posh school uniform. And I was caught by a policeman, big mistake. I didn't sleep that night, thinking I would be publicly humiliated by the headmistress at assembly the next morning. That put me right off.' I echoed his words.

'And were you publicly humiliated?'

'No, nothing happened. She never said a word. It was in the days when a policeman could frighten the life out of a youngster. Not today.'

'So, Miss Casey Jones, degenerate smoking schoolgirl, what else about your career of vice are you going to tell me?'

He was too close for comfort. This man had charisma in excess, such charm with that air of genteel kindness. There must have been a dozen good fairies at his christening, bobbing around on gossamer wings, waving their wands, trying to out-do each other with the magnificence of their gifts.

'The tests have come back on the blood found in Miss Ember's shower,' said Samuel, changing the subject. 'I took them ashore at Barcelona. They emailed the results.'

'Don't tell me. Yes, do tell me.'

'Animal blood, as I thought. Probably pig.'

'This gets worse and worse. I don't want to hear any more.'

'The engineers discovered that a pouch of blood had been attached to the head of the shower, quite cleverly, with a device for a slow drip. Hardly visible. So what do you make of that, Miss Holmes?'

'Nothing much, Dr Watson. Oh sorry, have I got the name wrong?'

'I'm flattered.'

'It's probably the bald patch, pipe and paunch.'

Later that night I bumped into DCI Everton. The detective was clearly lost, trying to find out where he was on the mini-sized deck plan issued to every passenger in their cabin.

'This is worse than the London Underground map,' he said, trying to work out whether he was starboard or port. 'Can you tell me where I am? Please help me before I end up in the cargo area or down in the engine room.'

'We don't carry cargo,' I said. 'Unless you count mountains of vegetables, booze and unwanted luggage. I'm Casey Jones, entertainments director. We've spoken before. I'm one of your suspects.'

'I know,' he said, nodding. 'How could I forget you? The woman with the radiant smile.'

'I can read maps, too.'

He stopped and looked at me. We were halfway along the corridor that housed a shuttered clothes shop and the closed Internet study. Nothing was happening at this time of night. He looked normal in a grey lounge suit, white shirt. I looked normal in my casual silk trouser suit. Not overdressed, minimal make-up, not too much wine.

'Miss Jones, can we talk? Is there somewhere we can go where we won't be overheard? I should like to talk to you. You seem to know everything that is going on on board ship. Or is it too late? I know you work a long day.'

'Sure, if I can be of any help,' I said, my heart thumping. 'There's always music until late in the Galaxy Lounge. We could sit far back, away from the dance floor, out of sight, a table in a corner.'

'Lead me on.'

'And you don't have to dance with me.'

'I should rather like to but I think it would be unwise, to be seen dancing with a suspect.'

I had no idea why I was doing this, except that it seemed

a good idea. I had nothing better to do. Maybe it was part of my job. We found a table, way back in a dark corner and a stewardess brought two drinks immediately. Wine for me and a scotch and soda for the DCI.

'So, Casey. May I call you Casey? Tell me all you know about this cruise and the various goings on.'

So I told him about Professor Theo Papados's death and the missing mobile, Miss Lucinda Ember's various dramatic problems, added Mrs Fairweather's kindness, Mr and Mrs Belcher's row and anything else that popped into my airy-fairy mind. It was a relief to offload it all on to him. He had broad shoulders.

I told him about the terrified Judie Garllund and her abrupt and unheralded departure. I mentioned the unknown celebrity who was supposed to be travelling with us and the extra passengers rescued from some clapped-out rowing boat in the middle of the night. For good measure I threw in Mrs Hilary Miles who wouldn't go ashore and Wilfred Owen, the retired theatre owner who had been one of The XYZ Factor judges.

'It makes my job seem almost humdrum,' he said, writing volumes in his notebook. 'And yet you look so calm, and always so confident.'

'It's only acting,' I said. 'I act being confident. I was once on the stage. I was a dancer until I had an accident, a nasty break that didn't heal properly.'

'Then you deserve an Oscar,' he said, his eyes suddenly bright and admiring. 'You're brilliant at it.'

'So how are your investigations progressing?' I felt I could ask, acting confident.

'I'm being buried under an avalanche of information. Sightings of the Belchers quarrelling or sitting in stony silence. Greg Belcher sightseeing on his own, or Dora on her own. Dora coming back to have her hair done. But so far, nothing adds up. Zip, zero, nada.'

I raised my eyebrows at the last phrase.

'Sorry,' he said. 'I watch too many late-night American cop shows.'

Now, I was halfway to falling in love with Dr Samuel Mallory, man of many charms and always kind to a stressed-out female. But a reluctance or weakness held me back. DCI Bruce Everton was different. He was ordinary, he worked on the street, he solved crimes, he was a basic, pizza-grabbing, pub-going copper.

This tall, perhaps lonely detective with cropped hair and nice manners did an unexpected somersault into my heart. I couldn't stop it happening. Maybe it was an excess of wine. Maybe it was his scotch after a long day.

'Would you like to dance?' he said.

'I'm a little rusty.'

'I like rusty.'

Now big men usually can't dance, but this one could. Perhaps it went back to his teenage days, dancing at discos or pubs. DCI Everton danced in a slow, careless sort of way, but it was in time to the music which always helps. He didn't step on my feet, just moved me about like in *Dirty Dancing,* a twirl here, a twirl there. I shut my eyes and enjoyed the sensation.

'Do you feel like a walk on deck?' he asked.

'For a bit,' I said. 'I have a busy day ahead and it starts early.'

'So have I,' he said.

So that's how I was seen on deck being thoroughly kissed by Bruce Everton. It was very nice kissing, not too much, no tongue in the mouth, fairly old-fashioned kissing, romantic and star-struck as was fitting for the velvet Mediterranean sky.

'A wonderful evening,' he said, coming up for breath. 'Thank you, Casey. You're not really a suspect, you know. You couldn't be.'

'I'm glad. I didn't do it. And thank you, too, for this evening,' I said. 'You are a most unusual policeman.'

This struck home and his hold tightened.

'Oh, Casey, if only you knew, if only I could tell you.'

I didn't want to know. I didn't want to know his baggage. He probably had six kids at home, a mortgage the size of Everest and a wife who nagged.

He let go of me and the warmth dissolved like ice cubes on a hot summer's day. It was not that he had stopped liking me, it was more that his responsibilities had reared up and hit him on the head with ice-edged sledgehammers.

'I'd better say goodnight,' I said hurriedly.

'Goodnight, Captivating Casey,' he said. 'I'll see you back to your cabin. I don't want anything to happen to you. And it might, if you are seen around with me. I'm dangerous company.'

I'd never been called captivating before. It was a moment to treasure.

# Sixteen

# Rome

Everybody had been to Rome some time or other. It was a city needing a hundred visits. No one could say they had seen all of Rome on a four-hour coach tour.

The pilot had come aboard early, at six thirty-six. We had to pass the breakwater and enter the harbour of Civitavecchia. It was a big 180 degrees swing of the ship before we came astern on to the berth. And it was windy, force five. Overcast with thunder and lightning in the vicinity. Not a good forecast, fingers crossed. Take a raincoat.

Tour sales rang me up in a panic. They had so many coaches booked for this city and not enough escorts. Could I please manage a few hours?

'Please? Please? Please, Casey, masses of photo opportunities for you,' said the manager, desperate. She could see tours being cancelled for lack of escorts.

'I can only do the morning. I can't spare any longer.'

'Thank you. There's a morning coach tour. We owe you a favour.' She'd probably forgotten the favour bit before she'd put the phone down.

It was impossible to see all of Rome's glories in one visit. No one could. It needed an extended weekend, at least four days, to take in everything. One day I would take some leave and spend it in Rome, exploring it on foot.

The *Countess* was berthed in a busy industrial port, Civitavecchia, and it was an hour's drive into Rome, quicker by train if you were an independent traveller. Some of our passengers had a free-roaming sense of adventure and train tickets were amazingly cheap.

My allotted tour was less adventurous. It was a morning-only itinerary that took us to all the most popular sites, stopped long enough for photo opportunities and a brief walk. It was merely a taster. No time for shopping or the cafe culture. Two comfort stops at roadside cafes where the quick-footed could buy an ice cream or a cold drink.

I checked everyone on-board, made a note of the numbers. Experienced guides counted the empty seats and where they were on the coach. But passengers had an unhelpful habit of changing seats so it was not a reliable record.

I found myself sitting next to William Owen, the retired theatrical impresario and one of our talent show judges. He was easy to get along with but spent much of the drive into Rome recording a commentary as his camcorder took in the sights. At first I thought he was talking to me. The avenue into Rome was particularly impressive, a wide, tree-lined approach with enormous ruins haunted by the sound of chariot wheels and the clopping of hooves.

Awesome Rome. Huge and beautiful ruins from different dynasties, defeating time. The Pantheon with its immense columns designed by Emperor Hadrian. The Spanish Steps, comparatively new, finished in only 1726. The huge Colosseum where gladiatorial combats gloried the spilling of blood until 404 AD. We got out and walked round the vast monument but were not allowed in because some private function had been booked. A stag party? Any spilled blood?

St Peter's Basilica, the largest church in the world, resting on over 800 pillars, the square a mass of people waiting, hoping for a glimpse of the Pope, whether it was his day to speak or not. We drove past, cameras clicking. The Trevi Fountain, site of romantic films, drop in a coin and your wish comes true. If only. I had a few wishes.

All these treasures were within walking distance of each other, with so many cafes lining the streets, little boutiques and small hotels. Everything was enchanting. I longed to stay, skip ship, immerse myself in roaming Rome. Of course, it would be nice to have someone to share in all these delights. Sharing would be part of the magic.

For a second, but only a second, I wondered if DCI Everton might be that person. I was trying to put those midnight kisses firmly out of memory. It had been a moment of madness, like fireworks going off. Glorious and heady, then fizzling out, sparks dropping into darkness.

I caught a glimpse of a handsome, dark head that I knew. He had got off a different coach and was listening to their guide, the usual group of ageing Barbie dolls clustered around him. For a moment it threw me completely off balance. Then I recovered. He was doing his job, caring for the physical and mental health of our passengers by being charming. I was the oddball. Book me an appointment.

He caught sight of me and immediately strolled over, scattering the entourage. I wondered what he was going to say. Something superficial?

'Was Professor Theo Papados a diabetic?' he asked. 'Can you find out for me from your general guest questionnaires?'

'What?'

'A diabetic.'

'What do you want to know for?'

'I took a sample of his blood and found a very low sugar level. Rather unusual.'

'I'll do what I can when I get back to the ship. We've got files. All this Roman culture comes first.'

'And history. The history of the whole world is out here.'

The sun bruised my eyes as I followed his tall figure walking back to his coach party. Then he was lost among the swirling masses. I didn't even know which coach he was on. Did I know what I was doing? I had to concentrate on my group, count heads, empty seats. Sometimes people took off on their own, left a coach, without telling anyone. Pass the headache pills. I was getting a familiar throb.

Our last highlight was the Sistine Chapel in the Vatican City with its famous frescoes of the *Creation of Adam* and *The Last Judgement*. No time to look at them, of course, but that's where they are, folks. There were a few grumbles, but I reminded them this was only a whistle-stop tour.

'You'll have to come back another time,' I said. Always the optimist.

William Owen was clearly tired by the tour, all the traffic and crowds, seeing so much of classical Rome crammed into such a short time. He put his camcorder away and shut his eyes, folding his hands on his stomach.

'You will excuse me, won't you, Miss Jones? Coaches always make me feel sleepy.'

'You have a nap, Mr Owen. You'll enjoy your lunch all the more.'

'Wake me up when we get there.'

We hadn't lost anyone so I could relax now, too, and enjoy the rural scenery between the city of Rome and the coast. There were acres of fields and farms and olive trees. It was dusty and peaceful. I thought about Dr Mallory's query. Why ever did he want to know if Professor Papados was diabetic? It would be on his personal details form. Anyone coming aboard to work had to sign a statement about their current state of health, allergies, medication. It was company policy. Managed diabetes would not be a problem.

'Ah, lunch,' said William Owen, waking up like clockwork as the coach rolled into the dockyard area. 'I'm looking forward to that. And a little pre-luncheon drink, somewhere in the shade. Would you care to join us, Miss Jones?'

He used the plural pronoun, us. That meant he had pre-arranged company for lunch. I wondered if it was his fellow judge on the show, the faded but once pretty lady. I'd seen them together several times.

'Thank you, Mr Owen. But another time. I have some work to do.'

Escort guides had a form to fill in afterwards and I was no exception. You had to report on the state of the loos used – as if you could personally check on the gents – cleanliness of coach, the local guide's knowledge and attitude. Also record any unscheduled incidents. We were incident free. I ticked off all the boxes and returned the form to the tour office.

'Didn't lose anyone,' I said cheerfully to the harassed staff. Port days were a nightmare for them. They hardly had time to nod, wave or smile.

'Good on you, Casey.'

I went to my office and switched on the computer, logging into the lecturers' files. It was a big file but I soon scrolled down to his name and brought up details on the screen. Professor Theo Papados was not diabetic. He listed no illnesses. Perfect health, he had written, in the comment space. I emailed the information to Dr Mallory. He might be on an all-day tour and not back for hours.

I had a replacement lecturer arriving from London this after-noon. It was rather late in the cruise for a lecturer on Ancient

Rome, so Head Office had gone for something completely different. Well, almost completely different. This man was going to lecture about antiques. He was an expert in the field. Field wasn't exactly the right word either. Most antiques are found in old houses, car boot sales, stacked in dusty attics. Perhaps the odd one might be dug up in a field.

There was a knock on my door. Most unusual. People usually breezed in and out as if it was a station terminus. I'd be issuing tickets soon.

'Miss Jones? The entertainments director? Is this the right place?'

'This is the right place,' I said. 'Come in.'

The door swung open and five foot eight of South American manhood walked in. He was wearing tight white jeans, a red striped shirt and cravat. He came over, flashing a million-dollar smile, took my hand and kissed it.

'Cavan Franetti, at your service, Miss Jones. I'm your new lecturer. Charmed to meet you.'

His smile was dazzling. I wondered if he could also sing.

Cavan had brought me a gift – possibly a bribe for a cabin upgrade, a reduced lecture load, invites to parties. It was a piece of Delft porcelain, blue and white, a sort of vase. I knew nothing about antiques.

'How lovely,' I said. 'That's a very kind thought. Entertainments directors don't get many presents.'

'But you should. You work hard to keep everything running smoothly. This is a ribbed beaker vase, a copy of Delftware dating from the eighteenth century. And I have brought a few other small things to sell, a few trifles,' he went on smoothly. 'Do I have your permission?'

'Anything for sale has to be sold through the shop, Bond Street,' I said. 'They take a small commission. I'll arrange for you to see the manager, Derek Ripon.'

He looked aghast. 'But they are valuable items, Miss Jones. I can't leave them in a shop. I couldn't allow it.'

'They will be perfectly safe,' I said, trying not to think of our shoplifter still on the loose. 'Mr Ripon will lock them away when we are in port and every night.'

'I should rather sell them at the end of each lecture,' he went on, determined to get his own way. 'People are always more interested then.'

'That isn't allowed,' I said. 'You have to move out of the lecture theatre, on time, to make way for the next lecturer or next event being held in there. You can't hang about, selling things.'

'This is very unsatisfactory,' he said, the warmth going out of his eyes. I wondered if he was going to take back his gift. 'I must think about it. Now which is my cabin?'

I gave him the number. It was Professor Papados's cabin, cleaned out, serviced and ready for a new occupant. Everything neat and pristine. Not a whiff of sudden death.

'I'm sure we'll work things out,' I said hopefully. This man wanted to make money on the side, selling his antiques to the passengers. 'I'll show you the lecture theatre. It's a lovely venue. You will be delighted.'

He did like the roomy theatre, stage and facilities. It seated a lot of people in a semicircle but was still intimate. He tested walking around and standing at a lectern, waving his arms about, throwing his voice to the back row, getting the feel of the place.

Dr Samuel Mallory returned very late from his tour. I saw the passengers rushing aboard, only minutes before all the pre-departure checks. The *Countess* was ready to sail and the lines let go at seven forty-two. We needed the aid of our thrusters and a tug secured aft. We moved off the berth.

Once clear of the breakwater we steamed into the Tyrrhenian Sea and headed towards Calvi and the Balange region.

'So?' It was Samuel on the phone. 'What have you found out? Tell me.'

'Professor Papapdos was not a diabetic. Why did you want to know?'

'His sugar level was very low. Most unusual. I had a hunt around. It's so unusual and easily missed. Perhaps he had been working on deck in his shirt sleeves. But there was the tiniest prick, minute, on his forearm.'

'So what might it be?'

'I'm guessing that someone might have injected him with one hundred units of insulin. The syringe looks like a fount-ain pen or a biro. You can get them anywhere, especially in India. They don't ask you for a prescription. Anyone could have bumped into him, accidentally, and injected him.'

'So what does it mean? If you don't have diabetes and are injected with insulin?'

'It means that your sugar level plummets and you die. And it looks like a heart attack. Insulin shock is when the blood sugar drops suddenly leading to unconsciousness. Professor Papados was in a diabetic coma which led to massive brain damage and death.'

I didn't know what to say. I was shocked and wanted to go home. Samuel seemed sure that he had found a mark on Theo Papados's arm. It could have been an insect bite, although we only get insects when near shore.

'What do we do now?'

'Not a lot. I'll report my findings to Richard Norton and Bruce Everton. It's lucky that we've got a DCI with us. Saves us a lot of paperwork.'

'So we've got someone on-board who stabs bare arms with pens and another who bashes heads with ashtrays. Better watch out for flying pens and ashtrays.'

'Or it could be the same person,' said Samuel.

That evening I wore long sleeves.

# Seventeen

## At Sea

Tonight's show was a compilation of numbers from Ivor Novello shows, *The Dancing Years*, *Perchance to Dream* and others. Those two titles had a special meaning for me. Everyone loved the show, all the melodies from their younger days. I noticed Miss Ember sitting in the front row of the theatre in yet another stunning outfit, a feathered silk dress with a beaded jacket. I couldn't put a name to the designer but it looked outrageously expensive. I hoped it wouldn't end up in our Bond Street shop window.

It was a wonder that our lower-paid crew were so good humoured and helpful when they saw so much opulence being paraded around – clothes, furs, jewels. They accepted the inequality of the world with stoic patience, sending home their pay. Perhaps they thought their turn would come in the next world. I sure hoped mine would.

Yet all I really wanted was to undo time. To go back to the days before I injured my ankle whilst dancing on stage. To go back to the days when I was whole and could dance two performances a night, and still dance on into the small hours in some dimly lit disco. The important things are sometimes too difficult to think about. I tried to remember that today is the only day worth living for. That there is no certainty of a tomorrow.

It was a strange feeling, introducing the shows, knowing that a murderer might be out there in the audience, sitting and watching. It chilled my bones to think that I could be smiling right at him. A murderer who might have a stock of insulin injection pens in his cabin. Perhaps he had a thing about lecturers in which case Cavan Franetti had better look out. He might be the next target.

I'd better warn him.

I was getting suspicious of everyone. What was Franetti trying to sell on the ship? Did he have some highly valuable object among the mediocrity? Say, a piece of a Chinese chess set from some imperial dynasty? We'd had enough of lost masterpieces on the last cruise. No more, please. This was supposed to be a holiday.

'OK, Casey?' It was Trevor, our stage manager, hovering behind me. 'You're looking a bit glum tonight. Where's your famous smile? The smile that launched a thousand cruises.'

'I left it in my cabin. I forgot to dust it off.'

'Go back and get it, girl. It's what the punters expect.'

He was right. The tenth point on my bullet list is smile, smile, smile. I had to think of all the good things around us – the sea, the sky, those fabulous clouds. The tireless wind that tempered the hot days.

I went on stage with renewed energy. 'What a fabulous city,' I said. 'Rome, the city of a thousand legends. I hope you all enjoyed your brief visit and will make another trip one day. And now, from not so far back in the past, tonight's spectacular, that master of story and music, the legendary Ivor Novello.'

I swept off, hoping Novello was listening and approved of my introduction. I wrote it. Was that a faint and distant hand-clap I heard? Or was he busy writing another musical with a celestial cast? No auditions needed. Just turn up and you'll get a part.

'How's my lovely MC?' It was Samuel Mallory, as immaculate as ever. Could be that in his student days he'd earned extra money as a male model, and the polish had rubbed off. His grooming was catwalk perfect. But I liked the look even more when he was tired and dishevelled.

'Shattered,' I said. 'How was your day?'

'Hectic. We only mislaid two passengers and a rucksack. Not a bad average.'

'What had happened to them?'

'The passengers attached themselves to a different guide from another group and wandered off with them. We found them about an hour later, quite unperturbed, in a café. The rucksack was never found. Probably being sold on Ebay at this very moment.'

'Pretty normal day, then.'

'Sure, you could say that.'

He grinned at me. The soaring music of Ivor Novello washed over us from the theatre. The words were poignant. *Perchance to dream.* Did Samuel have dreams? Would he ever tell me? He was an enigmatic mystery. I knew nothing about him except that he once worked in A & E in a Manchester hospital, and that he and his dad sailed boats.

'Time for a drink? My current harem is watching the show.'

'So I won't get my eyes scratched out?'

'Not if you are quick. But I do have a nifty line of eye patches in stock.'

'Would they match my outfit?'

'That could be arranged.'

We found a distant bar, little used. It was where the late-nighters stayed up till three in the morning, far enough away from everyone not to be a noise nuisance. It was dimly lit, with small candles in specially designed containers on every table. Fire at sea was the worst nightmare. No icebergs on this cruise.

Samuel came back from the bar with a dish of peanuts. 'I've ordered a bottle of Malbec Rose. It's an Argentinean wine, quite light, a new one. I thought you might like to try it for a change. If we don't finish the bottle, Joe will put it somewhere cool for us to finish later.'

Now that assumed we were going to meet again later. Dr Mallory was, as usual, taking a lot for granted.

'This is the second cruise for both of us, and I still don't know anything about you,' I said, ready to hear the worst. Three wives and an alimony case. 'Why don't you tell me?'

'Female curiosity is a curse. That's the one thing I really dislike about women. They always want to know everything about you. I take a size nine shoe. My prescription details are plus two point five for the right eye and plus two point seven five for the left. I don't dye my hair. I had a beard in my student days as I was too poor to buy razor blades. Anything else you want to know?'

'Teeth?'

'All my own, except for one crown. I broke a tooth playing rugby. I wanted to sue the chap who kicked me but the referee said it was my fault for getting in the way.'

The bottle of Malbec was brought to our table and his flow

was halted as the first glasses were poured out. It was intensely perfumed and a beautiful pale rose colour.

'Fascinating medical history,' I said. He was fobbing me off with trivia. 'And you used to go sailing when you were a little boy?'

'I spent my childhood messing about in boats. So graduating to a bigger boat is a natural progression for my sea legs.'

He wasn't telling me what I wanted to know. 'And you've had a lot of girlfriends?' I said, prodding deeper. 'You aren't telling me anything.'

'A prodigious number,' he said, tasting the wine with a straight face. 'I hold some kind of world record. Mmn, this is nice, refreshing.'

I was about to ask him if he had ever been married, when his mobile phone rang. He listened, not saying anything, his eyes clouded. He looked as if he had swallowed ground glass.

'All right,' he said with the deepest sigh. 'I'll be along immediately. Whatever are we going to do with her? Of course, she's more your problem than mine. I merely check her pulse and dose out the sedatives.'

He finished off his wine and got up. 'Sorry, Casey. It's your Miss Ember again. She is apparently having hysterics and the steward can't cope. He's reported that she's screaming her head off in her stateroom. Richard Norton is on his way to see her.'

'I'll come too, as after all she is my Miss Ember,' I said, getting up quickly. 'But I've no idea why everyone thinks she's my responsibility. Thanks for the wine, Sam.'

He nodded to Joe. 'Keep it for us, please.'

'Certainly, sir.'

Miss Ember could be heard over half the ship. That was somewhat of an exaggeration, but she could certainly be heard over several decks at that end of the *Countess*. Some passengers were hovering on deck, looking horrified, imaging a chainsaw massacre. But the majority were happily eating or in the theatre watching the show.

'What's that infernal noise?' said Commander Frank Trafford, stomping his way to a bar. 'Can't someone shut that woman up?'

'On our way,' I said sweetly. I didn't want to talk to the

retired commander. He was always so mean-eyed and bad tempered.

'What's it this time?' Dr Mallory asked, catching up with Richard Norton. 'A spider in her washbowl or a lizard down the loo?'

'It's somewhat worse than that,' said Richard Norton, puffing. He was out of condition. Too many four-course meals. He had a big frame to fill but I'd seen him tucking into a fried breakfast every morning.

'How much worse?' I asked.

'I don't think you should come in, Casey,' Richard said, as if I was six-years-old. 'It could be dangerous.'

'Miss Ember may need comfort,' I said. I sounded like a resident of Cranford, lavender and lace hankies at the ready.

Miss Ember's new steward was making tea. It was the panacea for every contingency. She was on the sofa, sobbing hysterically, clutching a cushion.

'I can't stand it, I can't stand it,' she shrieked. 'There must be someone on-board who hates me, who is making my life a misery. Everyone hates me. What will it be next? A dead b–body? My dead body?'

'Of course not,' I said, sitting down beside her. 'Dr Mallory is here and Richard Norton. You are quite safe now.'

'I'm not safe, I tell you. Something awful is going to happen to me. They want to kill me, kill me!' She was off again, sobbing wildly. 'Get rid of it, get rid of it, please, before it attacks me.'

Get rid of it? Get rid of what? We were hardly a floating zoo. I looked at Dr Mallory. 'Show me,' I said, firmly.

'You are such a forceful woman,' he said in my ear. 'Don't blame me if you faint. They've locked the door, very sensible.'

He turned the key in the door and took me into the bathroom. I'd seen these bathrooms hundreds of times before. They were luxuriously equipped, every mod con, everything of the highest quality. I gazed around, expecting dripping blood at the very least.

I gasped and stepped back. This was serious fainting time but I managed to control myself. No point in fainting when your impulse is to run.

It was in the Jacuzzi. It was an oval Jacuzzi with gold taps and small steps leading up and down into it. Curled around the bottom, looking decidedly lazy and comfortable, was a large snake. It was not asleep, its forked tongue flicking in and out, lidded eyes blinking.

'I can't stand snakes,' I said, retreating to the furthest wall, feeling the cold tiles. 'Is it poisonous?'

'We don't actually know,' said Richard. 'As far as I'm concerned, all snakes are poisonous. We're trying to find a crew member who knows about snakes. Some of these fellows have been handling them since childhood.'

'How about injecting it with a sedative?' Dr Mallory asked. 'If I could get near enough without being bitten.'

'Don't do it, Sam,' I said, words tumbling out. 'It's too dangerous. Give the sedative to Miss Ember. Let's get out fast and lock the door again. How on earth did it get in? These bathrooms are interior, no windows, no outer doors.'

'It's too big to have gone through the keyhole.'

'How observant of you. No wonder you are a doctor.'

'It's in my genes.'

I went straight to the balcony window. I found I was shaking and for once the sea did not soothe me. I really hated snakes. I didn't blame Miss Ember for screaming. It was a natural reaction. I felt like a good scream myself. But she would have to calm down before I escorted her to a different part of the ship. But where could she go?

There were no spare cabins anywhere, except the one she had turned down. Mr Belcher had moved back into his original cabin, now that DCI Everton was making other enquiries. Mr Belcher's bar alibi was rock solid, not only the barman's statement but also the timed bar purchases punched on his cruise card. They were irrefutable. The DCI was looking for someone else.

Dr Mallory joined me at the balcony window. 'I've given Miss Ember a sedative which should help her. It would be wise to move her from this cabin which seems to be programmed to upset her. Have you anywhere else she can go?'

'No, there's nowhere. She turned down the twin cabin that I offered her before. Of course, she might take it this time. But it's the purser's problem, not mine. Is that snake still in there? It can't get out, can it?'

'Don't worry. It can't get out. I can give her a private room in the medical centre if that would help. I could say that she needed overnight supervision?'

'How very helpful, thank you,' I said. 'I don't know how she would take the medical centre. Not exactly luxury standard. She's a very formidable woman.'

'So I've noticed. She even complained that I didn't know how to give an injection. She'll probably sue me for inflicted pain and humiliation.'

'Humiliation?'

'Having to say ouch in front of a steward.'

So there were two options. Overnight care and supervision in the medical centre, at no extra cost. Or the smaller cabin with fresh flowers, an open bar tab, and credit at the casino. I had noticed she liked a bit of a gamble. I went outside and phoned the purser.

'Not Dismember Ember again,' said the deputy purser who was on duty. 'She drives us all barmy. Nothing is ever right.'

'Which option shall I offer her?'

'Let her chose, then she can't blame us.'

'How much credit are you prepared to give her at the casino?'

He groaned. 'Make it a hundred. Worth every penny to keep her quiet for a couple of hours. Let's hope she loses it.'

I found Lee and asked him to take over the second Ivor Novello show. The steward and I trundled backwards and forwards, helping Miss Ember move into the smaller cabin. She grumbled the entire time. She could only move part of her vast wardrobe and she kept changing her mind about what she wanted to take with her.

'And where are the flowers you promised?' she demanded.

'The florist will bring them to you as soon as possible. It may be tomorrow.'

'I want drinks delivered now.'

'Of course, the steward will take your order.'

'That casino credit is pretty mean,' she went on. 'Can't you get them to increase it? I am being very reasonable. After all, it was a poisonous snake.'

'I'll see what I can do,' I said, dredging up the last of my patience.

We never did get to finish that bottle of wine.

# Eighteen

# Elba

One of the engineers was Spanish and knew a lot about snakes. He deserved a medal in my view or a standing ovation. He said it was a Montpellier snake, common in Iberia, one of the five poisonous snakes in Spain and of a ferocious appearance. He recognized it by the white underbelly, the yellow rim round the eyes and the ridge above, and the dark grey and green scales.

'It is poisonous,' he said, pleased to be airing his knowledge. 'But snake not kill humans. If bite people, only make lot of pain. It kill lizards and rats and small creatures to eat. It rears up and hisses like a cobra.'

No wonder Miss Ember was terrified.

'I will be able to transfer the snake into a sack because it is back fanged,' he said.

I didn't understand what this meant, but guessed it might mean that the poison shot out backwards?

He shook his head. 'No, the venom fangs sit at the back of the mouth. So you hold the snake so.' I tracked away fast. 'This snake like warm places so it will like Elba,' he said. 'No need to take it back to Barcelona.'

I thought this was a bit unfair on the lizards and other small creatures in Elba but I was not in the killing business, so I left it to others to decide. Dealing with the snake proved more straightforward than dealing with Miss Ember. Next morning Captain Nicolas asked me to go and see him in his quarters on the bridge.

'Miss Jones, please come in. Would you like some coffee? It's fresh. I understand Miss Ember is becoming quite a difficult situation.'

He had a machine that kept a jug of coffee hot.

'Yes, she is. Black, please, no sugar.'

He poured out two coffees. 'I need your help, Miss Jones. I need a brainwave to solve the problem of Miss Ember and the unfortunate snake. Apparently she refuses to go back into her stateroom and refuses any other accommodation. Not that we have much to offer. This cruise is full.'

I had a brainwave of sorts. 'You could marry her, you know, a shipboard romance, and then she could move in with you. A bit cramped after her luxurious stateroom but the status would be immense. She'd get to sit at the captain's table every night.'

His eyes twinkled. 'I thought I could rely on you for an imaginative solution, but I doubt if the current Mrs Nicolas would approve.'

'I do have another idea, sir,' I said. It came to me as I was thinking about Georgina Conway, the woman who inherited the Conway Blue Line from her grandfather and pioneered its expansion and modernization. 'A little bizarre, but it might work.'

'Try me.'

'I've checked on the position of the rest of the Conway fleet, and it might be possible to arrange for Miss Ember to be transferred to one of the other cruise ships. This could be easily done while both ships are in port, say here at Elba or Corsica. The purser's office would have to get the paperwork right.'

'Brilliant idea, Casey. Let's hope the *Countess Aveline* or the *Countess Stasi* have some spare accommodation that will please Miss Ember. I'll get the purser to email them right away.'

'Let's hope they'll take her.'

'I knew you'd think of something.'

'Thank you, sir.'

It didn't surprise me when I learned that the answer came back swiftly from both cruise ships, a firm negative. Lucinda Ember had cruised on both ships and been a perfect nuisance. They wouldn't take her. Not even as a favour to Captain Nicolas.

I started to wonder again. Passengers had been known to take the company to the cleaners over quite trivial matters. One woman tried to convince the legal department that the

ship's engines interfered with her hearing aid. For some it
became a sort of game, to see how much compensation they
could screw out of Conway.

Miss Ember had already been offered a free cruise which
was generous. What else could she want?

Dr Mallory was thinking along the same lines. 'I've
prescribed her a couple of sedatives. She refused accommodation in one of my side rooms in the medical centre and
refused the company of a nurse overnight. But she has come
up in a very nasty rash. She says she's allergic to reptiles.
That's a new one on me.'

'Look it up on Google. Reptile rash.'

'I certainly will. Are you going ashore at Elba?'

'I hope so. It's one of my favourite islands. Not so picturesque as Santa Margherita but all dusty and sun-baked.
Napoleon was lucky.'

'Lucky? He died there.'

'You have to die somewhere. But he didn't die here. He
was exiled on Elba. He died on St Helena, in the South
Atlantic, in 1821.'

'What a little Miss Know-All. I bet you got it from one of
your quizzes.'

'Passengers expect me to know the answers to everything.
I'm a walking encyclopedia. Try me.'

'Tell me, Miss Jones, does the ship generate its own
electricity?'

'No, we run on very large batteries.'

'So how far above sea level are we?'

'It varies on whether we are in dock or at sea.'

I wasn't the only one eager to see the rugged island of Elba.
There was a crowd of passengers up early and leaning over
the rails, camcorders at the ready.

I hadn't heard the ringing for the standby engines at six
forty-five a.m. but I did hear the anchor let go at seven twenty-
one. Later I watched them lowering the tenders into the water
ready for the continuous service into the small harbour of
Portoferraio. It was going to be a very hot day. The forecast
was thirty-two degrees Celsius, the highest temperature of this
cruise.

The young officer in charge of one tender was new. He

needed L-plates. He had three attempts at bringing the small vessel alongside the landing quay. The good-natured passengers gave him a cheer when he finally made it. He was red-faced and it wasn't simply the sun.

Heat rose off the cobblestones in quivering waves. Passengers hurried to the shade of cafes and shops. Portoferraio was the capital and main port of the island so it was a busy place and the second most fortified town in the Mediterranean. Malta is the first.

It hurt my eyes to look up to the star-shaped fort which dominated the town. I knew there were magnificent views from the fortress if you could manage to climb up a hundred and fifteen uneven steps. This was where I was going. It would be even worse coming down.

I heard panting and puffing behind me as I slowly climbed a steep and narrow cobbled side street, keeping to the shady side. You had to watch out for cars and taxis, as they seemed to do what they liked. I saw a car coming down a path and leaped out of its way.

'Nice one, Casey,' gasped a male voice, after a similar leap. 'No road rules on this island. Or they never get caught. Am I going the right way? Are you going to see the house of the great man?'

It was Richard Norton, taking some time off from being ship's security officer. I didn't think I'd seen him out of uniform before. He was sewn into that khaki outfit. But today he was in an open-necked navy T-shirt with fawn shorts and a wide panama hat. His legs were alabaster. He was going to get them burnt.

'Yes, it's this way. You don't often get ashore, do you?'

'Not this trip. But Detective Chief Inspector Bruce Everton is in charge of the murder investigation. I am no longer needed to preserve the security of the *Countess*.' He sounded completely fed up and cheesed off. Had he been suspended? Was I going to have to listen to a long line of grievances? Going to be a normal day, then.

'I'm sure the crew and the captain think otherwise. I know that the passengers are always reassured when they see you strolling about. Like a bobby on the beat.'

Not quite the most tactful thing to say, but the best I could do as the sun beat down and the oxygen got more rarefied.

Sweat was trickling down my nose and falling off. I flapped the hem of my shirt to get some air round my waist. It was almost impossible to walk upright.

'Of course, I'm still in charge of shipboard security, but I've been taken off the murder cases. The professor and the fishwife.'

'Fishwife? That's not a nice thing to call Dora Belcher.'

'Well, she was slanging him like a fishwife, I understand.'

'Were you there?' I knew he wasn't.

'Er – no.'

'Then it's pure gossip and surmise, isn't it? And it shouldn't be repeated without proof.' Again, not the right thing to say to poor old Richard. 'But who says the professor was murdered? It hasn't been confirmed. Cheer up, buster. We're nearly at the top and the view is worth the effort.'

We were approaching the Palazzina dei Mulini, the main residence where Napoleon had lived. It was a long, well-proportioned, pink-washed building with rows of tall windows. He'd had gardens for walking and palm trees for shade as well as a magnificent view over the bay. And the view in those days didn't include tankers in the port and new concrete buildings.

There wasn't time to join a tour of the faded pink palace although I would have liked to have seen inside. It's reputed to be a storehouse of treasures. It still has lots of beautiful furniture and paintings, silver and china, though many things have disappeared over the years. Don't ask me where they went. Some souvenir hunters have itchy fingers.

We leaned over a wall and took in the view before continuing the climb up to the Star Fort. Richard was getting his breath back now, looking less distressed. We took the last hundred yards easy, no point in pushing him. I wouldn't know how to deal with a heart attack. I had my first aid certificate but it wasn't something I practised regularly.

'Isn't this marvellous,' I said. 'Breathtaking. You can see the whole of the town, the bay, those mountains over there and even inland.'

'It's certainly worth the climb,' he said, offering me a mint. 'Thanks for letting me come with you. I needed some good company to cheer me up.' He took out some binoculars and started scanning the town.

'And I'm always very good company,' I said, sucking on the mint, enjoying the extra-sharp tang. 'See anything interesting?'

'I think I've seen Miss Ember going into a boutique carrying a parcel. Yes, it's definitely her. Not exactly a parcel, more like one of those plastic zip-up clothes bags.'

'It can't be the snake then. Show me, show me, please,' I said. Richard's got funny eyesight so I had to twiddle the focus dial till it was right for me. 'Where, where? Tell me. I can't find her.'

'A bit more to the right, down there, further down. No, not that way. The other way.' It was hopeless, trying to follow someone else's directions with binoculars. We lost her in the crowds.

My interest in the Star Fort evaporated in the heat. I wanted to follow Miss Ember and find out what she was doing. Perhaps that's what I had wanted to do all the time, but I'd not acknowledged it.

'Richard, if you'd like to stay up here a bit longer, that's fine. But I want to know what Miss Ember is up to.'

'Shopping,' he said. 'She went into a shop. That's what women do.'

How he ever got this job was a wonder to me. But to be fair, he didn't have to play detective and detect things. His job was security.

'I'm going down into the town to see if I can find her. What was she wearing?'

'A dress and a hat.'

I swallowed my impatience. 'Brilliant observation,' I said. 'I'll soon be able to spot her.'

The shorter route down to the main square was steep and scary. The huge slabs of cobbles were oily with heat. Motorbikes tore past me, sliding and skidding. This was the oldest part of Portoferraio, a street called Via del Amore. Not much *amore* about it today. Everyone was too hot for a dalliance.

The Sea Gate was ahead and the commercial centre of the town. The *Countess* tenders were waiting at the quayside to take passengers back to the coolness of the ship and a long iced Pimm's before lunch. It was a reassuring sight. Miss Ember was not in the queue, boarding the tenders. I checked with the crew that she was not already aboard. Her cruise card had not been scanned in.

A lot of passengers waved to me and said hello. 'Isn't it hot?' they chorused.

'Yes, really hot. It's lovely. Have you got enough water? There are some water coolers by the tenders. Help yourselves.'

I hurried back through the Medici Gate, making a quick scan of the shops and boutiques and cafes. Several familiar faces were eating huge slices of watermelon, spitting out the pips. A street market lured me and in thirty seconds I had bought six pairs of silky pants, lacy and embroidered, in black, pink and blue. I couldn't resist them. Nor the price. I could throw away my old white ones that were now washing sad and grey. I've often wondered why white things go grey.

I left the street market before I bought up the entire stall, and continued my tour of the expensive shops. Miss Ember would only shop expensive. No street market for her.

There were some lovely clothes, elegant furniture and household goods. You could start from scratch in Elba and furnish a home with style. But no need for duvets or curtains. Not in this climate.

I stopped in my tracks. In front of me was a white-painted corner boutique full of delightful accessories, belts, bags, hats and jewellery. The window had been dressed with Fifth Avenue flair. Everything was tempting. Especially the gown in the centre of the display.

It was a beautiful Chanel dress, the black and gold camellia dress. The one that had been in the wardrobe with the rat, in the ship's shop window with a pool of blood, and taken to a dry-cleaners in St Tropez from where it had disappeared. It was now in a boutique on the island of Elba.

That dress had certainly travelled.

# Nineteen
# Elba

I went into the boutique, checking first that I had enough time. This was going to be one fast interview. I prayed that the assistant would be able to speak English. There was no time for the dictionary.

She was very Italian. Olive-skinned with masses of black hair swept up into a chignon. She was wearing skinny clothes that probably cost a fortune. Her eyelashes were inches long, black as spiders' legs.

'Yes, madam?' she said, not looking at me, already bored.

'That dress in the window.'

'It is not for sale.'

Good start. 'OK, I don't want to buy it,' I came back fast.

She flickered a token look at me. I was of one per cent interest. She said nothing but turned what existed of her professional attention to an arrangement of jewellery.

'Where did you get the dress from?' I asked. 'I'd like to know.'

'I don't know.'

'Oh yes, you do. That dress came into your possession in the last half hour. And I have proof of that.'

It was a wild guess but fairly accurate. Miss Ember was seen carrying a clothes bag thirty minutes ago, now its contents were here in the shop window. The young woman looked a fraction disconcerted. She turned her attention to some fans.

'It was a private arrangement,' she sniffed.

I was surprised that she knew such a long word. 'So, tell me about it,' I said, eyeing my watch. It was worse than getting blood out of a stone.

'Please to kindly leave,' she said. 'I am busy.'

She certainly didn't know what busy meant. Swift action was required. I decided on shock tactics. I produced my laminated crew card which had a small photo on it, flashed it but didn't give her time to read the printing.

'This is a criminal investigation,' I said in a voice of authority. 'I am making enquiries into an international fraud which includes the acquisition of one black and gold Chanel couture dress. The description fits the dress in your window exactly. Now please tell me how you acquired it.'

The young woman crumpled. The sophistication diminished, flickered like a candle going out. For a moment I felt sorry for her. She had been hoping she wouldn't be found out, but alas Monster Truth had descended on her in the form of Ms Casey Jones, intrepid PI, but not yet registered.

'Tell me exactly what happened.'

At last she looked straight at me. She had the most beautiful liquid brown eyes. She must send the young men of Elba wild with lust for one look. And the older ones.

'This little old English lady came into shop,' she began. 'She very upset. She needed money for sending home to sick son. She said she would sell me very special dress for money. I see label. Chanel. Everyone knows Chanel label. It is very beautiful dress. I would look magnificent in such a dress. We have Gala Festival soon.'

I saw it all. She had paid Miss Ember for the dress out of the shop till, put it in the shop window, but planned to wear it herself at the Gala Festival whenever that was. Neat thinking and forward planning.

'How much did you pay her? This little old English lady?'

It was a lot of euros. I didn't have enough. No way. Miss Ember had walked off with a bundle. I was going to have to leave the dress, but then I caught sight of the handsomest head on the island of Elba. And not on the island for that long. Like me, he was a fleeting visitor. He was wandering along the street, on his way back to the tenders.

'Sam, please,' I said, rushing out of the boutique before he disappeared into the crowds. 'Can you lend me a lot of euros?'

'Of course, Casey, my dear,' Sam said laconically. 'How many do you want?' He took a wallet from his linen jacket and peeled off some hundred euro notes. He didn't ask what I wanted the money for. He didn't ask when he would get it back. He just gave it to me as if it was a couple of pounds. 'Will five do?'

'Yes, thank you. Perfect. It's a bit complicated but I will explain.'

'I shall expect a full explanation. In the Galaxy Bar, tonight at nine?'

I nodded. 'I promise.'

'And I know you always keep your promises. One of your most endearing traits,' he said, strolling on, by himself, amused by his own company. He tipped his hat, very Jane Austen.

I went back into the boutique where the young assistant had regained some composure.

'You can't have it back,' she argued. 'It belong shop now.'

'Oh no it doesn't and oh yes, I can,' I said. 'Or you will be charged with receiving stolen goods and may even go to prison. Now take the money and find something else to wear at the Gala Festival. I'm sure you will look stunning. You would look stunning in a sack.'

It was not an easy transaction but I got the dress back and she put it in one of their classy gold and black boutique bags. I also got a photocopy of the receipt which Miss Ember had signed and I got a receipt for the euros which I paid for the dress. I was hoping that Conway would eventually repay me and then I could repay Sam. It was a chain of repayment. It might take years. It probably would. We would both be old and grey. Miss Ember had made a profit. Conway Blue Line would lose out.

Still, the thought of knowing Sam when I was old and grey was comforting. He would look distinguished but I would look, well, old.

I put the dress in a safe place in my cabin, in the wardrobe behind the life jacket, in classy boutique bag. I told my steward, Ahmed, not to let anyone into my cabin.

'No matter what they say. No one, Ahmed.'

'Yes, Miss Jones. No one.'

'Only you, the doctor, the security officer or the captain. No one else.'

'No one else.' He looked bemused.

'It's very important.'

Lee was glad to have a few hours ashore. I was back on-board in time for a salad lunch in the Terrace Café. I threw in a few prawns for protein. Later I went to Richard Norton's office. He was sitting despondently behind his desk, shuffling papers, sipping water. His knees were red.

'Cheer up,' I said for the second time that day. 'I have recovered the Chanel dress that Miss Ember sold to a boutique this morning. It's the same dress that went missing after dry-cleaning at St Tropez. Same dress that was draped in the Bond Street shop window on board the *Countess* dripping blood. Same dress that was in the rat infested wardrobe. It has a history.'

'So, what am I supposed to do with it?' he asked, bewildered. He was lathering his knees with after-sun lotion. A bit late.

'Keep it as evidence,' I said, sadly realizing that Richard Norton was not *au fait* with this kind of swindling. 'Miss Ember is obviously up to some trickery and you should find out. You are employed by Conway Blue Line and it's your responsibility to investigate the matter.'

'Shall I put the dress in a secure place?' he said, surfacing through a fog of indecision and painful knees.

'Excellent idea, but I have put it in a safe place. And the fewer people who know the safe place, the better. It may be needed as evidence.'

I left him to wallow in despair and smarting knees.

Between checking rehearsals for tonight's show, I tried to locate Dr Mallory but he was nowhere to be found. More casualties on those steep steps? He was an expert on sprains.

Miss Ember was also nowhere to be seen. I had almost forgotten about our missing non-entertainer, Miss Judie Garllund. But I did meet Detective Chief Inspector Bruce Everton. He was strolling the decks, looking ashore enviously.

'This is the life,' he said. 'What a beautiful island.'

'It certainly is,' I said. 'As long as you don't get murdered on-board.'

'I apologize for not having more time to talk to you, Casey. Have you ten minutes now?'

'As long as you promise not to sweep me off my feet and kiss me in front of several hundred returning passengers,' I said.

He grinned. 'I should very much like to do that, but since you are hoping to keep your air of cool elegance, I promise not to. It will be difficult, but I'll do my best.'

'Thank you,' I said, hiding a smile. I had changed out of my crumpled shore clothes and was back in uniform. 'Let's go to my favourite place and have a cream tea. Very English and sustaining if you miss a few meals.'

'I've missed a lot of meals. I can't get used to the times. I always turn up just as some food outlet is closing.'

Food outlet. Head Office would love that.

The Terrace Café was empty. Most passengers were still ashore. Elba was a novelty and they were making the most of the time. I collected a tray of tea, home-made scones, jam and dish of cream. Bruce Everton had spotted a free table on deck but in some shade. It was still very hot and the sun was a furnace. We had a view of the harbour.

'This is perfect,' he said with a grateful smile. 'Thank you. Everyone is so busy on board. You are always so busy. It's nice to find an oasis of calm.'

'Have you felt neglected?' I asked.

'I feel neglected, in the way, and a nuisance. Death isn't taken seriously on board this ship. It's as if it's another diversion, but nothing that must interfere with eating or entertainment.'

I was shocked at his sarcasm. 'No, surely, not as bad as that. That's awful. The passengers were naturally upset about Mrs Belcher. Many knew her. The professor was different. They hardly knew him. They don't get to know our lecturers that well until further into the cruise.'

'I've been interviewing everyone who knew Mrs Belcher, all the passengers with cabins along the same section of the ship, also their table companions. All I've got is that they argued a lot. I've interviewed all the other lecturers and your arts and crafts people. Nobody knew the professor. He had a cabin to himself and was not much of a mixer.'

'You might as well interview every single passenger on board. And the entire crew and the stewards. Everyone is a suspect. I guess I'm still a suspect but you are kind enough to pretend that I'm not.'

'I could demand that the whole cruise is called off and the ship and passengers return to Southampton for investigation,' he said, biting into a scone heavily laden with jam and cream. 'Then they might take some notice. They regard my questions as an intrusion on their holiday.'

'I understand your feelings of frustration,' I said, stirring my tea. I wanted to drink and drink. I was dehydrated. 'But the killer is still on board. You have more chance of arresting him at sea than you have in Southampton. He'll disappear in minutes once we dock. He'll slip away and you'll have no

chance of finding him. Why not hold a meeting, all the officers, heads of departments, and hammer home how important
this is? They might take some notice then and come up with
titbits of information that'll help you.'

'I'll think about it,' he said. He was a nice-looking but
ordinary man, yet his eyes were full of honesty like beams from
a lighthouse. They were pale blue, dancing with light, outlined
by fair eyebrows. Eyes are the mirror of the soul. I'd read that
somewhere. I could see his soul but I couldn't read it.

'Do you want to hear what else is happening?' I said, letting
the cream and jam pack calories into my gut. 'We've the
ongoing Ember saga and the missing singer.'

'Sounds intriguing,' he said, letting some of the frustration
roll off him. 'Why don't you tell me? I might learn something from your methods of deduction, find them instructive.'

So I unburdened my soul and he listened. He listened like
a policeman, not like a soul mate or a friend. But it was good
because he did not interrupt or make me feel like a fool. He
did ask leading questions.

'This Miss Lucinda Ember,' he said. 'Has she got a criminal record?'

'Heavens, I've no idea and no way of finding out. I only
know that the other cruise ships of the Conway Blue Line
were not eager to have her company. In fact, they refused to
take her on board.'

'I can find out for you,' he said. 'I've got my laptop with me
and can access most of our databases. Of course, it might only
be a few parking tickets, but it all helps to build up a profile.'

I liked that phrase. Building up a profile. It summed up
what I did most of the time for passengers, entertainers and
some of the crew. But Dr Samuel Mallory was still a mystery
to me. I couldn't build up anything about him.

'Thank you. That would be a great help.'

It was not long before all the tenders were secured back
on deck, and the usual announcements were made for missing
passengers. Miss Ember was not missing. Then the *Countess*
weighed anchor, swung off her anchorage and proceeded out.
We set a westerly course, heading towards Calvi.

'There's a legend, you know,' I said finishing the last of
the tea. 'That Christopher Columbus was from Calvi. At that
time it was part of the Genoese empire.'

'Almost every port in the Mediterranean claims Columbus as its famous son,' said Bruce Everton, grinning. 'His mother certainly got around.'

'And we don't even know who she was.'

'That's history for you. The unknown Mrs Columbus. Mary was the only mother ever to became famous. Every other mother has vanished into the mists of time. Thank you, Casey, for a pleasant and informative afternoon. Can I call you Casey? Miss Jones is rather formal.'

'Only call me Miss Jones if you are coming to arrest me.'

'I'll remember that,' he said solemnly. 'But I doubt if it's a possibility. You are transparently honest.'

It was a nice compliment but not entirely accurate. I knew I could lie like the best of them. Sometimes it was necessary to lie. Social lies I call them. We all need them at times.

'Dora Belcher came back to have her hair done,' I said. 'Wasn't that a little strange?' I asked. 'Especially when she'd had it done the day before.'

'The ways of you ladies are a mystery,' said Bruce.

Dawn Charmans, the dance captain, was racing across the deck towards me, blonde hair flying. She could move fast when she had to. There was a show starting in about twenty minutes. I had to change too, into some glad rags. Something cool and floaty for tonight.

'Case, hang on a minute, girl, I got something to tell you.'

'Can't it wait? We haven't time to talk. You're cutting it fine. We're both cutting it fine.'

'I can get into my first costume, slap on some make-up, and be on stage in ten minutes flat. It's checking the others wot takes the time.'

'So?' I was itching for a shower, literally itching. Elba was a dusty island. I hadn't decided what to wear yet.

'That non-appearing artiste, the so-called famous cabaret singer, Miss Judie Garllund. Well, I've found her. Howd'ya like that? Got time for me now?'

'Right. Talk as we walk,' I said, heading her toward the theatre.

# Twenty

# Corsica

There was no way I was going to get ashore on Corsica, not after the information that Dawn gave me yesterday. I had to stay on-board while we entered one of the most beautiful gulfs of the Mediterranean, and anchored half a mile north of Calvi harbour.

So no long and cool swim for me at the town beach which was tantalizingly close to the harbour. Such clear blue water. It was only a twenty minute walk, along the front, through palm-lined gardens, past small shops and hotels. The last time I was there, I burnt the soles of my feet on the hot sand.

It was time to help Detective Chief Inspector Everton. I had discovered some clues, including the whereabouts of Miss Judie Garllund. But for the time being, she could stay where she was, out of sight, out of trouble. She was not likely to surface. My chatting around would not attract any attention. I was always talking to people, on deck, below deck, state-room or my lady's chamber.

No one had discovered a motive for the death of Professor Papados. Dr Mallory had assumed it was natural causes although he had that theory about an insulin jab. At least that's what he told me, but then he did not always give me straight answers. Protecting me from the truth, he called it.

I went into the bar where the professor had collapsed. It was a small side bar without a name, where passengers went for a bit of peace and quiet, wanting to escape from the masses. The barman was an amiable Irishman with unruly dark hair called Paddy. No one knew his real name. He sailed all the cruises. I don't think he had a home to go home to.

'Hi, there, Paddy,' I said. 'How are things?'

'Quietened down a bit now, miss,' he said. 'We were on

the sightseeing circuit after the poor professor copped it, here on the floor. A real gentleman, he was. Didn't even need to clean the carpet.'

'I'm sure the carpet was cleaned,' I said, not sure if this was an obscure Irish joke. 'How did he seem before he died?'

'Not himself, miss,' said Paddy, polishing some glasses till they sparkled. He didn't hold with our newfangled dish-washers. There were always smears. 'He didn't seem all there which was unusual in such an educated man. Like he'd lost his sense of reality.'

This was a strange thing for Paddy to say.

'Did he look any different?'

'He did, miss. He was very hot.'

'But it was getting hot.'

'This bar is air-conditioned and his face was bright red. He was drinking a lot, had got awful thirsty all of a sudden. Normally he was a one drink man and he made it last.'

'Alcohol?'

'No, it was coke. One bottle after the other. He said his mouth was dry.'

'Was there anyone with him?' I asked.

'No, he was on his own, as usual. Except that singer woman was with him for a bit, earlier on. Judy Garland, as she calls herself, same as that famous star. She came in here, all dolled up, trying to chat him up but he'd have none of it. Sent her packing quite sharpish.'

'Judie Garllund? Are you sure about that?'

'Perfectly, miss. She was chatting away to him about nothing, trying to cadge free drinks, for sure. I know the type.'

'What happened then?'

'Nothing really, except that he got even more hot and angry and dry. He was quite aggressive before he collapsed, not like his normal self at all. It was very strange.'

'Was Miss Garllund still with him?'

'No, she'd gone before then.'

Paddy poured me an orange juice, added ice and a few slices of fruit, and pushed it across the counter to me. I thanked him.

'Did he happen to mention Miss Lucinda Ember at all?'

'Funny you should ask that, miss, but he did,' said Paddy. 'He asked me if she ever came into this bar. It was as if he didn't want to see her. I told him she never did. He was safe from her in here. He looked relieved and asked for some water. He said he was very hot. Suddenly he sort of staggered and collapsed, unconscious like, and the doctor came. It was touch and go. The good doctor almost saved him, the blessed man.'

'I know. Dr Mallory was pretty upset about it. One other thing, do you remember if the professor had a mobile phone on him when he died?'

'That was another thing he was going on about,' said Paddy. 'Somehow he'd lost his phone and he was annoyed. Said it had some special photos on it that he wanted to get printed out for you. That's right. He said you had to have them. It was important, he said. Don't reckon nobody's getting them printed now.'

I felt a tremor of apprehension and it wasn't only the clinking of ice at the bottom of the glass. The professor's mobile phone was missing. What else was missing? It was like a jigsaw puzzle with half the pieces gone astray. A motive was missing for a start. But something weird was nagging my memory and I didn't know what it was.

I thanked Paddy for the juice again and left the bar. I passed the Bond Street shopping gallery and stopped at the window where the Chanel dress had draped the model. If only that model could talk. She had her head back on now and was wearing a shore-going outfit. Blazer and cotton trench jeans, jaunty cap.

Richard had traced the photo of Lucinda Ember on the model back to the ship's photo gallery. They always displayed recent photographs taken by the ship's photographers for passengers to buy. Someone had lifted a head and shoulders shot of Lucinda Ember and glued it to the model's face.

Suddenly I saw something that I hadn't noticed before. The beauty counters were laid out right behind the window show case. There were several gilt-edged mirrors so that shoppers could try out the various cosmetics.

What was intriguing was that the mirrors were angled, so they also reflected people standing in other parts of the shop. What if Professor Papados had noticed that, knew that his photos of the dress also contained the reflection of someone in the shop? Someone you would not expect to see there. Someone who should not have been there?

It was a possibility and an intriguing thought. It could also be a motive for getting rid of the professor before he told anyone. Why did I keep saying 'get rid of' when he had died of a heart attack, a natural death? It was not a comfortable thought. I had to tell someone my suspicions.

But who should I tell? Collision course, Casey.

Morning surgery was still busy. Passengers were waiting outside the doctor's consulting room, idling through current glossy magazines, renewed each cruise. No dog-eared, out of date publications on the *Countess*.

'A quick word, please' I said to the nurse receptionist. 'I'm not a patient. I need to give Dr Mallory some information.'

'I'll fit you in as soon as this patient comes out.'

'But I've been waiting a long time,' said Frank Trafford, whose hearing had picked up our exchange. 'She's not going in before me.'

'Staff do have priority,' said the nurse. 'Unless you are an emergency, Mr Trafford?'

'Commander,' he snapped.

'Thank you.' I smiled around at the waiting passengers. 'I'll be double quick. Promise.'

'Miss Jones,' said Dr Mallory, not even looking up as I went into his surgery. 'I don't seem to have your notes. What is it this time? A nose job, ears pinned back or the morning-after pill?'

He could really make me mad. But this was not the time or the place for banter. I had promised those people waiting outside. Commander Trafford was probably timing me, right now.

'I've been talking to the barman in the side bar where Professor Papados died,' I began.

'Paddy.'

'Sure, Paddy told me that before he died the professor was hot, thirsty, red in the face and aggressive. Thought you ought to know. Also that Miss Judie Garllund was in the bar before he was taken ill, chatting him up.'

'Enough to make any sane man hot, thirsty, red in the face and aggressive.'

'I thought you ought to know.'

'Thank you, Miss Jones. Keep taking the tablets.'

'And I have information about the missing Miss Garllund.'
'Riveting news. Next patient, please.'

Lee had gone ashore for a couple of hours. Security on the card scanner at the top of the gangway confirmed that Miss Ember had also gone ashore. I had a feeling that this was my only chance. But I did need a terribly good reason for looking round her stateroom. More mice? Something a little more serious, say another rat?

Like the one I was smelling?

Her new steward was not keen to let me in.

'I have been told that no one, absolutely no one, is to be let in. Even myself am not allowed in,' he said staunchly.

'But that doesn't mean me,' I said, digging in my heels. No, I wasn't wearing heels. 'I am not no one.'

'You are Miss Jones, worthy entertainments director. Very clever. Very pretty.' His dark brown eyes twinkled for one and a half seconds, then blanked off.

'So you will let me in?'

'No.'

'So I will have to go and get Richard Norton, the security officer?' The last person I wanted to speak to. He'd try to chat me up. I didn't have the time or the inclination.

'Yes, miss.'

'You are wasting my time.'

'Sorry, miss. I know, absolute pain in the rear.'

I wondered where he had learned that. Come on, Casey, think up an alternative argument that will floor him. But there was no need. Dr Mallory came sauntering along the corridor, waving a piece of paper in his hand.

'Health and Safety check,' he said. 'Door, please, steward.'

'Yes, sir, doctor.'

We were both inside in seconds. I didn't know what to do or where to start. I didn't know exactly what I was looking for either.

'I hope you realize that I'm risking my reputation,' he said. 'I could lose my job and my licence over this. Getting access to a stateroom on false pretences is no mean matter. Dawn said you might be here.'

'But you said Health and Safety.'

He waved the piece of paper in front of my nose. It was a

sheet from his prescription pad. It said six Dramamine. They were motion sickness tablets.

'Looks perfectly authentic to me,' I went on.

'Made out for Minnie Mouse?'

'We'll put them in a trap. New method of rodent catching. Let them sleep it off.'

'I suppose we should ransack cupboards and unpick hems of clothes,' Sam said, wandering into the bedroom. 'That's what they do in films.'

'Slash the cushions and pillows. Sniff all the bottles.'

'You've less of a clue than I have. Sitting area, bedroom, bathroom and balcony. In that order. Let's go. What are we looking for?'

'Sorry. I don't know.'

We didn't do any slashing or sniffing, ransacking or unpicking. I was never any good at hems at school. We turned everything over and back again, under drawers and cupboards, on top of shelves and storage spaces, felt along hems. There was nothing unusual or suspicious.

'After all, if there was some incriminating picture on the mobile then whoever took the phone, wouldn't have it any more.'

'Meaning?'

'They would have thrown it overboard instantly, pronto, at the double.'

'Some whale has gobbled it up, photos and all.'

'Moby Dick with indigestion.'

'Sshh.'

I heard it too. A minute sound, like the scraping of a chair leg on the deck. We still had the balcony to check. The private balconies on the *Countess* were all reached by sliding doors. We could see two sun loungers and a table. Miss Ember had draped a beach towel over one of them, to dry in the hot sun.

Miss Ember? She hadn't come back from Calvi yet and was still residing in the twin cabin, running up a bar bill and casino losses. And I could hardly imagine her swimming from the public beach at the far end of the harbour. Anyhow, used towels were dumped on the bathroom floor and replaced with fresh ones by the steward on his next round. But Miss Ember wasn't using this stateroom, except to collect clothes.

Sam crouched down silently, balancing on his heels and squinted under an edge of the towel. He unwound as silently and stood up.

'She's going to get dehydrated and cramped hiding under that lounger,' he whispered. 'A Deck is rather high for a freedom jump. I'd better call Richard Norton.'

'Who is it?' I asked, even though I knew the answer. But I let him have his moment of glory.

'The shoplifter, with or without an Equity card.'

# Twenty-One

## Calvi

It was the bangle on the wrist that gave her away. The engraved silver one costing £175 that the shoplifter had taken along with the stand. Derek Ripon had shown me a photo of it in a catalogue. I went down on my knees and peered at the glimpse of wrist underneath the towel.

'Definitely the stolen bracelet,' I whispered. 'Unless Mr Ripon buys them in bulk.'

'We must stop her jumping,' said Sam. 'She might panic and jump. Both of us together. One, two, three, go.'

We slid open the door to the balcony, tipped the lounger towards the railing, and blocked her, all in one swift coordinated movement, so that she had no chance of getting away. The female figure was curled up on the decking in the fetal position. She looked up at us, shocked, dismayed, and speechless for once.

'So we've found you at last, Miss Garllund,' I said, picking up the towel. 'What a merry chase you've led us. Just in time to do your first show in the Princess Lounge. They've made you a lovely balcony.'

She went white beneath her sunburn. She'd been doing a lot of sunbathing out on this balcony.

'Don't hurt me,' she mumbled, crossing her arms over her chest. 'Please don't hurt me.'

'Don't be silly,' said Sam, in his best bedside manner. 'Of course we are not going to hurt you. Get up and don't attempt anything foolish. It's a very long way down.' He took her arm and escorted her inside.

'How did you find me?'

'We won't go into that now. What's more important, what are you going to wear tonight for your show? Have you got a decent dress?'

I wasn't going to tell her that Dawn had seen her sunbathing on the balcony. And Dawn wasn't going to tell me what she had been doing visiting the next-door stateroom. Purely platonic, a social call, she said.

Judie looked at me, aghast, horrified that I might be serious. 'B–but I haven't rehearsed anything. I can't sing without rehearsal.'

'You've got plenty of time,' I went on. 'Everyone has gone ashore today. You can have the theatre to yourself for the afternoon.'

Sam was on his phone to Richard Norton. 'We've found the missing singer, Judie Garllund as she calls herself, in stateroom 212 on A Deck. Miss Ember's stateroom. She's also in possession of stolen property, the silver bangle from Bond Street. You'll probably want to question her.'

I could imagine Richard's surge of elation. A crime solved, two in fact, if you count one a missing person and two a shoplifter, even if they were the same woman. And both despite the presence of Scotland Yard's most elite detective, flown out at great expense. Richard was grinning as he entered the stateroom, some minutes later, wearing his official flat cap. He must have taken several short cuts. It was a wonder he wasn't carrying a truncheon and handcuffs.

Judie was by now sitting on the sofa, weeping into her mascara, being made to drink a glass of water by our handy resident doctor. She didn't need medical attention. She was wearing black trousers with silk braid down the outside and a man's white T-shirt, concealing but too heavy for today's temperatures. Unless they were a disguise of sorts. Maybe she had been going around dressed as a young man. Her hair was pulled back in a skinny pigtail. Tuck it under a baseball cap, wear a loose jacket, and she could pass as a youth.

Black trousers? They were probably Lee's trousers, the ones that were stolen while he was pressing his dinner suit. He wouldn't want them back now. We'd get him a new pair. It would be a legitimate expenditure. Then I noticed something glinting round her neck. It looked to me like Miss Ember's Byzantine necklace.

'Ah, Miss Garllund, perhaps you'd like to explain what you are doing in Miss Ember's stateroom and how you came to possess that silver bracelet.'

Judie Garllund was recovering fast, regaining her composure, crossing her legs. 'Why, Miss Ember invited me to share her stateroom to keep her company, after all the dreadful things that have been happening to her. Disgraceful, I'd say. She didn't want to be in here alone. As for the bracelet, it's beautiful, isn't it?'

'Where did you get it from?'

'Miss Ember gave it to me as a gift. She's such a lovely lady. It's a thank you present for a few favours. She's a really generous person.'

'But Miss Ember isn't here. She's moved to another cabin.'

'She said I could stay here.'

'Don't believe her,' I said sideways to Richard, under my breath. 'Ask her when she got the bangle.'

'It's very pretty,' said Richard. 'Did she give it to you after you collected her dress from the dry-cleaners?'

Good one, Richard. On the ball at last. She fell straight into the trap.

'Yes, that's when she gave it to me, right after we left St Tropez, and I brought her dress back. She was so grateful.'

'How did you manage to get the dress from the dry-cleaners? You didn't have a receipt. How did you know which cleaners?'

'I happened to see you go in,' she said. She'd been following me, she meant. 'You looked laden so I thought I'd help out. I told the manager I was Miss Ember's assistant and he gave me the dress. Such a nice man. That's why Miss Ember gave me the bangle, to show how pleased she was to get the dress back safely.'

'Funny way of showing her gratitude,' I said. 'The bangle was stolen from Bond Street salon several days later. It was still on display, chained to the jewellery counter long after we left St Tropez.'

Judie coloured, realizing that she had been a little too eager in her explanation. 'I may have got the days mixed up,' she said. 'I have been ill, you know. The doctor knows I've been ill. Too much sun. And food poisoning. All the stress of rehearsing.'

'I'm so sorry to hear you have been unwell,' I said. 'It would have been courteous to have let me know that you were not well enough to go on stage. We had to put together a last-minute show from scratch. Fortunately it was very good, but you might have left us in a disaster zone.'

'I'm sorry, Casey. I didn't think. I was too ill.'

'And since then?' said Dr Mallory. 'You have apparently recovered but still sent no word to Miss Jones.'

'I forgot,' said Judie. 'I have a terrible memory.'

'Early onset Alzheimer's?' I suggested.

'I think you have conveniently forgotten a great deal,' said Richard Norton. 'Please come with me to my office. I want to take a full statement. But first, I have a list of items missing from the Bond Street salon, and I should be obliged if Miss Jones would have a look around for them.'

I took the list and made for the bathroom and the bedroom.

I found the Dior perfume straight away. It was still in its silvery grey box and cellophane, unopened. They would be able to check the barcode to see if it was the stolen perfume. It would be difficult to identify the cosmetics and the clothes. There was a lot of stuff strewn over the bedroom with *Countess* logos and labels. But much of it was definitely not to Miss Ember's taste. It was too young and casual to belong to the older woman.

I put all of the cosmetics into a plastic bag. Many were brand-new and unopened. There was a pair of sunglasses with the price tag still on them, so they went into the bag, too. It was filling up. I was beginning to enjoy myself. Our little excursion had not been wasted.

'What's going to h–happen to me?' Judie began to worry, biting on her lip.

'I shall take a statement from you. Of course, it would be easier all round if you simply confessed. You will be restrained for the rest of the cruise in the brig. We have a small cabin that is perfect for people like you. Unfortunately it is an interior cabin. If you insist that you are innocent, then every item will have to be flown back to Britain for forensic examination.'

'Either way then, I won't be able to do a show on stage this evening?'

'I doubt it,' said Richard. He had played right into her hands. She thumped the sofa with relief. 'The acoustics from the brig are rather restricted.'

'Well, thank goodness for that,' she said. 'I loathe going on stage, I can't sing in tune and I hate audiences. I'm never going to go anywhere near a theatre, ever again in my life. I'm finished with it.'

This didn't sound like one of our normal entertainers. Nerves, yes, they all got nerves. Who didn't? But they loved doing what they did. They loved singing, dancing, telling jokes, playing the fiddle, reciting Shakespeare, whatever. Performing was a joy that they lived for, despite the hard work, the endless rehearsals, the touring and often not much pay.

'I'm curious,' I said. 'If you dislike going on stage so much, then why are you here? Your agent recommended you. Your CV is modestly enthusiastic. You've had a lot of experience in the provinces, Manchester, Blackpool, Portsmouth, pantomime, cabaret.'

'It's lies, fabrication, fiction. I made it all up. The agent has never heard of me, never heard me sing. It was a con. I had to get on this ship, that's all.' She said it loudly, barely hiding her triumph that she had duped everyone.

Dr Mallory refilled her glass with cold water. 'I think maybe we are now getting nearer the truth.'

'Why did you have to get on this ship?' I asked.

'What do you mean, you had to get on this ship?' repeated Richard.

Suddenly she clammed up, fastened her mouth with Velcro. She'd let that slip, wasn't going to say any more. She asked to go to the bathroom and I had to go with her, in case she was about to swallow the contents of a bottle of Valium. It was so embarrassing. She started crying again, her face getting red and swollen. She came out and threw a few things into a holdall.

'What's this brig place like?' she asked, sniffing.

'Down in the depths, cramped, cold, wet. Infested with vermin, I expect. I don't know. I've never been there. It's certainly not five star accommodation. There's no cabin enter-tainment. Better take this portable radio with you, or did you pinch that, too?'

'No, excuse me, that's mine.' She was actually indignant.

'Take face cleanser and moisturizer. This jar of Nivea is probably yours. You could give yourself some facials to while away the time. It'll be a week before we are back in Southampton,' I said.

She began to weep again. Perhaps it was all that water the good doctor had been pumping down her. 'I want to go home,' she wailed.

'You are going home,' said Richard sternly.

We might have found the shoplifter but we were no nearer to solving the two murders. Mr Belcher's alibi at the bar, with the barman and his bar purchases, all computer logged, was absolutely watertight. He was nowhere near their cabin when his wife was murdered and then, somehow, her body transported to the interview room.

He had been interrogated by DCI Everton several times but stuck to his story. He seemed genuinely upset by his wife's death.

'We'd quarrelled all day, on and off, about the bloody packing. I was sick of it all,' he said, morosely, but still emotional about Dora's death. 'So I decided to drown my sorrows and let her come to her senses. I wish I hadn't. If I hadn't left her, she might be alive now. Ready to rip another strip off me. But even that would be better than this, being a suspect, people thinking I did it, when I didn't. I would never kill her, never. And I've got to tell her children, her family.'

'Her children?'

'She was married before and has two children, a boy and a girl. Grown up they are now, married themselves, but I've still got to tell them, haven't I? They'll probably blame me. I seem to get the blame for everything.'

'Funnily enough, I believe him,' said Bruce Everton, relating that part of their conversation to me. 'It was a second marriage for both of them, and Greg Belcher was beginning to regret it. The constant rows, the arguing, the bickering. It was no way to live. If he had murdered her, then he'd hardly tell me all that, would he?'

'Could be a double bluff.'

'I don't think he's that clever. How could he have fixed the computerized card purchases at the bar? Now that would be clever.'

'Got someone else to do them for him? Paid somebody.'

'What about the signing of each chit? I've checked the signatures on the receipts. They are all his. He was definitely in that bar, drowning his sorrows in Scotch. Besides Paddy confirms it, and Paddy has no reason to give him an alibi.'

'No reason we know of,' I agreed.

'At least your shoplifter is behind bars for the time being.'

'In the brig. It's the only secure area we have on-board. Not exactly luxury accommodation but certainly a cut above a prison ship.'

Passengers were beginning to return from their excursions. There were few cultural destinations on the island, but the stunning scenery and picturesque villages were worth a visit. My favourite was Sant' Antonino, the oldest village in Corsica, which was perched on top of a mountain. It had vaulted streets and narrow, winding passageways, full of ghosts and mysterious deeds. The island tours drove through deep forests of chestnut and pine, deep mountainous passes, fruit orchards, swathes of vineyards and olive groves. It wasn't how people imagined Corsica. They only remembered tales of brigands and pirates and underground passages leading to the sea.

But not for me, today. Perhaps on another cruise. And not apparently for Mr Belcher. I found him leaning on a rail, watching the coaches disembark their passengers and join the long queue for the tenders back to the ship. He looked grey and seemed to have aged, deflated somehow.

'You didn't go ashore, Mr Belcher?' I asked.

'No, I didn't feel like it. Even though the wife and I were chalk and cheese and quarrelled a lot, she was good company when she was in a good mood. I don't feel like going on my own. I'm not being kept on-board or anything,' he added hurriedly. 'That detective chap said I was free to go ashore anytime, as long as I left my passport with the purser. Seemed fair enough to me.'

'Seems very fair,' I said. 'After all, you are not under suspicion. Did you have a hangover after all that drinking in Paddy's bar?' The bar now had a name. I must tell Paddy of the promotion.

'No, I didn't,' said Mr Belcher. 'The moment they told me about Dora, I stopped drinking and I was stone cold sober. I couldn't believe she had gone. I was angry again, not with her, this time, but with the bastard that did it.'

'Have you got any idea who might have killed her?'

'No, no idea at all. Could be anyone. If I didn't know he

was halfway across the world, sailing the Pacific on a merchant ship, I'd say it was that violent first husband of hers, Frank. He was that annoyed when we got married. He caused a scene outside the church and had to be escorted away. I never saw him but I did see the damage he did to the wedding car after he threw a bucket of tar all over it. Can you believe it? Couldn't get the stuff off. The car had to be resprayed. And I had to pay for it.'

'Would he know you were on this ship?'

'No, he couldn't know. We never kept in touch.'

'I understand Mrs Belcher came back to the ship early to have her hair done. Do you know anything about this?'

'No idea. Always having her hair done. That's nothing new.'

I meet hundreds of people on board ship and it's impossible for me to remember all their names. But this scenario was ringing a loud bell. Bad-tempered, naval connection, Frank? We had a bad-tempered Frank on board. But it was a bookie's sure bet that it wouldn't be the same person. If her first husband was travelling on the *Countess*, he would surely have used an assumed name.

'Sorry, but I have to go now, Mr Belcher. Are you with nice people on your table in the dining room?'

'Yes, they're really pleasant. I'm lucky in that respect. They make it easy for me to join in the conversation and I like that. No Mrs B to nag me, or contradict me, or tell me to shut up. It makes a change. A bit on the quiet side, actually.'

I left Mr Belcher leaning over the rail. I had a lot to do and not much time. But where to start? Some of the jigsaw was falling into place.

# Twenty-Two
## At Sea

The manifest contained over a thousand names, a list of passengers and crew. I was up half the night, scanning the Christian names. There were four Franklins, five Frankies and eight Franks. There was one Franklyn and one Franky. Sometimes Francis was abbreviated to Frank. At this point, I gave up and went to bed.

I had even missed the *Countess* leaving Corsica and I always made a point of being on deck for a departure. She backed off her anchorage without incident and once clear of the land set a south-westerly track towards our next port of call, Gibraltar. The famous monkey mountain was not one of my favourite ports and I could happily give it a miss. It was a duty-free haven of alcohol, leather and perfume if you were into a long walk to town and marathon shopping.

Judie Garllund, or whatever her real name was, had gone into refusal mode. She was refusing to say anything. She would not give any information about herself, not her name, address, age or occupation.

'She can sit there until we reach Southampton,' said Richard, clearly riled. 'I wash my hands of her.'

Miss Ember was also refusing to say anything beyond confirming that she had invited Judie to share her stateroom. She was ruffled at being interviewed again.

'Why didn't you tell us?' I asked, keeping my calm. 'We've been doing our best to find something that suited you.'

'It was none of your business. You people seem to have had it in for me throughout this whole cruise,' she said, looking even more scrawny than ever. It was as if she was determined to show that the smaller cabin didn't agree with her. 'I can't do anything without all these questions from you lot. I've been victimized from day one by everyone, even the captain. He's never asked me to sit at his table. You're a lot of interfering, official busy bodies. I shan't let it rest there. Head Office are going to hear about this.'

I could see another letter on the way. She must use up a lot of complimentary stationery.

'We are simply trying to find out the truth of the matter,' said Richard, his expression betraying how fed up he was.

'Apparently Judie had been turned out of her cabin so that it could be fumigated. Germs in the air conditioning,' she said. 'The poor girl had nowhere to sleep.'

Another story on the wild side. Judie had disappeared from her cabin. It had not been touched since. But once we neared Southampton, a stewardess would pack all her belongings so that the cabin could be cleaned and made ready for the next occupant. I hoped it would be an entertainer who actually liked singing, dancing, balloon blowing, anything as long as the contracted person went on stage.

I phoned up Karim, the head steward, and suggested that the cabin packing could be done earlier, to save time in the last-minute rushed turn round. Judie was unlikely to return to her cabin. He seemed to like the idea. Anything to save his staff valuable time.

'I will get one of my best stewardesses to do it,' he said. He didn't know the exact circumstances. 'Would you like her to pack a small bag of warmer clothes for when we reach Southampton? The English climate is always a shock after the Mediterranean.'

'Yes, please. A good idea. That would be so thoughtful, thank you.'

Judie would probably be taken straight into custody for appearance at a local magistrates' court, on the shoplifting charge. I wondered if Miss Ember's generosity would stretch to bail?

It was still warm on deck but there was a force two to three wind, which caught a few hats and sent them overboard. I rescued one straw hat with its ribbons caught against the railing, and nearly fell when grabbing the ribbons. It was a graceful slide along the decking, but the wrench on my ankle nearly resulted in a less than graceful, primeval yelp.

'Rescuing errant hats is not in your job description,' said

Samuel Mallory, helping me to my feet and heaving me to the nearest deck chair. 'Have you hurt the ankle? It's the injured one, isn't it?'

'It's always the injured one, dammit,' I said. 'I never hurt the other one.'

'It's the good one that keeps you going. Your injured ankle wouldn't be able to support you if you hurt the good one.'

Convoluted, but I knew what he meant. It made sense. 'I suppose not.'

'You missed our walk last night. I waited for you on deck. The crew were taking bets on how late you would be. Then they decided you had thrown me over and our romance was finished, kaput.'

I was feeling mildly homicidal with the pain. 'Firstly, it isn't *our* walk, as you put it. I never said I would be there so I wasn't late. Thirdly, I haven't thrown you over because fourthly there never has been any romance to throw over.'

'What a long speech, Casey,' said Dr Mallory, sitting in the chair next to mine, and holding my hand under cover of taking my pulse. 'I'm absolutely delighted to hear you say that you haven't thrown me over. So there's hope for me, yet? I take heart from this statement. You are still considering me for a light-hearted shipboard romance?'

'Don't bank on it.'

'I feel we both need a little romantic interlude after all the heavy drama of the last few days. It hasn't been easy.'

He was laughing at me as usual, but beneath it was a genuine concern. It was difficult to resist him when he was being sympathetic. He called over a hovering stewardess. She darted forward as if on springs.

'A Pimm's for Miss Jones. Purely medicinal. And an orange juice for me.'

'Orange juice?' I asked.

'Yes, I'm operating in half an hour. A passenger came aboard with stitches in a hernia wound and they have gone septic. It all needs tidying up. As far as I can see, a botched operation. One of these in and out in a day jobs.'

'Sounds nasty. Before you go, Sam, tell me what you think Miss Ember is likely to get from Conway Blue Line in the way of compensation for these various, what we might call, mishaps?'

'Every case varies according to the circumstances. But I

should think she'll get her money back on this cruise and the offer of an alternative cruise some other time, completely free. Conway are very generous. Two cruises for nothing.'

'Could she also sue for nerves or something?'

'If she has nerves or something, I suppose she could. The reptile rash, or whatever it was, has cleared up despite her scratching it raw with her nails. Is she thinking of suing the company?'

'I don't know. It's all horrendous, if you think back. The snake, the rat, the blood coming out of the shower. I suppose the dress in the Bond Street window was a joke of some sort, but it all adds up to some very unpleasant experiences.'

'You sound as if you are on the lady's side now.'

'I am trying to be fair,' I said, downing the ice-cold Pimm's. I began to feel even fairer. 'Even if she does annoy me and is so rude every time we meet.'

'Better go and scrub up,' said Sam, getting out of the chair. He finished off the juice. 'See you around, Miss Jones. No more hat rescues. It's bad for trade.'

The passenger whose hat I had saved was grateful. It was Hilary Miles, the woman on my table who never went ashore. 'It was bought for me in Calvi,' she said. 'I think it's a little too big for my head.'

'So you didn't try it on?'

'No,' she said, shaking her head. 'I didn't go ashore.' She paused, struggling, wondering whether to tell me. 'You see I have agoraphobia and claustrophobia, both at the same time. One is the fear of public spaces, the other is the fear of small places. It makes going anywhere, even a lift, a nightmare. It was hard enough coming into the dining room for the first time. I don't know how I made it.'

'I noticed that you weren't very happy.'

'Happy? I was terrified. I couldn't leave fast enough.'

'I admire you for coming on the cruise at all,' I said. 'Being on board ship itself is a big step forward, surely? This huge deck is like a market place.'

'But it has perimeters. All the rails and doors and lifeboats and deck furniture make it seem much smaller, but not too small. It seems like it's divided into manageable sections. Am I making any sense?' Mrs Miles was hanging on to her hat as if it was the only stable thing in her life.

'Yes,' I said. 'If I had realized earlier, I could have helped. At least we dock alongside at Gibraltar, so no tenders involved. We could walk down the gangway together and you could step on land for a few minutes. That would be something, wouldn't it? Even if all you do is wander round the few shops on the dockside. Then you can come straight back on board and sit on the deck watching everyone stagger back with their duty-free haul.'

She smiled at me and the hesitant smile changed her face. 'I'd like to try that. But no promises, Miss Jones. I might chicken out at the last moment.'

'And put some milliner's elastic inside your hat so that it hooks round your hair,' I said, rubbing my ankle. 'That's what our dancers do if they have a big hat to wear on stage. I'll get you a bit from wardrobe.'

'You're a mine of information,' she said. 'Thank you.'

This is what I should have been doing, helping Mrs Miles from the start. But I'd been too busy trying to solve things which were none of my business.

I was bone weary with a painful ankle, but still mystified by the strange happenings around Miss Ember, my thoughts tumbling around spin-dryer fashion. Why couldn't I forget it all and let Richard Norton sort out the puzzles? It was his job, not mine.

When I got back to the office to finish returning calls, there was an email from Karim, the head steward, marked urgent.

*Miss Jones. Stewardess clearing out cabin in hysterics. Please to come.*

I hurried along to the cabin which Judie Garllund had once occupied. Karim was standing guard outside, looking grim. The ashen-faced stewardess was being consoled by another woman and sipping water.

'I tried to phone you. We have not touched anything,' he said. 'You must see it as found.'

The cabin had been half cleared. Two big wheelie cases were full of folded clothes. The stewardess had been using lots of new tissue paper as we always instruct. One of the Conway touches.

On the desk were two plastic pouches containing a dark red liquid. I didn't need to touch them. They were blood, but not real blood. They were labelled 'Fake Blood' from Max

Marks Magic Shop. This was getting interesting. What else did she have in store?

'Surprise, surprise,' I said. 'Well spotted.'

But why the hysterics? Nasty shock perhaps, but producing nothing more than a few gasps, surely?

'Please to look in refrigerator,' said Karim, standing back to allow me through. Like mine, the cabin had a small refrigerator under the desk. Hers was no exception.

I opened the refrigerator door, expecting the usual row of mineral waters and an ice bucket. Instead, on the shelf were two plastic bags, both sealed. One contained two dead rats and curled in the other was a very nasty-looking snake. It was either dead or hibernating. I did not investigate.

'Anything else?' I asked faintly.

He opened the wardrobe door very slowly, his kindly face concerned. 'Please, Miss Jones. Take care. Do not have the hysterics.'

I thought I might well have hysterics. In the circumstances, I felt I was entitled to have full-blown hysterics. But Dr Mallory was operating on a septic hernia scar and it wouldn't be fair to disturb him.

I sat outside for a few minutes and the two stewardesses gave me sips of water and patted my shoulder sympathetically. This was going to be a great story for them below decks in the crew cafeteria tonight. It was *Coronation Street* and *EastEnders* rolled into one. Their moment of gory glory.

'Thank you,' I said. 'I'm feeling a lot better now. Lock the cabin, please Karim. I'll get the security officer to take over. It's his responsibility. I'll phone him straightaway. Sorry my phone wasn't on before.'

Richard Norton was not pleased to hear from me. 'Really, Casey, I've enough on my plate as it is, without you phoning me every five minutes.'

I ignored the exaggeration. 'Well, here's something more for your plate. Not exactly John the Baptist's head, but near. Go to Judie Garllund's former cabin and look in the wardrobe. Take strong smelling salts.'

'I haven't got time for jokes, Casey.'

He put the phone down on me. That is something I do not

like at all. Grown men acting childishly. Let's see how he handles the wardrobe.

I went up on deck for some fresh air, letting my brain free itself of the images. I wanted a blank screen. Judie Garllund was not going to haunt me with her weird collection of souvenirs. There was no other word I could put to her choice of memorabilia.

The discovery of these items put this Judie person firmly into the Lucinda Ember box of tricks. This couldn't be a chance encounter made during the cruise. You don't bring dead rats, a snake and fake blood with you on the chance of going to a Dracula fancy dress party. The blood dripping from the shower had been pig's blood. Sam was not likely to make that kind of mistake. The fake blood was obviously back-up or for some other planned nightmare. Perhaps Lucinda was going to be smeared with blood and didn't fancy pig's.

I tried to get an email through to the agent whose name had been on her fake CV. But it kept being returned. They either didn't exist or their email address was no longer valid.

Lee was concerned. 'Are you all right, Casey? You're looking a bit upset.'

'I'm not upset,' I said, wearily. 'A little stressed out. There have been some new complications. Don't you worry about them.'

'Can I help? There must be something I can do.' Lee still had a sad look in his eyes but he was enjoying his job, and I didn't want to change that. I wanted to keep him on the team.

'Yes, there is something you can do. I'm looking for a passenger called Frank with naval connections, who could be travelling under an assumed name. He might be in the merchant navy or the Royal Navy. No real information about him. In his fifties, I should think.'

'Sure, I'll ask around. Make out it's for a quiz question.'

'Good idea. But be careful. Don't let him know that you are making enquiries. You might find yourself being tipped overboard.'

'I'll be extra careful. Put your feet up for ten minutes, Casey. You don't look as if you have eaten today. Shall I get you something from the Terrace Café?'

'No, thanks. I don't want any food,' I said. The contents of the wardrobe had completely put me off eating.

I truly couldn't remember when I had last eaten. The events of the last few hours had concertinaed into a horrible messy collage. My head needed washing out and freshening up. Perhaps a swim in one of the *Countess*'s pools would help. I rarely went into the ship's pools. Four strokes and you bump your head. But this felt like an emergency, like I needed the cleansing ritual of water.

There was a spare swimsuit in the office. It had been there days, waiting for me to take it back to my cabin and rinse out. It had dried stiff and smelt of salt.

I used the changing rooms next to the indoor pool. It was flanked by the gymnasium. None of the bikes or walking machines were in use at the moment. I couldn't see the point of walking on a machine, when you could walk in the fresh air on deck. The pool supervisor was not about, which was unusual. Perhaps he was having a quick fag on deck.

The pool was empty making a pleasant change, no stately matrons in big swimsuits doing one and a half lengths before dinner. I decided to swim round and round anticlockwise. Don't ask me why. It was the way I struck out. The water was soothing, cool and sparkling with lights. They had artificial sunlight playing on the surface to make people think they were outside. I wondered which boffin thought that one up.

Rolled up at one end of the pool on a long spool was a length of heavy green netting. This was stretched over the pool at night or when it was dangerous to use the pool. If the sea was rough and the ship was pitching, they closed all the pools to passengers, and emptied out some of the water. I've seen the pool water lurching from end to end in waves, splashing over the tiled sides, drenching the artificial palm trees.

It was a lazy sort of swim, not for exercise but simply to empty my mind. My brain had too much baggage. I felt the tension easing from my shoulders and the rhythm of the strokes becoming stronger. Someone was moving about, out of my vision, probably one of the gym instructors putting away equipment or tidying up. I vaguely heard an odd rattle but took no notice of the noise.

Something flopped down over my head and my outstretched fingers went through mesh, getting caught. It caught me by surprise. I rolled over, to push it off but there was a dragging sensation as some floating stuff wrapped itself round my body. I could feel heavy yards of something and started fighting to get it off me. But it was round my legs as well as my body. It was the weirdest sensation, frightening, like being encased in prickly wire.

I knew what it was now. It was the green safety netting. Somehow it had got loose and fallen on me. I struggled to get out of it, but the more I struggled the more I got entangled.

A surge of fear panicked me. This could be dangerous. It was heavy stuff, especially when wet. I heard another noise, like a grunt.

Someone was there. Vaguely I saw a figure at the side of the pool. Someone had thrown the netting over me and was even now dragging the edges around, trapping me like a fish. I tried to see who it was but the trawl tugged me over, mesh hard against my nostrils and my eyes. Another grunt and then a door closed.

I started to thrash about, choking, gasping for breath. There was no one around. I had to get out of this on my own. Already I was tiring. Polar bears, penguins, what would they do? They'd float. I only hoped that the weight of the netting would not drag me under first.

I managed to reach out and grasp the side rail, trying to keep my head above water, but the heavy netting was pulling me under. Keep calm, Casey. I told myself to take small, rapid breaths. I didn't know why, perhaps conserving energy.

Surely whoever was in charge of the pool would come back soon. And where were the attendants anyway? It should never be left unsupervised.

Now I was getting very cold. The heating had been turned off. I couldn't move to keep myself warm. I tried to clench and unclench my fingers and toes but I was trussed in the netting like a Christmas turkey.

I tried to laugh but it was no laughing matter. My feeble laugh echoed round the tiled pool house. The laugh came back at me. The place echoed. A thought surged into my head. I had to use the echo. It was worth a try.

'Help, help,' I shouted but my voice had no strength. 'Help, help me.'

Courage, Casey. I remembered Brownie camping, sitting round a flickering fire singing, eating burnt sausages and toasted marshmallows.

'Ten green bottles hanging on the wall,' I started singing. It was the only song I could remember at that moment. We used to sing it, my brothers and me on childhood journeys to Cornwall.

'Ten green bottles hanging on the wall, and if one green bottle should accidentally fall, there'll be nine green bottles hanging on the wall. Nine green bottles hanging on the wall . . .' The words echoed round the tiles. I had a backing group.

Then I sang *One Man Went to Mow a Meadow* all the way through, *Oranges and Lemons, The Twelve Days of Christmas, A Hard Day's Night, Yellow Submarine.* The water was getting colder. My fingers were pruned. I couldn't feel my toes.

I ran out of words and there was nothing for it but to start all over again. The words were becoming difficult, slurred. I was tiring fast. I'd got as far as three g–green bottles h–hanging on the wall, when I heard footsteps running along the outside corridor and a door being wrenched open. In moments, arms were in the water, pulling me out of the pool. I recognized the pool attendants. They were wrapping me in towels, trying to rub some life into my arms and legs and trying to get me out of the netting, all at the same time.

'S–someone tried to d–drown me,' I spluttered, coughing up water.

I was shivering badly when Dr Mallory arrived with his bag of magic potions. I couldn't speak, a lot of netting still tightly wrapped round my body.

'Let's get her out of this stuff. Careful, now. Cut it if you have to. Gently does it.'

'How d–did you k–know?' I asked incoherently, trembling, when my face was finally free.

'You were spotted on a remote CCTV,' he said. 'When I was told there was a singing whale in the pool, I knew it could only be you.'

# Twenty-Three
# Gibraltar

There would be an enquiry, of course. There's always an enquiry. It was discovered that the pool attendants had been summoned to a departmental meeting which they couldn't locate and the call was untraceable. The heating had been turned off by a person or persons unknown.

'Do you know where you are?' Dr Mallory asked.

'Of course I know where I am,' I said. 'I'm not confused or disorientated and I don't want you sticking a rectal thermometer up me.'

'Excitability is the first stage of hypothermia,' he said.

'I got cold and wet and very frightened. If you want stage of torpor, I can do stage of torpor.'

'I think she's all right,' said the doctor, closing his bag with a snap.

'Who knew you were going for a swim?' asked Richard Norton. He was a little put off that the interview was being held in my cabin, and I was in bed, wrapped up in blankets, sipping hot milk. I didn't think the hot milk was necessary but my steward had insisted. Ahmed had read somewhere about English ladies liking hot milk. He really was a poppet.

'No one. It was a spur of the moment thing. Maybe Lee Williams. He might have seen me getting my swimsuit out of the filing cabinet. I'm not sure. I thought he'd gone on deck by then.'

'You keep your swimsuit in a filing cabinet?'

'Of course. Doesn't everyone?'

'So Lee Williams is a suspect,' said Richard.

'No way,' I said, shaking my head. My hair was drying out into an absolute bird's nest. End of any possible romance with the security officer if I'd ever wanted one.

'You're not being very helpful,' said Richard.

My temper was heating up. It must be the hot milk.

'And you are being completely ridiculous. Lee wouldn't try to drown me. He has no reason to drown me. Miss Ember has more reason to try and get rid of me.'

'Miss Ember may have a good reason but she certainly hasn't got the strength to drag a heavy net over you and manage to twist it round your body. You may recall she is only five feet tall.' This was said with heavy sarcasm. The man was an idiot.

Samuel wanted to leave a nurse with me but I refused. It was a waste of her time.

'I'm all right,' I insisted. 'I'll be fine on my own. If I feel in the slightest bit woozy, I'll phone you.'

He put my mobile by my bed. 'Promise?'

'Promise.'

'And lock your door.'

As soon as the mob had left my cabin, I snuggled down into the warm blankets for a few moments, letting my brain return to an even keel. It had been unnerving but I was safe now. Somehow I was getting near the truth and that made me dangerous.

I staggered to the bathroom and put some moisturizer on my face. The swim had played havoc with my skin. A touch of eyeliner and lip gloss and I was ready. I phoned DCI Bruce Everton.

'I have some information,' I said. 'My cabin is 414 E Deck. But the door is locked so you must say who you are clearly.'

'I heard what happened,' he said. 'How are you?'

'Warming up.'

'Do I need a password?'

I was beginning to like him very much. 'Definitely. It's hippopotamus.'

'I'll be right over.' He didn't waste words. I wiped off the lip gloss. No need to go over the top. He was only a policeman, not a rock star.

Bruce Everton was at my door in five minutes. He knocked on the door and gave the password without the slightest embarrassment. He had a bunch of yellow roses, bought at the florist's shop in reception. I thought this showed style.

'Come in,' I said, flopping back into bed, swathed in

blankets. 'Sit down. Dr Mallory turned the thermostat up. You can turn it down if you like.'

'I'll suffer,' he said, putting the roses into a jug of water. 'It's more important that you thaw out.'

'Thank you for the roses. They're lovely. A kind thought.'

'I thought you have suffered enough because of my incompetent handling of this case. I'm sorry. I never realized how difficult it would be to sort out information about all the passengers on board ship. They are everywhere, doing this and that, all of the time. It's a nightmare. I'm making a grid.'

'I have several bits of information to give you about Mrs Dora Belcher's death. I've recently found out that her first husband, someone called Frank, may also be a passenger. Their marriage was also full of bad feeling, acrimonious divorce, etc. She should have stayed a spinster.'

'And do we know who he is?'

'No, not yet. I've a list of passengers with Frank or Frankie as a Christian name. He may have changed his surname.'

He nodded. 'Criminals often don't change their first name. It makes life easier.'

'Miss Lucinda Ember is most certainly out to file a fraudulent claim on the company, to take Conway to the cleaners. But we have discovered that one of my entertainers, the so-called singer, Miss Judie Garllund, along with Miss Ember, actually brought items aboard to provide evidence of mismanagement and set the scene for trauma, nervous breakdown, or whatever Miss Ember was about to stage.'

'Tell me.'

So I told him about the sachets of fake blood, the dead rats and the snake in the refrigerator. I also told him what was found in the wardrobe of Miss Garllund's cabin. Even he was shocked.

'Jesus,' he said. 'More work for forensics.'

'We all thought Miss Garllund had gone ashore at Monte Carlo. The scanner had swiped her card, but she hadn't gone ashore. It's easily done. You say to the security officer, oh dear I must pop to the loo first, and they let you. People who are going ashore often make a last-minute visit as a precaution. No one wants to be caught short in a foreign country.'

'Where did you find her?'

'Under a lounger on the balcony of Miss Ember's stateroom. She'd been holed up there for days. In the stateroom, not under the lounger.'

'So Miss Garllund is not who she says she is. She could be anyone Lucinda Ember picked up in a pub, advertised for, bumped into on the street?'

'Absolutely. It's a conspiracy to file a compensation claim against Conway Blue Line. Hundreds of thousand pounds. I've seen claims that size. You know what the claims market is like these days. And Judie was going to get her share.'

'Don't I know it? Scotland Yard is snowed under with huge claims for hurt feelings. And that's officers, not victims of crime. Is there anything else you want to tell me, Casey?'

He was looking at me with those nice eyes, not policeman's eyes but honest man around town eyes. I felt he was trustworthy. He'd guard me, protect me, escort me across busy roads.

'Are you married?' I asked suddenly. I don't know why I overstepped a boundary. I couldn't stop myself.

'I was. Not any more,' he said.

'I'm sorry.'

'So am I,' he said. 'My wife was run over by a drunk driver. She was on her bicycle. She'd been to a Spanish evening class. Debbie was hooked on further education and we were planning a holiday in Spain.'

I didn't know why I asked him such a personal question. 'I'm so sorry,' I said. 'That was unforgivable of me. I shouldn't have asked.' He leaned over and touched my hand.

'I want you to know,' he said. 'You're such a lovely lady.'

I wanted the blankets to swallow me. I felt two inches high. This nice, top Scotland Yard detective actually liked me. I had to change the subject before I started to cry.

'Professor Papados. I think he was murdered because of photos he had taken on his mobile phone. I don't know if he ever had time to get them printed, but his phone disappeared after he died. The photos had evidence about the planting of Miss Ember's Chanel dress in the Bond Street shop window. I think there's a reflection of someone.'

'That's interesting,' said Bruce, letting go of my hand. It was a reluctant movement. 'I thought he had a heart attack or a stroke.'

'He did but Dr Mallory felt sure he had saved him. Then something else kicked in that paralyzed the nervous system.'

'Defibrillation doesn't always work,' said Bruce. 'Television programmes give us the wrong idea that it saves lives all the time. But the percentage is actually quite small.'

'This Garllund woman, the one in league with Miss Ember, had been talking to Professor Papados in Paddy's bar not long before he started acting strangely.'

'And why are the photos significant?'

'Because behind the shop window are the beauty counters and they have several mirrors. Maybe there was a reflection of someone in one of those mirrors, someone who didn't want to be seen. And the reflection showed up in the photos.'

'Such as who?'

'Miss Ember herself? I think Miss Ember put the dress in the shop window with her own photo on the model's face, and tipped fake blood over the feet. Don't ask me why. Part of this crazy compensation scheme?'

'I suggest you know far too much for your own good,' said Bruce Everton, rising to his feet. 'You should stay in your cabin and let no one in.'

'But I've work to do.'

'Work can wait. We nearly had a third victim, remember?'

There was a knock on the cabin door. I looked at Bruce and he went over to listen.

'Who is it? Identify yourself.'

'It's Lee Williams, deputy entertainments director. Casey knows me. I'm her right-hand man and I've got some information for her.'

I nodded. 'Lee's OK. I trust him.'

Bruce Everton raised his eyebrows. 'You can't trust anyone.' But he opened the door and Lee came bouncing into the cabin.

He looked round. 'I've never been in your cabin before,' he said. 'It's the same as mine, only everything is the other way round.'

'They are all the same,' I said, suddenly weary.

'I heard about, you know what, the marathon swim,' he began. 'Are you all right?'

'I'm very tired,' I said.

He looked uncomfortable. 'Sorry. I'll be quick. I think I've found the man you were looking for. Christian name Frank, naval connection, as you said.'

'Well done, Lee. Good work. Where did you find him?'

'He was in the library. Commander Frank Trafford, retired, he says. But I think he's lying about the rank. Some fast self-promotion on the passport application. I tripped him up on a couple of nautical questions. And there was something else that was funny.'

'What was that?'

'The hems of his trousers were wet.'

Greg Belcher agreed to go with me to the library to identify Frank Trafford as being Dora's first husband. I dressed quickly in a tracksuit and trainers, hair tucked in a bandeau. Props lent me a pair of brown-rimmed spectacles. I could be anyone, streets away from the elegant Miss Jones.

'I don't want you to speak to him or indicate in any way that you know him,' said Bruce Everton firmly. 'All we want you to do is identify him.'

'And I want to catch the bastard,' said Greg Belcher. 'My lovely Dora . . .'

Dora had become a lot lovelier in the last few days. He was forgetting all the quarrels and arguments. She was being elevated to matronly sainthood.

'Are you sure he won't know you?'

'He's never met me, even at the wedding. But I've seen photos of him, and the ones in the newspapers when he was given a six month non-molestation order. He wasn't to go within a hundred yards of Dora, or she was to call the police. He'd been bashing her up. That's when she filed for a divorce.'

'So he won't recognize you?'

'Not a chance.'

Funny how women go for the same kind of men, time and time again. Dora Belcher had come aboard with a black eye.

There was only one entrance to the ship's library and DCI Everton and Richard Norton stationed themselves outside it. Lee wandered along the book shelves with me at his side. He said he wasn't letting me out of his sight. Greg Belcher was a few steps behind us, peering at the titles on the sleeves.

'Have you read this one?' said Lee, taking down a gory-covered thriller. 'He's a good writer, fast and furious. Never a dull moment.'

'I like a story that's a little more relaxing,' I said.

'So did my Dora,' said Greg, completely forgetting his instructions. 'Dora loved a good book. Never happier than when her nose was buried in a book.'

Lee nudged me and whispered. 'Over there by the desk. Fawn trousers, navy blazer, short grey hair.'

Greg Belcher heard the whisper and spun himself round. His eyes widened. 'That's him,' he shouted, pointing. 'That's the murdering bastard.'

Commander Trafford moved like lightning, but so did DCI Everton and Richard Norton. It was a clash of the Titans.

There wasn't room in the brig for another prisoner, so Petty Officer Frank Monk (alias Commander Trafford) had to be secured in crew quarters, down in the depths. He denied he had smashed Dora Belcher on the head with a heavy crystal ashtray from the Galaxy Lounge, then somehow transported her body from the cabin to the interview room.

But when charged with attempted murder, that of wrapping me up in heavy netting, hoping I would drown, he went strangely quiet.

'I'm not saying anything,' he said. 'I want a lawyer.'

'I reckon he'd been among the crowds that witnessed the row between Dora and Greg Belcher and decided it was a good opportunity to put the blame on her husband's shoulders,' said DCI Everton later. 'But it didn't work because of your computerized billing system. You can fool people, but you can't fool a sophisticated machine that records every penny you spend, when and where.'

Lee was conscious-stricken that he might have alerted Frank Trafford in some way. He admitted that he'd been talking to Kristy, the dancer, for quite some time before he came looking for me and heard about the incident in the pool. He hadn't realized that the man might be dangerous.

More flowers arrived for me, freesias from Lee and a huge bouquet from the stage company. My cabin was beginning to look like a florist's shop. Another bouquet was delivered, signed from William Owen and Jeanne. I didn't know who Jeanne was, but I could guess.

'I go find more vases,' said Ahmed, grinning.

Dr Mallory stood in the doorway, taking in the flowers, his face contrite, floppy hair falling over his brow. 'Sorry, Casey, I didn't have time to buy flowers.'

'It's OK, you don't have to give me flowers. Saving lives is more your scene.'

'But I should have. I didn't think. I was too busy with something else. Can I come in?'

'You're my doctor, aren't you? I want to get back to work. It's safe now, isn't it?'

'I suppose so. Both Judie Garllund, or whoever she is, and Frank Monk (alias Commander Trafford) are in custody. There are more guards on their doors than stewards serving drinks. They won't get out until we reach Southampton.'

'Oh dear, they'll miss Lisbon.'

'But you won't miss Lisbon. I've arranged that Lee will stay on-board and you are having a day off, a whole day ashore.'

'Right bossy boots, aren't you? I'll run my department as I want to. It's for me to say who gets shore leave.' Talk about Miss Attitude. I needed counselling.

Sam ignored me. 'I thought you might like to know that I have discovered something interesting about Professor Papados's death. It wasn't totally natural causes, but it wasn't insulin as I first thought. He did have a weak heart and had had surgery. True, he could have gone any time. But traces of atropine were found.'

'Atropine? What's that?'

'Di-hyscyamine or Hyoscine, in the book. Eye drops to you and me. They are used for pupil dilation and are not for consumption. A few drops would be lethal in about six minutes. The circulation and respiratory systems collapse, paralysing the nervous system. The victim is hot, dry, red-faced, with aggressive behaviour, just as Paddy described.'

'He was poisoned?'

Sam nodded. 'That's the probability, but we need more tests. I can't do them here. I checked on his bar billing, and apparently he signed for two drinks some minutes before he collapsed. Time enough for a couple of drops to be squirted into his drink as he signed the chit for one beer and one vodka and dry ginger. Apparently she only stayed to drink half of the vodka. Paddy remembers her having to leave for some rehearsal.'

'Rehearsal,' I said drily. 'She didn't know the meaning of the word. And the eye drops?'

'Anyone could bring them on-board. Normal medication. It could still be in Lucinda Ember's bathroom, looking quite harmless.'

'Or it could have been tossed overboard, to give the fish a headache.'

'How did you find out?'

'I sent some samples to a colleague of mine in London. He's emailed me back with this information. They'll have to run more tests, of course. But it does look as if the poor professor was poisoned.'

'And all for taking a photograph.' I was stricken now. It had been my fault. He'd still be alive if I hadn't asked him to take some photos.

Sam went over to my cabin window to distract my attention. 'Look, we're coming into Gibraltar Bay. Only the afternoon here. Quite long enough to stock up on booze.'

'That doesn't sound like you,' I said.

'I didn't mean me, I meant the passengers. There's only time for a fast trot to the Main Street shopping centre or a cable car ride up to the top of the rock and the apes' den. I'd rather see the great siege tunnels.'

'I'd rather stay on-board.' But I was remembering my promise to Hilary Miles. I had to keep it. 'I have to see a passenger down the gangway. Then I'll come back.'

'As your doctor ordered. Shall I see you this evening?'

'What about your harem?'

'My harem has lost interest. Doctors don't make as much money as company directors and property magnates, even the bald, paunchy ones.'

I showered quickly, dressed in casual three-quarter length trousers and a sleeveless shirt. I wanted to catch the last of the sun before we started the voyage back to cloudy England. It was a fine, clear day and still warm.

'We wondered where you were last night,' said several couples. 'It was an excellent show.'

I thanked William Owen and his companion, Jeanne, for

the flowers. They looked very happy together. Sometimes cruises did work a magic. They were in no hurry to go ashore, no shopping, no rock, no apes.

'The name's Arabic, isn't it?' said William, stopping at the top of the gangway. The *Countess* was berthed in the vast dock area.

'Yes, from Jebel al Tariq. You can just hear the name in the middle. He was a general who conquered Spain in 711.'

'Before my time,' said Jeanne.

'Tariq ordered his men to burn their battle ships behind them, which meant that they could only conquer or die,' I went on.

'So "to burn your boats" means not to give in or look back,' said William.

'Something like that. A rather harsh order.'

'Those were cruel days,' said William, taking Jeanne's hand as if to reassure her. 'Let's have a stroll ashore, my dear. Stretch our land legs.'

Their happiness was so acute, it made me catch my breath.

Hilary Miles arrived at the top of the gangway. She was looking nervously at the expanse of dockside below. 'I don't like this,' she said.

'A few minutes ashore, that's all,' I said. 'Nothing more. Let's go together. I'll go down first. Just look at me, my white shirt, nothing else. Ignore Gibraltar. Pretend it's not there.'

It wasn't easy for her. She was shaking as she went down the gangway and clutched the rail as if she never wanted to let it go. She was helped down the last step by a member of the crew.

'A quick look at the souvenir shops and then back,' I said. I heard footsteps behind us, hurrying. It was Cavan Franetti, the antiques lecturer, looking suave and debonair. He tipped his hat to Hilary Miles with a gallant bow.

'I hope to see you at my lecture tomorrow,' he said. 'It is about beautiful things. So it would suit you.'

It was a hammy compliment but she seemed to like it and raised half a smile. I noticed that she gazed after him as he hurried into town to shop.

'That wasn't so bad, was it?' I asked.

'It was all right,' she said.

\*     \*     \*

I wore my favourite dress that night. It was a pleated, silk-crepe, full-length, strapless gown by Valentino. I dare not tell anyone what it cost, even second-hand. The original owner only wore it once, to a film premiere. What a waste. It floated round me like a crimson flame.

Tonight's shows were based on Jules Verne's classic novel *Around the World in Eighty Days*. It was an ambitious programme of musical numbers from shows, films, operas and variety. Lee was the MC, looking very smart in a new dinner suit. Derek Ripon even gave us a discount. We assured him that the stolen items would eventually be returned to him and he was in a good mood. The late-night film was *Bridges of Madison County* with Meryl Streep and Clint Eastwood. I'd be there for that.

There was a liberated feeling about the ship that evening. Both prisoners were secured. We were all safe. No more nasty happenings. We could enjoy the last few days at sea and the last port of call, Lisbon.

And Sam was with me. He sat beside me in the dark of the cinema, and when I shivered in the air-conditioning, he put his jacket round my shoulders. Meryl Streep never had it that good.

# Twenty-Four
# Lisbon

L isbon was different; Lisbon I loved. It was a spectacu-
larly hilly city with cobblestoned streets, baroque and
beautiful buildings, a stately city with classical squares and
boulevards, ancient castles and cathedrals.

The approach to Lisbon was fascinating – a slow progress
along the River Tagus, past villages, scorched fields and vineyards. I stood on deck, watching life on the banks carrying
on as if the majestic, gliding, white *Countess* was nothing
more than a paddle steamer. I was not the only one skipping
breakfast. The first view of Lisbon was something special.

DCI Everton joined me on deck to watch the passing scenery.
He was wearing a London suit and a tie. At his feet was a
soft zip-up holdall.

'I've come to say goodbye and to thank you,' he said. 'I've
checked out,' he added, as if it was a hotel.

'You're leaving us? Surely not? You've only been on-board
five minutes.' Suddenly I didn't want him to go. He was something stable in a mad world.

'We've decided that Frank Monk and Judy Street should
be flown back to the UK today from Lisbon. They are too
much of a liability to remain on board. I can't expect the crew
to take responsibility for keeping them secure.' He wasn't
looking at me, his gaze intent on the passing scenery.

'I can understand that, but I'm sorry you're going,' I said.
'Judy Street – is that her real name?'

'Apparently. Or it's one of her names. She changes her
name as regularly as she changes addresses. Our database is
miraculous. I tracked Lucinda Ember to Holloway Prison of
all places, where she shared a cell with a prisoner called Judy
Street for several months. It seemed too much of a coincidence.

Miss Ember had been found guilty of credit card fraud, not surprisingly, and Judy Street for a shoplifting spree in Oxford Street. She stole on a mammoth scale, several thousands of pounds worth of stuff. Your Bond Street salon was peanuts to her, a few practice runs, keeping her hand in.'

'Good heavens,' I said. 'So it does seem possible that they cooked up this whole fraud scheme while sharing a cell? It must have helped to pass the time. Maybe they were going to go halves on the payout. But why aren't you taking Miss Ember back with you?'

'Because, so far, she hasn't actually done anything wrong. She may decide to abandon the whole idea if Judy Street splits on her. There's no proof that she or Judy fixed the shower, or put the dead rat in her wardrobe, or that Judy bought a doped snake in Barcelona and smuggled it aboard. It all depends on whether Miss Ember pursues her compensation claim.'

'She may drop it now that she knows Judy Street is going to be charged.'

'It alters the whole scenario,' he agreed. 'I'm taking the old shower head back with me for forensic tests. Something may show up.'

'So you are going?' I didn't want him to go. I felt safe with him.

'Yes, Frank Monk is too volatile to be left here. He is a man with a dangerous temper, out of control. So we have him on a count of murder and a second count of attempted murder.'

'Attempted murder?'

'He was going to leave you to drown, Casey. The netting would have dragged you down overnight. The lighting is timed and goes out. The CCTV would not have picked you up then. You had a lucky escape.'

I shuddered. It did not bear thinking about. Change the subject, Casey, quick.

'Has he confessed to murdering his ex-wife, Dora Belcher?'

'No, he denies everything. But apparently he had arranged to meet her for a drink that evening. It could have turned into a row and he hit her with the crystal ashtray in a violent temper.'

'So that's why she had her hair done again. She had a date with her ex.'

'But he's insisting that he didn't keep the arrangement. That he forgot all about it.'

'Forgot? You don't forget about murdering somebody.'

'Well, quite.' Bruce smiled, his eyes warming up. 'I'm going to miss talking to you, Miss Jones. You're the only person I would ever talk to about anything.'

It threw me, of course. I hoped I still looked the immaculate entertainments director, not some soft, knee-wobbling female. 'So you are going?'

'Yes. There'll be a police escort for the prisoners to the airport. You'll see the vans when we dock.'

'Vans?'

'Armoured police vans. No windows.'

Bruce Everton suddenly went silent and remote as if someone had altered the scenery overnight. He took a card out of his pocket and scribbled something on the back. He weighed it in his hand as if a lot depended on it.

'This is for you,' he said.

'For me?' The art of conversation seemed to have disappeared.

'I want you to have my office email address,' he said. 'If you ever need help of any kind, please get in touch with me, straightaway. No hanging about, Casey. And here is my private email address, as well, in case.'

'Thank you, Bruce. How very kind,' I said, tucking the card into the pocket of my cut-off white jeans. I didn't know what to say. I was wearing the plain navy and white nautical outfit that Sam liked. I was going ashore at Lisbon today. It seemed a long way ahead.

'You might fancy a meal one evening or to go to a show,' Bruce went on diffidently, strangling the words. 'Hell no, I forgot, you get enough of meals and shows on-board.'

'Are you asking me out?'

'Sounds like it. Sorry, I'm not very good at this. I'm long out of practice.'

'Thank you, Bruce,' I said again, not sure what to make of it. He'd thrown me completely off balance twice today. 'That would be lovely. One day, I don't know when, maybe. I'd like to go on the London Eye sometime. And long out of practice is OK with me.'

He grinned like he'd had a personal sunrise. At least I hadn't chucked him overboard. Email is a wonderful thing and he would make sure we kept in touch.

'Take care, Miss Jones. No more detective work, please. Stick to shows. It's a lot safer.'

'I'll try to remember that, Detective Chief Inspector Everton.'

Then he was striding away, desperation written into every inch of his ramrod back. The man was lonely. Everyone around him had been enjoying themselves and it made him realize that it was time to set himself free from the past.

I moved away. I didn't actually want to watch him leaving.

It was all the little details that I liked most about Lisbon. Mosaics in pavements, hand-painted tiles on walls, decorative street signs. Coming into the harbour was to discover a magnificently majestic slice of history. Explorers and traders had set out from this harbour to discover the world. Prince Henry the Navigator and Vasco da Gama were still remembered by the proud Portuguese.

The *Countess* came into the dockside and made fast among all the other shipping. A line of coaches was waiting to take passengers to the delights of the hills, to Sintra, to Estoril. At a discreet distance I spotted several police cars, two vans and uniformed officers. DCI Everton and his prisoners would leave from the lower level crew gangway, long before any passengers went ashore.

I turned away. I didn't want to witness the event. Frank Monk had battered his ex-wife to death and had tried to drown me. I didn't want to lie awake at night, thinking about him. His face had to be forgotten.

'Ready to go ashore?' said Sam. He was admiring my outfit, conservative and modest to suit the Portuguese temperament. 'Like the gear. Where would you like to go, Casey? Cathedrals, palaces, cafes, shopping?'

'I'd like to go for a tram ride through the old town,' I said. 'How does that suit you?'

'Perfect,' said Sam. 'We'll get a taxi to Black Horse Square and hop aboard a tram.'

'We could walk it.'

'Even better.'

'And while we are walking, you can tell me all the things

that I want to know. I don't understand why I'm not given any straight answers. It's infuriating and frustrating.'

'You already know far too much for your own safety,' he said complacently.

'For instance, I saw people being smuggled aboard, in the middle of the night. I'm not stupid, I know what I saw. Yet everyone denies it. Who were they and what were they doing? Richard refuses to say anything.'

'As he would, being strapped by red tape. It was, you see, strictly against company rules and he would not want to even know about it. He might lose his job.'

'But I want to know,' I persisted.

'You were probably imagining it, Casey. Ghostly shapes in the dark. A little too much brandy at the last bar.' His grey eyes glinted with amusement. 'I suggest you forget about it.'

'I was not imagining it and I refuse to forget about it.' This was not a good start to our day together. The situation needed to be defused or I would be taking that tram ride by myself.

'Casey, I am not going to say anything. But let's imagine a fairly domestic sort of scenario. Perhaps a member of the crew and his pretty stewardess girlfriend, were too much in love to check the time, had been so immersed in each other on some park bench or on some beach. Then they saw our great ship sailing away without them. Panic set in. They'd lose their jobs, their pay, their possessions. What would you do? Apart from leaping aboard from the pilot's launch, I mean.'

'I'd hire some sort of boat.'

So that was it. Two members of the crew crept back aboard at night, helped by other members of the crew. Somehow they'd got hold of a boat to come out to the *Countess*. They would be in dead trouble if the truth was known. Too much in love? As if I knew.

I sobered down. 'And the corpse in the yacht. Who was that? No one will tell me about those poor remains.'

'Quite right, too. The less anyone knows about that individual, the better. I am presuming that it was some sort of Mafia killing. Some cousin, brother or uncle, getting rid of another rival cousin, brother or uncle. A gangland killing. The Italian police refused bluntly to say anything. Even poor old Richard was kept in the dark. He wasn't at all happy.'

I was beginning to feel somewhat better. A brightly coloured bird from ashore fluttered on to our rigging, scenting break-fast crumbs. There were explanations and the good doctor was treating me like another adult, giving me nearly straight answers at last. But there were still other aspects that needed clearing up.

'How did that . . . that thing, that rotten thing, that crawling thing get into Judie Garllund's wardrobe?'

'I should imagine she stole it from the butcher's area of the kitchen. She's good at nicking things. They probably use it in making their delicious minestrone soup stock. And the snake, which you are probably going to ask me about next, was bought in Barcelona, maybe at a market, and smuggled on board, half doped. Perhaps bits of the butcher's special ingredient had been used to feed the snake. I don't really know what they eat. Insects, isn't it?'

'I don't know what you are talking about. Please explain.' The conversation was getting out of control and the private screen of my brain was overloaded with flashing lights and zigzag snow. The aerial was pointing the wrong way.

Sam took my arm and headed me towards the gangway. 'Enough of all this interrogation. Now have you got your hat, water, sunglasses, crew card, factor thirty-five? I'm not taking you ashore in Lisbon unless you are a good girl and promise to behave nicely.'

'I promise,' I said, putting on the straw hat. 'No more questions. Oh sorry, there is one more.'

He stopped, a look of weariness crossing his face. 'No more, I refuse.'

'The celebrity who is supposed to be on board. Is it a pop star, a football millionaire, a cabinet minister? Their disguise is absolutely perfect. Come on, tell me. Do you know who it is?'

'Miss Nosey Parker Casey Jones, yes, I do know who it is and you are the last person I would ever tell. You'd have them up there on that bloody stage of yours, doing a spectacular, making speeches, handing out the dance prizes.'

'It's royalty!' I said triumphantly.

'I'm not telling you.'

We went through the security scanner and began to descend the gangway. Lisbon in all its perfection lay before us. Bird of Paradise flowers and palm trees and wide avenues awaited our inspection. I was wearing comfortable shoes.

'Look,' I said, stopping. A couple were walking ahead of us. 'There's Hilary Miles and Cavan Franetti going ashore together. It's a miracle. He's managed to get her ashore.'

'Is that interesting?'

'It's amazing. One day I'll tell you about it.'

Lisbon was already weaving its magic spell. I began to relax, the knots easing from my still-sore shoulders.

'I'll let you into a little secret,' said Sam, stifling a yawn behind his panama hat. He waved to some female passengers who were boarding a coach. They waved back, beckoning, inviting him to join them. 'We have a new stowaway on board.'

'Good heavens. Have you reported it?'

'I have indeed. All properly logged by Captain Nicolas. He was really chuffed. Six pound ten ounces of baby boy getting his first taste of cruising. Mother and son doing well in the medical centre. Probably be on deck by the time the *Countess* leaves Lisbon.'

He'd been up all night and yet he still arrived for our date, immaculate and on time. The man had stamina.

'Champagne tonight,' I said hopefully. 'The perfect reason to celebrate. We don't get many babies born on-board. Let's hope the Bay of Biscay is calm for him.'

'He'll be getting his sea legs by then.'

Sam handed me down the last step on to land. I could see now that he was tired. No more questions. The one I really wanted to ask him could wait, but I held on to his hand, in case he fell asleep walking.

'What are they going to call the baby?'

Sam groaned. 'Can't you guess?'

# Twenty-Five

# At Sea

Richard Norton could not resist having a full departmental meeting to report to everyone on the success of the investigations. *His* investigations as they were now, since DCI Everton was no longer on board and in charge. He had to invite me as I was so mixed up in it all, although I'm sure that he would have preferred it if I was absent.

Captain Nicolas had laid on coffee for us. We sat round a long table in the small conference room. The room was sometimes used for club meetings or small publicity events and was tucked away behind a bar on the top deck.

Richard Norton opened the proceedings by making a lengthy speech that nearly sent everyone to sleep. If it hadn't been for the coffee, I'd have nodded off. Only good manners kept an alert expression on my face. He was not going to give me any credit for my help in any way, but I let that pass. It was not a problem. My ego was intact.

'I want to thank everyone for their cooperation during a very difficult time during the last few days and weeks,' he went on. 'I really appreciate the way you have backed me up in all my endeavours to bring these investigations to a successful conclusion.'

He then went on to thank everyone personally. It took ages. Derek Ripon, Karim, the purser's office, catering, the library, Dr Mallory, Uncle Tom Cobbley and all.

'And we should not forget Miss Jones,' said Captain Nicolas, interrupting the flow. 'Who was, at times, in great personal danger.'

'Of course, Miss Jones,' said Richard hurriedly. 'Who discovered a few things in the course of her normal work.'

I didn't put him right. The captain knew the truth and that was what counted.

'What about Miss Lucinda Ember now?' the captain asked. 'Has she quietened down?' I was about to answer when Richard leaped in.

'Nothing further on that front,' he said. 'She has returned to her stateroom and as far as I know has kept a very low profile. There was nothing we could actually charge her with. It all depends on what she does when we reach Southampton, if she starts any claims for compensation, etc.'

He was quoting DCI Everton, almost word for word. He continued with a lengthy description of Judie Street and Frank Monk being taken to Lisbon airport on an accompanied flight to London, which everyone already knew. We'd all be comatose if he went on much longer.

Suddenly, the door to the conference room was flung open and Dr Mallory entered, still in his surgery whites. 'Sorry to be late everyone, Captain Nicolas, Richard. Patient problem. Have I missed anything? Is that coffee still hot?'

'No, you haven't missed anything that you didn't already know,' said Captain Nicolas before Richard Norton could open his mouth. 'Come and sit down. Pull up a chair.' A stewardess immediately put a cup of coffee in front of him.

'So, I was just saying that the complicated investigations are complete and I was thanking everyone for their help and cooperation,' said Richard, determined to get his word in.

'That's good,' said Sam. 'So the shoplifter has been taken back to England and the unpleasant faked claims are no longer an issue, am I right?'

'That is correct.'

'And the man who tried to drown our lovely entertainments director is also in custody in the UK?'

'That is so.'

'What about whoever murdered Dora Belcher? Have I missed that? Who has been arrested for killing her?'

There was a tiny silence. Surely the good doctor knew? The medical centre wasn't exactly the Outer Hebrides. Richard cleared his throat and tapped his notes with his pen.

'It was Frank Monk, or Commander Frank Trafford as he liked to be known on-board, a naval man. He's been charged with killing his ex-wife. It was an open and shut case.'

Dr Mallory looked up sharply, almost spilling his coffee. 'Open and shut case? What do you mean, an open and shut case? I can't believe what I'm hearing. What proof was there that Frank Trafford murdered his ex-wife?'

'I gave DCI Everton all the evidence. The crystal ashtray which will no doubt have his prints on. Evidence that he had made arrangements to meet Dora Belcher the evening she was murdered. He was insanely jealous of her second marriage. A clear case of revenge. Crime of passion.'

'I'm sorry to burst the bubble of your carefully constructed evidence,' said Samuel Mallory with the faintest touch of irony. 'But there is no way that Frank Trafford could have murdered his ex-wife that evening. When he returned from his trip ashore at Monte Carlo, he came straight to the medical centre where I operated on him, some half an hour later. And he spent the night there, sleeping off the anaesthetic. Dead to the world, if you'll pardon the expression.'

The meeting broke up in a shambles. I felt sorry for Richard Norton in a way. DCI Everton had been misled by the evidence produced but what worried me even more was the fact that we still had a murderer on board the *Countess*. And that was a frightening fact. If Frank Monk didn't kill Dora Belcher, then who had?

Dr Mallory immediately took the medical records to the captain's study. All times and dates were logged meticulously. He then emailed DCI Everton, not once asking how it was that I knew the detective's Scotland Yard email address.

I went on deck, pulling on a sweater. There was a northerly wind, six to seven force, buffeting the ship as we continued to track along the western side of the Iberian Peninsula. Later today we would round Cape Finisterre to begin crossing the Bay of Biscay. Nearly home.

The doctor joined me at the rail, watching the choppy sea and the white-topped waves as the *Countess* ploughed through them. We were going to have a very rough crossing if this wind didn't drop.

'Are you annoyed with me?' he said at last. 'You haven't said a word.'

'I'm not annoyed with you,' I said. 'I just don't understand how you didn't know that Frank Trafford had been charged with the murder of Dora Belcher. Everybody knew.'

'Nobody told me. Nobody thought to tell me. You are not the only one kept in the dark half the time. Though I am surprised that DCI Everton accepted such circumstantial evidence, as he did. Perhaps he was told something else which he couldn't check. Why didn't Frank Trafford deny it?'

'He did deny it. He then refused to say any more. Why didn't he say that he was in the medical centre?'

'I know why,' said Sam. 'Because he reckoned he'd be safer in custody in the UK than still on board ship. Maybe he thought he was the next on the hit list.'

'That's awful,' I said. 'Any of us could be on that list. It's frightening.' My face went white with fear. I could feel the blood draining.

'Don't be frightened,' said Sam. 'I've my own theory about all this. Remember, Dora Belcher came on-board with a black eye. She was in a violent relationship. A domestic. They were on the edge of getting divorced. And she was after her fair share of the goodies, the house, the savings, whatever wealth Greg Belcher had accumulated.'

'But the computerized bar bills. Greg Belcher has a water-tight alibi. He couldn't have done it.'

'Somehow we've got to break that watertight alibi. The answer is there somewhere.'

I hesitated. I knew all about medical confidentiality but I was dying to know. And I couldn't stop myself asking. 'Sam, I know this is against the rules, but why did Frank Trafford come to see you after Monte Carlo? Can't you give me a hint?'

Sam laughed and pulled me against him, shielding me from the wind. 'You and your female curiosity. It's not exactly breaking any rules. That famous bad temper of his. Remember how grumpy he was all the time? The poor man had chronic toothache and an abscess on the root. He went to a back street dentist somewhere onshore and they broke the tooth and made a right mess of his mouth.'

I gasped. 'It was toothache.'

'He came to me in agony. I'm not a dentist but I had to do what I could to help him out. So I gave him a hefty local injection and a few whiffs of nitrous oxide because he wouldn't keep still. There was no way I could sort out the abscess and the broken tooth with him fidgeting and trying to tell me what to do.'

'I didn't know you knew any dentistry.'

'Neither did I.'

The Officers' Mess was full and they gave me a welcome as I went in. Some wags started whistling *Ten Green Bottles* but I let them have their joke. I was after the carrot and coriander soup. I'd got chilled on deck.

'Tell me,' I said, slurping soup in a matey manner. 'You know those two who were smuggled aboard at midnight? Was it before or after Palma? Now, I know it happened so don't start denying it. Nobody is going to get into trouble, especially not through me.'

I could tell by their faces that the male bundled aboard was one of their own. An officer. Hence the brick wall. But the girl? They might be less protective.

'I only want to speak to the girl for a few moments. Something you fellas wouldn't understand. A girlie thing, you know?'

I could talk rubbish when I had to. Sometimes I was ashamed of myself. The officers didn't understand a word but pretended they did.

'If that's all it is,' said one of them, cutting himself a huge hunk of Stilton. 'It was one of the Thai bar stewardesses. Lovely little thing. I wouldn't have bothered coming back at all.'

They all laughed. Ha, ha. The male group bonding.

'What's her name?'

'Leila,' someone said but was then shut up by a fellow officer. But I had heard and that was all I needed to know. Half a salad later and I was away to find Karim. He told me that I could find Leila serving at the bar on A Deck.

'Very nice girl,' he said, cautiously. 'Good worker. You not getting her into trouble?'

'No,' I promised. 'I only want to ask her a couple of questions. Don't worry. Her secret is safe with me.'

Leila was indeed a lovely girl. One of those tiny Thai women with long black hair and a twenty inch waist. She served me an orange juice.

'Miss Jones,' she said shyly. 'Karim says you wish to ask me a few questions. I am happy to give you answers if I know them.'

'Thank you,' I said. 'I know about you and your friend both coming aboard, late at night. I was there on deck and I saw you. It must have been terrible in that little rowing boat.'

She shook her head, her long hair swishing like a curtain, looking down at the deck. 'It was bad dream.'

'A bad dream you will want to forget. But before you forget, tell me if anyone else came aboard with you? Were there just the two of you, or was there a third? Another person?'

'Yes, the man who rented us the rowing boat, he came too. He said his boat was too damaged to row back to land, so he came on with us. He said he would get off at the next port of call and be no trouble. We never saw him again.'

'Was he English or was he Spanish?'

'He was big English. He said he had to leave England in a hurry for some bad reason. He was making living with boats. I was frightened of him.'

I leaned forward and smiled. 'Thank you, Leila. That's all I wanted to know.'

I took a cashmere jacket with me and went looking for Sam. He was in the Galaxy Lounge bar with a shrunken harem. The rough weather was taking its toll. He was buying the ladies double brandies but they still didn't look too happy. It was difficult to look alluring if your stomach was churning your supper. Their eyes flickered venom when they saw me.

'May I have a word, on deck,' I said, not standing too close.

'Of course, Miss Jones. Excuse me, ladies.'

I shrugged into the jacket as the wind buffeted the door opening on to the deck. It would have to be a brief talk. Any minute now and the decks would be cordoned off as too dangerous. My hair whipped away, out of its careful chignon.

'Hold on to me,' said Sam. 'Twenty stone is enough ballast, surely?'

'I'm not that heavy.'

'Combined weight. Just guessing. Let's find a sheltered corner.'

I loved rough weather but I knew this was getting to be

unsafe. We stood in the shelter of a doorway and lifeboat, protected by the worst of the gusts. The only place to be alone and not overheard.

'Why do you think Frank Trafford wrapped me in heavy netting, hoping I would drown?' The thought of that watery grave still made me tremble. 'What had I done to make him hate me so? Was I close to a solution, that drove a nervous killer to the surface?'

'It was enough that you jumped the queue in the surgery. He's one of those vindictive people who never forget, no matter how trivial the annoyance. He wanted to teach you a lesson. He never thought of the consequences.'

'Time to circle the wagons then. But I think I've broken Greg Belcher's bar alibi, in a way,' I said. 'Lateral thinking.'

'Brilliant. My clever girl. I adore you.' He kissed me with enthusiasm on the cheek. Not exactly loving, more like boisterous congratulations.

'I said sort of, not actually broken. Greg Belcher could have hired someone else to do it. His bar alibi is ninety-nine percent foolproof. But what if there was an extra Englishman on board, that no one knew about, someone who had to leave the UK in a hurry? Maybe an ex-con? There are a lot of those about. He could have been hired by Greg in the UK or Greg Belcher met him on board and took advantage of the situation, paid him to kill Dora. Remember the black eye? The killer's probably gone ashore by now, with the money.'

'You're not fooling me,' said Sam, shielding me from the wind. It was strong enough to flatten his body against the wall. 'What do you really think, Casey?'

'Don't you believe me?'

'No, I don't. You said his bar bill was ninety-nine percent foolproof. So, tell me about that one percent flaw.'

I knew Sam could read my mind. 'He was drinking beer with a whisky chaser. Now that's a lot of liquid to hold. At some point in the evening, Mother Nature had to be obeyed.'

'Naturally. She who must be obeyed.'

'I got copies of all his bar receipts. As you know, they not only have the date on, the barman's name, the bar venue, and the time the receipt was issued. Practically *War and Peace*. I put them in time order and there was one thing no one had noticed.'

'What was that?'

'Roderic. Paddy took a ten minute break and Roderic stood in for him. There's one receipt headed Roderic with his service number. Maybe Paddy went to fetch supplies, maybe something was slow in being delivered. But he left the bar for ten minutes. Greg could also have slipped out.'

'And you timed the distance?'

'Yes. I did a late-night run. It was possible in ten minutes. Pretty fast work but just possible.'

'Adrenalin,' said Sam. 'So these mathematical logistics will be passed to the right authority and you'll let them sort it out?'

'Yes, let them sort it out. It's their department, not mine.'

'Casey Jones, you are a wonder. Whatever should I do without you?'

'I don't know. Chat up lonely female passengers. Pull a few teeth.'

He folded me into his arms. The Bay of Biscay was ahead, a trough of chaos to be survived. But Sam was with me and that was all that mattered.